Make Me Exhale

COAL HAVEN, BOOK 5

MARIE JOHNSTON

LE PUBLISHING

Copyright © 2023 by Marie Johnston

Editing by Evident Ink

Proofing by MBE, Judy's Proofreading, and Deaton Author Services

Cover by Shanoff Designs

 Created with Vellum

Trust fund? Check. Plans to restore an old train foundry into a brewery? Check. Grumpy project manager? Sigh . . . check.

If I wanted to deal with a man just like my uptight dad, I would've told my parents what my brewery plans were. Only I didn't tell anyone. I waited for my trust fund to deliver once I turned twenty-five, and I bought the old train foundry I'd been eyeing for years. Then McCoy Cunningham shows up.

I'm told he's the best. He's older than me and knows both sides of the business—the restoration and the brewing. But all I've gotten from him are scowls and dismissive grunts. McCoy might think he's the expert, he might look at me like I should be in diapers with pigtails, but he's wrong if he thinks he can bulldoze me.

All it takes is one look. One time I catch him eyeing me with something other than disdain. One conversation where we're geeking out over yeast strains and hops. One kiss that leads to more.

I promised myself I'd never settle for a guarded man who thinks he knows everything, especially one who won't put me before business. And after what McCoy's been through, he's all about work. No personal entanglements. The last thing I need is to be left with flat beer and a broken heart.

One

ISLA

It wasn't every day a girl got a trust fund and bought an old train foundry. And it wasn't every day that a twenty-five-year-old got to drive to her old building and picture the brewery and event center it was going to turn into. Okay, that part was every day. I'd been here daily since I closed on the property a few weeks ago. My family didn't know yet. Only my real estate agent, my lawyer, and the contractors I'd hired to restore the building and build the brewery.

Really, it was a miracle the deal was kept quiet, but I had insisted on discretion. No one else needed to be involved in my business unless I invited them in. I learned that lesson from my family. No one was allowed in a Barron's business —not even other Barrons.

I kept my gaze on the highway and called my brother using Bluetooth. "Can I use the zero turn tomorrow?"

"Dad's mower's not working?" Stetson asked.

"No. It's for the old foundry outside of town." I bit my

lower lip and went for it, my hand tightening around the wheel. My stomach roiled. I couldn't believe I'd kept my plans to myself for this long. Now it was time to face my family, and I'd start with the easiest first. "I bought it."

I would've told Lyric first, my best friend and new sister-in-law, but she was a new mom who'd gone back to work full-time. She had enough going on, and I was in the foreign territory of not knowing when I was bothering her.

An odd feeling. I'd never withheld parts of my life from her. In my family, secrets were best left unspoken—even if the whole town knew about them anyway. Lyric was who I turned to, and now she was in a different stage of her life, while I still lived with my parents to save my trust fund for my building plans.

"You did what?" he asked almost absentmindedly, like he couldn't possibly have heard me right.

"Used my trust fund money to buy the old foundry off 200. It'll be an event center and brewery."

I chewed my lip through his silence. Stetson was my doting older brother, but sometimes I wondered if he did so much for me because he didn't think I could handle the work or responsibility myself. I was afraid to ask. I guessed I would find out now.

His tone was almost neutral, but he couldn't suppress his astonishment. "Serious?"

"Dead."

"Mom and Dad don't know?"

"Not yet. I'll talk to them tonight, but the project manager is arriving soon, and I want to tame the weeds around the place."

"You've already . . . shit, Isla." He didn't sound disappointed, but he'd be shocked for the rest of the day.

Hurt dimmed my sunny mood. Did he think the foundry was an impulsive purchase? That I hadn't thought it through? "I've been planning it for a while. All I needed was the money to make it happen."

"Yeah, okay." I could picture him taking his ball cap off and wiping the back of his wrist across his forehead with a stunned look on his face. "Sure. You, uh, need me to bring it by?"

And there was the rub—other than his disbelief. I owned the place, but that was about all. I didn't have a pickup, lawn care equipment, or even a simple push mower. "No, I can meet you any time that's good for you."

"Not a problem. Lyric works tomorrow, so I'll have Rina with me, but I can bring it—"

"I'll do it."

Stetson had a big heart. He'd take over, and I'd let him. But I wanted to care for *my* place. "I can grab the pickup and trailer from your house and bring it back, if that works."

"Depends." Humor crept into his voice. "You gonna take out a hundred yards of fence?"

I chuckled, but my smile died quickly. He meant well, and he was only teasing. But the fence incident during my teenage years when I'd been helping cut hay had haunted me and was another reason Dad and Stetson hadn't asked me to help around the ranch. "I can't promise I won't hit unexpected litter in the grass, but I'll replace anything I break. Promise."

"I'm not worried, Isla. Come by whenever."

He was sort of worried. He'd never admit it, but I was me. There wasn't a curb in town that didn't have black smudges from my tires. I'd like to think I've matured, but it wasn't my opinion I was trying to change. "Thanks."

I hung up and opened the window. The noise from highway speeds kept me from delving too far into Stetson's reaction and worrying about how my parents would respond. The smell of wildflowers wafted in the window. I'd love to close my eyes and soak it in, but I was driving. I was nothing if not the dutiful, responsible daughter I was raised to be.

Trying to gather my excitement from before the call, I thought about my future brewery. The reconstruction would cost a fortune. Installing the fermentation tanks and the production line. Perfecting my recipes on a large scale. A microbrewery was nothing like the home brewing I'd been doing, and I'd learn soon enough.

Outside the window, pastures with grazing cows flew by until the foundry was visible around the trees surrounding the property. *My* place. The business plans that would catapult me into adulthood—at least in everyone else's eyes. I'd known what I'd wanted for years. I just knew I'd get railroaded if I told anyone.

Did that make the train foundry a metaphor?

I didn't have time to ponder as my gaze landed on a white pickup. There was a placard on the side, but I couldn't read it. Movement beside the building told me that whoever was there was walking around the place. The sale was done. The place was inspected. The insurance adjuster had already been out. Who could it be?

I was tempted to drive away since I was by myself. I wouldn't call Dad, but I could check with Stetson, see if he could drive out and face the stranger with me. But he had a baby with him, and I wouldn't ask him to put my niece in a precarious position. Besides, I was the owner. I couldn't call for help every time I was unsure of someone.

Ugh. The decision between competent businesswoman and savvy girl on her own shouldn't be this hard.

I had my phone in my hand, ready to hit the emergency button, as I used the other to maneuver the steering wheel. I saw the bold letters of McDaniel Contractors written across the white topper. I sagged against the wheel, relieved. I'd hired them out of Denver. A comprehensive company that would do the consultation and planning through the design and build phase. I didn't want to use an out-of-state company, but the owner had been my point of contact, and she'd promised to use local subcontractors whenever possible.

Sylvia McDaniel had said the project manager in charge would be down earlier than the crew to look at everything and get pictures and measurements before the engineers and architects came. This must be him. McCoy Cunningham.

Excitement rose. I wiggled in my seat. This was happening. The project manager was here to begin the process of turning my hunk of coal into a diamond. I hadn't found out much about McCoy online, and his photo wasn't on the company website. Still, Sylvia had spoken fondly of him, and the woman had won me over during our first conversation. She'd continued to treat me like a competent adult. A trait that was lacking in people around Coal Haven.

I closed my window and parked next to the truck. Getting out, I looked around. Bugs buzzed in the background, and the wind ruffled my hair. It was the middle of June, and the sun was high in the sky. The temperature was hot but not smoldering, and there was still a cool hint to the breeze. A final sign of spring that would fade to sweltering heat in a few weeks. I loved this time of year.

I didn't believe in omens, but it was a perfect day for the project manager to show up.

Shoving my long braid over my shoulder and pushing my sunglasses up, I walked over the broken concrete path that had long since succumbed to wild grasses. I couldn't see the man who must be McCoy. Stepping into the tall grass, I waded through the wild growth to the side of the building.

The foundry towered over me. It encompassed the term

"open floor plan." It was two stories tall, with offices built on the opposite side of where I was. Eight-foot-high windows graced the wall that faced the road and the outside was old brick.

It would be gorgeous when it was restored.

Foxtail grass brushed my thighs. I should've worn pants, but I'd only meant to come and gawk at my purchase as I'd done every day since I'd closed on it. "I'm gonna have to check myself for ticks," I muttered as I turned the corner.

I nearly ran into a broad chest. I yelped, and the man held his hands up.

"Whoa. Who are you?" His voice was deep, pleasing.

"What?" I'd heard him, but nothing was registering when I was faced with . . . *him*.

His expression bordered on hostile, and the rest of him was as hard as his voice. His rumble sank into places in my body I didn't know existed. I shook my head and blinked. I didn't do well getting surprised. Conflict and I were acrimonious acquaintances. I avoided it, and when faced with a disruptive situation, I tripped over my words and couldn't form coherent thoughts. Usually, I was as sweet as a milkshake and tried to win people over to prevent an argument.

I wasn't sure how to act now. Words vanished off my tongue. The guy with the granite jaw full of dark stubble had flinty, amber eyes and shoulders wide enough to block the sun. I was used to being around big men. I was tall, for one. Stetson was well over six feet and Dad was only a few inches shorter than him. My male cousins were in the same range. But this guy was intimidating.

"Who are you?" His growl should've scared me. Deep and grumbly, it was reminiscent of the trains that still traveled past the foundry. "This is private property."

"Yeah, I know." I spoke without thinking, still stunned but also irritated. He was challenging *me*?

I wasn't used to that. I was Isla Barron, and people gave me a wide berth to spare themselves animosity from my parents. And my spoiled ass was used to it.

"Then why are you here, little girl?"

I sputtered out a laugh. Young lady, maybe. I didn't wear much makeup. For my mom, it was like armor every morning—cover every flaw so no one could comment on anything but how stellar she looked. She'd had me using face cream with SPF protection since I was five. Her acne regime could make us millions, but half the ingredients were probably banned.

My skin was flawless, and with my light eyelashes and brows, I glowed like a Hollywood starlet. I also had to show ID everywhere outside of Coal Haven because no one believed I was over twenty-one.

The stunned humor passed and indignation rose. I hadn't owned this property for a month yet and I was already being questioned. "I'm not a little girl."

A cocky brow arched, a dark slash I didn't think could shift into a position that wasn't a scowl. His gaze raked down my body, practically stripping me as he went.

I forced myself to hold still, but I bunched my fists as he took his time stroking up my bare legs to the high waist of my jean shorts, the strip of skin bared by my crew-necked, fitted tank top. I gulped when his gaze stroked over my breasts. I wasn't a large-chested woman, but I did okay. My bust had more curves than my hips. Every year, I committed to a squat challenge and quit after the third day, figuring that I'd rather walk without pain than have a social media–worthy behind.

I swallowed hard, and a hint of sardonic amusement touched his lips.

His gaze clashed with mine. "Lemme guess. You just graduated college and you're bored. There's nothing to do in this tiny-ass town, so you're snooping but calling it a hike?"

I reared back. Whether I was exactly what he said or not, his vitriol was uncalled for. "Excuse me?" Anger loosened my tongue, and words and an attitude I rarely entertained spilled out. "Are you some washed-up corporate guy—wait." I tapped my chin. His jeans were splattered with white paint, and his shirt had a small hole under the armpit, made visible by his pretentious, hands-on-his-hips stance. "Washed-up artist. You're bored, nothing to do, your wife left you, and you're roaming old properties wondering if you can get back to the glory days or if it all went to shit because of you?"

My heart hammered, and I wanted to grab every word that left my mouth. I was alone, six miles out of Coal Haven, with a stranger who looked like he could twist me into a pretzel—and not in a fun way. I'd forgotten he was likely the McCoy Cunningham Sylvia had gushed about. It was too early to burn bridges.

His face blanched, and it was his turn to recoil.

I pressed my fingers to my forehead. "God, I didn't mean to—You're here with McDaniel Contractors?"

His brow furrowed, and his gaze traveled to the pickup I'd parked by. "You can read."

This couldn't be the guy I had to work with. He was rude. "What's your name?"

"Who's asking?" His hostility was roaring back after my retort had seemed to drain him of energy.

"The owner of the property you're standing on," I snapped. I was channeling way too much of my mother today. I worked hard to be nicer to others than her, but this guy had asked for it. Which made sense. His righteous, entitled expression reminded me of my dad.

His expression went blank. "The owner? Izla Barron?"

I indulged in a smug smile and stuck my hand out. "Isla —the *s* is silent."

He blinked at my outstretched hand. Did I out-stubborn him and wait for him to shake it?

Muscles popped on the sides of his jaw. "How old are you?"

Refusing to justify myself, I smiled sweetly and kept my hand out like I expected him to shake it. "Does it matter?"

The cocky brow lifted again. His eyes narrowed, but he engulfed my hand with his. I held in a shiver. Warm and big, his grip oozed strength. His biceps flexed and his forearms— dear Lord, forearms weren't supposed to be sexy, but his were cut with prominent veins I could trace with my tongue.

When he slid his palm off mine, I almost groaned. His rough, calloused hands made flashes of bare, sweaty skin and dark rooms stream through my mind.

He broke my impromptu fantasies when he spoke. "McCoy Cunningham. Sylvia gave me this little project."

The building was almost twelve thousand square feet. The peak of the roof that ran the long way down the middle of the long building was twenty-five feet high. It wasn't Union Station, but it wasn't exactly little. Dick. "I'm sure you'll do fine."

His eyes narrowed again. Did the man only talk when he was insulting me?

I pushed my sunglasses into my hair and mimicked the way he propped his hands on his hips. "So? You have any questions?"

"No, but I'll need to set up a time to meet with the point of contact and your financial people to get a sense of your budget."

"Uh, me and me."

He sucked in a measured breath and failed to contain his annoyance.

"Is that going to be a problem?" I asked, deliberately channeling Naomi Barron. Mom could always make people quake using her most conciliatory tone.

"You have no one else working on this?"

His question shouldn't have gut punched me. It shouldn't have prompted the burn behind my eyes.

I would not cry. He meant a team to help with this project. Not my personal life. Not the friends I had who were barely more than acquaintances and not my best friend, married to my brother, with a bouncing baby girl. The best friend I used to see a few times a week and who I now had to share with two other people.

I wasn't going to be selfish. I was happy for Lyric. Ecstatic. And she married my brother. How lucky could a friend get?

But still. It only showed me how isolated I was, and that wasn't her fault. Neither was it what McCoy was asking. I lifted my chin. "It's just me. Rest assured, I'll be as professional and knowledgeable as possible. I'm a quick learner." I shouldn't have been the only one making assurances and promises. I summoned my dad for that comment. *Don't be afraid to show them who's in charge. Sometimes, the earlier, the better.* "I can expect the same from you? I won't have to be making calls to Sylvia for a new project manager?"

"She won't fire me."

I meant replace him, but his frank tone gave me pause. He wasn't smug about it. Almost . . . resigned. "Why?"

"I'm the best one for the job. I know both sides of the project, and I have experience running multiple teams." His jaw clenched, and it was like the next thing he said was spoken with a knife to his throat. "And she's my mom."

* * *

McCoy

Well, it was out there. I was a nepotism baby, and this young thing now knew it.

I didn't know why it bothered me this girl—*Isla, the* s *is silent*—knew. I hadn't cared until this project whether anyone knew I was the boss's kid. Mom wasn't just the boss; she was the owner. I hadn't worked for her for years, but things had changed in my life. Yet here I was.

Isla blinked, and I was drawn to her hazel eyes, a stunning blend of sparkling blue and gold, like the two colors had started out fighting and decided to swirl together. "She's your mother?"

"I'm between jobs at the moment." Even using broad, vague language brought the sting back. More than that. The fury. "Sylvia thought it'd be a good project for me."

I didn't mention Mom spoke annoyingly fondly of Isla. I hadn't paid attention to the details, not even to her name, only accepting Mom's encouragement—nagging—to get me out of her house and distract me from the train wreck my life had become. Ironic the site is an old train foundry. Parts had been cast and engines used to be repaired here, and Mom had sent me here to repair myself.

Of course the first person I ran into was a bright young girl who looked like she could conquer the world with a smile. No . . . she looked like the world would just hand itself over for a grin. My mood had darkened as soon as I'd seen her, and I'd tried to drive her off.

Only to learn she was the one in charge.

Fuck me.

"You call her Sylvia?" Isla's innocent amusement

combined with genuine curiosity would be endearing to the less jaded. I could see why Mom would like her. An ingenue like she had once been.

"I get taken more seriously when I'm not calling her Mom." And guys were more honest with me when they didn't know who I was.

I couldn't believe I'd told Isla, but I couldn't have her calling Mom and complaining about me. I didn't need to be nice to do the job. Professional, yes, but I'd never been an ass-kisser. Mom knew it, but she'd taken to Isla, and I couldn't add getting canned by my mom to the list of shit I had to deal with.

"I get that," she muttered.

I dimly recalled Mom saying something about Isla's family and how they were prominent around Coal Haven. Why did it matter? There were a few thousand people in this little North Dakota town in the middle of nowhere.

I'd prepared for the Great Plains, but Coal Haven was just west of that region. The landscape was lined with as many fields as grazing pastures, but the rolling hills were broken up with blunt buttes. At first glance, it wasn't as breathtaking as the mountains of Colorado. But the gentle hills were green, the fields lush, and after where I'd been living the last few years, it was . . . peaceful.

The quiet had seeped into my bones as I wandered the property. Getting interrupted had burst the calm bubble I'd formed around myself, temporary and fleeting, and I'd lashed out.

Getting taken off guard by younger, seemingly innocent, and stunning women seemed to be a talent I couldn't ditch. It'd cost me everything already.

"I came to look at the property, but I haven't gotten settled in town yet." It was the closest to an apology I could get. "I planned to get in touch after my lodging was taken care of."

"Are you staying at the motel?"

"I'm at the Northern Lights."

Her plump pink lips curved into a smile. "It's the only one."

"Sure." I'd noticed that when I booked the room but chose proximity over comfort. I hoped I didn't regret it. "I'd better go check in."

"I'm around tomorrow." She tightened her lips as if that was a bad thing. "So, give me a call or just stop out."

Her informality was refreshing but a sign that she was inexperienced as fuck. Did she know what she was getting into? And where did she get the money for this place?

Isla Barron. I hadn't done much research before I'd gotten here. More had been on my mind, but tonight I'd remedy the situation. I'd pore through Mom's notes and search all things Coal Haven and Barron online. "I'll stop out, then. Afternoon?"

She shrugged, yanking my attention down to the way her top molded over her tits. "If I'm not out here, I can meet you."

She was several inches shorter than me but still tall for a woman. Her legs went for miles and were bronzed. Her hair was braided, and the last thing she looked like was a businesswoman. I'd expect to see her in the bars, not brewing the beer behind them.

But then she might hire the brewers, bring on managers, and be nothing but the owner. Still. Where did she get the money? Maybe it was the history with my ex talking, but who'd Isla use to get what she wanted? There weren't many self-made millionaires at her age. Investors? A sugar daddy?

I didn't realize I was staring until she shifted her stance

like I was making her nervous and she asked, "Do you have my number?"

Crap. I had to get hold of myself. She was gorgeous, but I wasn't usually swayed by looks. Only once, and it had been more than enough. "Yeah." Probably. Mom had sent me all the information, but I wanted this conversation done. I needed to center myself. To remind myself to be professional. Isla was not Hannah. She was young and had that eternal optimism vibe about her, but she wasn't my ex.

"Okay." She backed up and turned, calling over her shoulder. "Talk to you tomorrow, then."

I watched her go, my gaze dropping to the way her ass swayed in her jean shorts. I scratched the back of my neck. Was it just me, or did her visit not make sense? "Did you get what you came out here for?"

She stopped in the middle of the overgrown lawn. She said *she* would be mowing the grass. Didn't she have a groundskeeper either?

"I, uh . . ." Her gaze darted around and softened when it landed on the building. Genuine affection shone in her eyes, and I almost—almost—wondered what it'd be like if it was ever aimed at me.

Ridiculous.

"I like to periodically stop out here." She nodded like she was convincing herself. "You know, empty buildings can be tempting to the wrong people."

She was right, but this place had stood empty, probably with no security, for years. The old foundry was likely such a mainstay of the land people forgot about it. It was like the trees and the river—just there.

She flashed a tight smile and finished walking to her— fuck, was that a Range Rover? I expected a flashy car. A Lexus, an Audi, or a BMW. A car.

I had a soft spot for a Range Rover. I had bought one as

my first *I made it* purchase. And then I'd lost it. If it wasn't for the work truck, my ass would be walking.

She drove away. I watched until she was out of sight, disappearing around a curve on the highway.

I shoved my hands through my hair. Could I be any more of a creeper? I stomped to the pickup. My mind was fried, and I could only get so many ideas from the outside of the building.

Jumping behind the wheel, I gave the old foundry one last look. Years ago, people built shit to last and this place was no different. I couldn't wait to get inside it.

The brewery part . . . that I could wait for. At least I was a few steps removed from the process.

My phone rang, and I hit answer on the steering wheel so I could talk and drive. "Yeah?"

"Is that how you answer the work phone?" Mom's partially amused voice filtered through the cab.

"I knew it was you." I hadn't. And yes, that was how I answered the phone. After the last fifteen months, she should be glad I didn't answer with a "Fuck right off." She was one of the few in my life who didn't deserve that from me.

"Have you made it to Coal Haven yet?"

"I'm just pulling into town." The crowd of trees ahead and the scattering of houses on the side of the road told me I wasn't far away. "I stopped at the jobsite."

"Is it as nice as the pictures?" Only Mom would see the treasure in an old relic.

"Better. I didn't get inside of it, but I think it's got good bones." I cleared my throat to confess. Better to have it out there in case Isla complained. Mom needed to know I was competent. I'd let myself down; I wouldn't let her down. "I ran into Isla."

"Oh, you met her? What a dear."

A hot, sexy one. A doe that looked like she'd startle in a heartbeat but possessed some hidden steel to stand up to me. "I thought she might be trespassing at first."

"Coy." There was the warning tone. "You weren't an ass, were you?"

"She looks like she should be getting ready for rush week."

"She's done with college. She's been nothing but professional."

If she'd been professional, she wouldn't have latched on to my mother like a lost kitten left on the side of the road. I was thirty-six. I didn't talk to Mom for the last twenty years about my emotions and how I felt at work. We talked shop. What jobs she was doing, her opinions about them, the same on my end. She didn't treat me any differently than everyone else. She was different with Isla because Isla was a different client.

"It's fine. It'll be fine. We're meeting tomorrow so I can get some more information."

"Keep me in the loop."

"Will do." I hung up and frowned. I'd stayed on the main road and now the trees were thinning and the highway stretched in front of me.

Did I already drive through the whole town?

Dammit. I pulled into the end of a long driveway and looped around to head back. I'd missed the motel, but there weren't many signs scattering the side of the road. The largest neon signs were for the gas stations. Another shorter sign for the farm and tractor supply place stood next to a bar's neon lights. The grocery store was a block off the main road.

Where the hell was the—

I almost missed the flat, long building lined with doors

by a building that looked like a clinic or therapy place of sorts.

I parked by the small, square office. Inside, an older woman with gray hair pulled into a bun was folding towels. She pushed her glasses up her nose. "You must be McCoy. I'm Karla." She slapped a key on the counter hooked to a gaudy red plastic key chain almost as long as my phone. "You're in five."

I paused, reaching for my wallet. "Don't you need to see my card? Get my license plate?"

Her gaze went out the window. "You got the white pickup?" She grinned like it was an inside joke, and maybe it was. This place was so small there was no missing I was the stranger. "No wild parties, but I imagine you'll be busy all day. What are you working on?"

"The old train foundry." Did it have an official name? I'd have to ask Isla.

Her brows popped. "Who bought that? The last owner couldn't even afford to mow the lawn."

I would've thought the purchase would be bigger news in Coal Haven. "Isla Barron."

Her mouth formed an *O*, and she didn't speak for a few moments. I'd shocked her into silence. Should I have kept my damn mouth shut? It wasn't like it'd be a secret once the engineer, architect, and contractors started milling around the property. Half of them would probably have to book a room at the motel.

"I'll be," she said. "Isla, huh?" She dropped the white washcloth she was folding. "Must be that oil money."

"Oil money?" I was being nosy, but if the rest of the town was in Isla's business, I could be too.

"Yep." She pushed her glasses up again and crossed her legs like I should settle in for a long story. "The Barrons are big landowners around here, and in the seventies, oil was found on their land." She gave me a knowing look that could only say *big* money. "Rumor has it, the kids got all the land and they get the money from the oil wells, but the grandkids got trust money. I imagine it's when they hit twenty-five, as that's gotta be how old Isla is." She rolled her eyes to the ceiling, her lips moving through calculations. "Yep, she's a year ahead of my grandson."

I wasn't far off with my bored-college-grad guess. Just like Isla had hit too close to home with hers.

Karla flipped the washcloth and folded it with tighter seams than I could frame into a wall. "Holden and Stetson are close in age and they built houses around the same time. I imagine that's when their trusts came through."

"And Holden and Stetson are . . ."

"Stetson's her brother. Holden's a cousin." She gave me an indulgent smile. "You might as well learn them all. They're all in town." A beat of sadness crossed her face. "Well, not all. Derek and Evander are Isla's cousins. Bruce's kids, but Evander's been gone with the military since graduation and poor Derek died a few years back."

"He must've been young."

"Too young," she agreed. "Holden and Nora are siblings. Kira's kids. Good kids. Kira . . . eh." My lips quirked as she continued. "And then there's Archer and, gosh, I don't know his brother's name. They weren't raised in North Dakota, but Archer lives here now."

I wasn't interested. I wasn't. "Who are their parents?"

She had to think for a moment. "Allan? Yes, Allan. Never met their mom, but Allan was a few years older than me."

I filed away all the names. Doing business in a small town came down to the people. "So the oldest generation is comprised of Kira, Bruce, and Allan?"

"And Cameron. Isla and Stetson's dad. Cameron and Naomi. Hopefully you can steer clear of them."

I chuckled at her boldness. Cameron and Naomi earned a warning, Kira a shrug, and Bruce must be decent. Allan still lived out of state. "My business is with Isla."

Her snort turned into a snicker. "Your business is never with just one of 'em, and definitely not with just Isla. Cameron would never let her take on a big project like that by herself."

The surprises kept coming. Mom never mentioned Isla's parents, just that her family was prominent. What were the dynamics like? "Interesting."

"I'll say. The Barrons are synonymous with Coal Haven. If you're going to be here a while, you'd better learn who they are."

I had enough personal drama; I didn't need to get embroiled in small-town bullshit. "I'll keep that in mind."

She smiled. "Welcome to Coal Haven."

Two

ISLA

I woke up early to load the mower and get most of the lawn care done before I met with McCoy.

McCoy Cunningham.

Warm tendrils curled through my belly, but I scowled as I finished getting dressed. It was nothing but a physical reaction. The guy was gruff, more than a little entitled, and he hadn't apologized for insulting me when we'd run into each other.

Maybe I should be grateful he was protecting the place, but I was also tired of people not taking me seriously. Or talking over me to my parents or my brother. I hadn't realized how bad it was until I left for college and returned home and the pattern resumed.

With my cousin Derek's death, I hadn't argued the point. I hadn't wanted to disturb things more than they had been. And then the half brother I wasn't allowed to acknowledge moved back and ended up married to

Derek's widow, and I'd continued to lie low through that drama.

I'd had nothing else to do, but I'd been busy planning. Being the farmers' market director had been more of an annoyance, something my parents had pushed me into to give me experience. The market was considered my little project.

So patronizing. Like McCoy had been, but I couldn't think about him right now. I'd dwelled on his scowly features enough yesterday. I needed to focus. My family didn't react to drama well.

Like when my long-lost cousin Archer moved to town after being born and raised in Texas. Or when Holden met and married a single mom of four. I couldn't believe Aunt Kira was still talking to him. Then there were Lyric and Stetson.

Things in the family were smooth now. Leave it to me to unsettle it all with the foundry. My name was the only one on all the papers, and it was time to tell Mom and Dad. If they heard from anyone else, there'd be hell to pay. In the Barron household, hell was an icy silence full of disappointed looks and pointed comments meant to hurt like physical barbs.

I brushed my hands down my old black basketball shorts and navy-blue Coal Haven Drillers T-shirt that I'd ripped the sleeves off of to make a tank top. I packed a change of clothes so I could meet with McCoy in something that didn't smell like cut grass and mower exhaust.

Tossing the bag over my shoulder, I jogged upstairs and found Mom in the kitchen. She sat at the island, enjoying her morning routine of reading the paper and drinking coffee. I liked to sit on the deck beneath the large picture windows that gave the house an owl look, but Mom wasn't an outdoorsy gal.

"Morning." The warmth from earlier turned to lead crystal in my gut. "Is Dad around?"

Mom took off her silver reading glasses and scrunched her forehead, but it barely creased thanks to the doctor's appointments for Botox in Bismarck she thought no one knew about. "He's getting dressed. What's wrong?"

"I just want to talk really quick before I run to Stetson's."

"I'm here." Dad rounded the corner, buttoning the sleeve of his white dress shirt. His trousers were black, and before he left, he'd throw on a suit coat and his cowboy boots. Western chic CEO was how I described his look for his job at the oil refinery a few miles out of town. "What's up?"

His color was better than it had been a few months ago. His chronic leukemia was responding well to treatment, and to anyone outside the family, he looked hale and hearty. How he preferred it. It'd kill his pride if anyone thought he was sick.

"You guys asked what I planned to do with my trust fund," I started, wishing I could put this talk off. But McCoy was in town. I'd told Stetson. If my parents learned from someone else I bought the foundry, they'd be hurt. And when my parents were hurt, they lashed out, and their grudges were legendary.

Mom lifted her chin and her eyes narrowed. She knew something was up. I could never hide my feelings from her. She was too shrewd when it came to reading people.

Dad tilted his head, his expression almost identical to Mom's. "I take it you've decided?"

His tone clearly asked why I hadn't consulted them. I wasn't ready for that conversation, but I might not have a choice. "I bought the old train foundry on Highway 200." Stunned silence descended, and I wanted a shell to retreat into. "I'm going to turn it into a brewery and event center."

"Isla." Mom blinked, and she pursed her mouth. "We need to talk about this."

"There's nothing to talk about," I blurted and internally winced. Her idea of talking back was what most people considered a discussion. "The sale is done, and I researched contractors and—"

"When did you do all this?" she snapped.

This wasn't going well, but it was just as I expected. They were shocked, and they thought they should've either talked me out of it or brokered the deal. I glanced at Dad, but his expression had stuck on concerned and confused. "I, uh, I've been doing research over the last couple of years. Since college . . ."

Mom's brows popped as far as they were able. The effect made her appear less surprised and more upset. "For the last three years you've been planning this?"

She couldn't claim I rushed into my decision. "A nice long time."

"Without discussing it with us?" Her voice pitched up. That wasn't surprise. She was growing angry.

"You two had other things going on." The argument was lame, but there it was.

"Isla." Disappointment oozed from Dad's tone. "We're always here for you."

A little too much. That was the problem. They would've taken over the project. This was to be my career. Not a *little distraction to keep me busy* like the farmers' market. "I know, but I wanted to do this. On my own."

There. I'd said it. Would they lash out?

A deceptive mask of calm descended over Mom's face. "Well," she huffed. "Three years."

I nodded with enthusiasm I didn't mean for her to see. I

was passionate about the old foundry, but she might think I was thrilled I'd eluded her for so long.

"All that silly brewing in the basement and you think you can turn into the next Anheuser-Busch?"

I stiffened against her nasty tone. My hobby was a passion. I'd gotten good at home brewing, but like everything else, I had kept it under my belt. Lyric would taste my beer batches. Sometimes Stetson. And Lyric had known I'd traveled around the state visiting breweries and asking questions, making contacts. There'd been nothing silly about it. Mom and Dad had sampled my first brews, which of course were hoppy and thick and not good, and relegated it to a silly hobby.

"And the sale is done?" Dad asked like he struggled to understand. He would be acting more like Mom if anyone was around. But at home, he could be a befuddled parent.

"Yes. The project manager arrived yesterday, and we're going to get started on the design. The crew will arrive in a couple of weeks, and—"

"God, Isla," Mom barked. "And you didn't think we'd want to know? That we were too busy? You bought an abandoned building that no owner has been able to do a damn thing with since the railroad was done with it. How do you know this person, this company, is trustworthy? How do you know . . ." She shook her head and moisture gleamed in her eyes.

"I'm sorry." I was only sorry I'd hurt her. I tried to be gentle. "But I'm twenty-five and in charge of a lot of money. I didn't want anyone to step in and take control."

She pushed away from the island and rose. "So you lied?"

"I didn't lie about anything."

"What research?" Dad asked, probably unable to resist his curiosity about the business side.

"I toured breweries, studied other places that have done the same thing, and looked over various business plans while I designed my own."

He nodded approvingly, but his expression shut down. "And you thought we'd muscle you out? You thought your mother and I would have time to interfere?"

I shrugged. Guilt gnawed at my insides. Dad sounded like I hurt his feelings, but I couldn't lie to them. Mom had a way of talking me into a corner if I didn't tell the truth.

"Dammit, Isla." Mom crossed her arms, her gaze assessing. "I guess since you're so keen to prove you're all grown up and can do things by yourself, you might as well find your own place to live."

"What?" She was kicking me out? I had yearned to live on my own since I finished college, but I'd bided my time until my trust fund landed in my account. Since then, I'd saved money. I wasn't financing the restoration and I planned to make my living with the brewery and events center. A bit of a risk, but I was determined.

After college, I had helped around the house and half-heartedly looked for jobs, but they'd discouraged me. Dad didn't ask me to help with special projects around the ranch, but I still did chores for the horses. When he'd been going through treatment, I pitched in with Stetson. I chalked up what I did as room and board, took the farmers' market director job when they asked, but they were just ways to control me. Since my brother had proven resistant to their tactics, they focused on me.

When Stetson hadn't quit dating Lyric at their insistence, they'd pushed him out of the family business. Stetson ran this ranch. He did all the work. And they'd used it to control him. Until Stetson walked away to be with Lyric. I didn't think Dad would've relented, but his illness had changed his perspective.

Now it was my turn.

"You can find your own place." She looked down her nose at me. "Spread your wings. You must've planned to support yourself at some point?"

Dad gave Mom a measured look, but he wouldn't disagree. Maybe he wanted me gone too. He was the CEO of one of the biggest employers in the area, and I hadn't gone to him for advice.

He met my gaze and his eyes softened, but he nodded. "I'm sure you won't have an issue finding somewhere to stay."

"The Northern Lights might have an open room," Mom said flippantly. "Use some of that oil money before your purchase drains you dry."

The motel. I could be McCoy's neighbor. The experienced project manager who thought I was a college kid killing time would see me moving in next door. What would I tell him? My parents kicked me out? That wouldn't help the first impression he'd gotten of me. I didn't know him, and he might try to walk all over me.

Maybe moving was for the best. I wanted to be viewed as an independent woman. I had to act the part. "I told Stetson I'd swing by this morning. I'll have my stuff out by the end of the day."

Mom blinked. Did she expect me to beg to stay?

"There's no rush," Dad said. No matter what, I was his little girl. Yet that was part of the problem. He ran the farmers' market even though my name was down as director. I'd be in the middle of dealing with an issue and then I wouldn't hear from any of the parties involved because he'd intervened. It was embarrassing and infuriating, and there was nothing I could do about it.

"I know." I shrugged. "But it's time." I gave them a sunny smile and breezed out of the room, keeping my smile in place so I wouldn't tremble. I was on my own, but scary or not, it was time. I'd be fine. Finding a place shouldn't be hard and—

"Isla," Mom called just as I was about to step out of the door. "The vehicle is ours too."

My heart sank and my throat grew thick. I wasn't attached to the Range Rover. Though silly me had thought it was a college graduation gift, their names were on that too. I'd been as naive as they had thought. "Okay. I'll find another car by the end of today too."

I pushed out the door and hopped into my ride. I blinked back tears and ignored the burn in my chest as I snatched up my sunglasses. Holding my breath, I drove away and then let the hyperventilating begin.

I did it. I lost a lot, but then it had never been mine in the first place. A few minutes later, I pulled into Stetson's driveway. He already had the mower loaded on the flatbed trailer and had strapped it down.

Sucking in a few long breaths, I parked and got out just as he sauntered out of the garage. I summoned another bright smile, but he scrutinized me.

"What's up?" he asked, his tone concerned. He patted the bundle strapped to his chest. Rina's fuzzy head stuck out of a baby wrap, and she was snoozing. The look fit Stetson better than him sitting in Rattler's having a drink and picking up women.

I glanced around. The garage doors were open, and Lyric's car was gone. Normally, she'd be the one I cried to, but I didn't want to break down in front of my brother. Proving I was capable and independent didn't include bawling in front of people. "Nothing. Thanks for letting me use the mower."

"Isla. It's eight in the morning, and your face is all blotchy. Was it Mom or Dad?"

I scrunched my nose and went to sit on the bottom step of the stairs that led to his front door. The drawbacks of being transparent. I couldn't shut down my expression like our parents. I'd settle for telling him what happened without sobbing. "I just told Mom and Dad, and they were pissed I kept it from them."

"You didn't want them talking you out of it."

Grateful he saw the situation I would've been in, I nodded. "I didn't want them taking over. They still see me as the little kid running outside barefoot."

"I get it. Can't say I'm surprised they didn't take it well."

"Mom kicked me out, and she's taking the car away."

"Whoa." Rina stirred, and he gently bounced from side to side. "Just like that?"

"I guess it's about time." My throat thickened, but I swallowed. The feelings clogging my chest made me feel ten years younger. "I'm old enough. I shouldn't be living with my parents."

"But they could've been more understanding. They can't just cut off a kid whenever we don't do what they want."

They could, and they would. Maybe I'd feel differently if I'd learned my daughter was using me and keeping secrets. That was how it had seemed to Mom. I wanted to change the subject to lighter and more necessary topics. "Know any open rentals?"

I'd helped Lyric look for an apartment before she moved in with Stetson. The options hadn't been exactly dismal, but I needed something now and I couldn't be picky. Still, I also didn't want to take the first thing available and end up with a crappy landlord or a long lease.

"Take the cabin," he said.

"You and Lyric are going to use that this summer."

He patted Rina's back. "Not if you need it. Seriously. If

you go to the motel, the whole town will start talking, and you need time to look for a decent place." He shrugged like that was the end of it. "Let me get Rina's car seat, and we'll head out with the mower."

"I can do it."

"It's no problem."

There it was. Helpfulness was a part of his personality, but he didn't see how he coddled me. "Stetson." He paused, half turned to the house. "You're doing it, the same thing Mom and Dad do."

His eyes widened. "Oh, shit. I am. Lyric calls me on it sometimes, you know."

I smiled. I missed her, but her support meant everything. "Can I borrow your pickup too? I'll bring it back as soon as I'm done." Then I would buy a pickup for my next purchase and some lawn equipment for the foundry. I had budgeted for it. Sort of. Restoring a historic building would need a lot of padding and emergency funds.

He gave me a steady look that said he knew exactly what I was thinking. "Would I be overstepping if I looked at what's available for used trucks in town while Rina naps?"

"Not if you ask first like you just did. But you don't have to."

"I know. Looking's more fun when I'm not the one buying." He handed over the keys. "Try not to crack the windshield."

"That happened once, and it wasn't my fault." Another vehicle had kicked up a rock on the highway.

"Grain truck. Right." He smirked and started for the garage. Before he disappeared inside, he turned. "What's the name of your new place?"

I'd given this subject too much thought and had what I considered the perfect name. But I wanted to hang on to it a little longer and wait for a time when I wasn't looking for a place to live and a new vehicle to drive. "I'm not sure yet."

His smile slipped, as if he knew I had a name in mind and didn't want to share it. But unlike our parents, he wouldn't force the issue. "Better make it good," was all he said.

* * *

I'd lost count of how many times the sound of metal blades whacking and scratching a rock's surface interrupted the steady drone of the engine. The next time Stetson took this mower out, his lawn was going to look like a frayed green sweater thanks to dull blades. Rocks littered the land like icebergs, with only the tips sticking out. When landscaping was done, I could have them removed and use the rocks as decoration. An artful pile by the entry or on either side of the sidewalk to the door.

I rushed to finish before McCoy arrived. I had the zero-turn mower back on the trailer, but Stetson had been prudent enough to load the push mower in the bed of the pickup. That had taken more muscle to lift down, and I was covered in grass shavings and grease streaks.

I should've worn pants, but I'd foolishly thought I'd whip the mower around, listen to some Cole Swindell in my Bose headphones, and be done. Thanks to the rocks, I couldn't use it for as thorough of a job as the lawn needed. Instead, my legs were red and bumpy from getting pinged with the debris shot out of the mower.

Leaving the machine by the pickup, I grabbed the Weedwacker and raced around the building to tidy up its appearance. News would spread, and people would see it knowing Isla Barron was in charge. My parents would drive by, and I couldn't give them more ammunition to think I couldn't do this.

If my legs had been battered before, they were full of welts now. Note to self—only jeans from now on for yard work.

Working on the edge of the sidewalk all the way to the parking lot, I cut the motor at the end and turned around. McCoy was leaning against the front of his pickup, his arms folded across his chest. He was wearing similar clothing to yesterday, only his faded blue shirt was emblazoned with Denver across the front. His jeans molded around his thighs, and I was glad I couldn't see his ass. He probably had a spectacular one—that I had no business thinking about.

Proper businesswomen didn't frolic with the first person they officially met from the company they hired.

I puffed a hunk of hair out of my face. The strands fell back over my eyes, full of bits of dried grass. "Hey. You're early."

His biceps flexed, but he didn't push off the hood. "You really do your own lawn care?"

"I have nothing else to do." Crap, I hadn't meant to hint that I was a spoiled girl with nothing going on. Only now I was homeless and without a vehicle. Which brought me to why I should've rescheduled this meeting. But I couldn't bring myself to put off what I had to do with the foundry to tend to my sudden mess of a personal life. McCoy had come all the way from Denver, and he'd arrived early.

He only tilted his head slightly. "Is this a bad time?"

"No. I just wanted this cleaned up so you can get a good look at everything."

He slipped his phone out of his pocket. "I'm going to grab some pictures while we're here and send them to the *A* and *E* team."

"*A* and *E*?" I hated my own ignorance, but the term sounded too generic to Google.

"Architect and engineer. I'll get some dimensions too." He straightened and went to the bed of his pickup, and I held my breath. The glutes flexing under the denim were a better show than I could've imagined. Thick and round, it wasn't just his ass but the way his broad back tapered to his hips. His shoulders were even wider.

The temperature was barely over seventy, but I had the urge to fan myself.

I trudged to Stetson's pickup, hoping I didn't have sweat rings around my pits. Setting the Weedwacker in the bed of the truck, I eyed the push mower. How much did I want to flex in front of McCoy? Because grunting and cursing while I tried to lift the machine and use my hips to bump it into the bed of the pickup didn't feel like showing off. I'd done it enough to know it wasn't my most graceful moment.

Why did I care about how I looked around McCoy?

"Need a hand?" he asked from behind me.

I yelped and jumped back from the open tailgate and into a hard chest.

"Whoa," he said like I was a pony ready to bolt.

When I turned around, I gulped. While I smelled like gasoline, sweat, and cuttings, I got a hit of woodsy citrus from him that reminded me of Blue Moon on tap, poured into a frosty mug with a fresh orange slice.

"Didn't mean to scare you." He took a deliberate step back. God, did I smell that bad? "I know you're probably used to throwing that thing around, but do you want a hand?"

I stuffed my hurt and embarrassment away. His words robbed any defensiveness rising in me from his offer. "Yeah, you mind?"

"I wouldn't have offered if I wasn't serious."

I sighed and almost—*almost*—stomped my foot. An unfortunate habit from when I was a kid that made me look spoiled when I was frustrated, but I knew better than to say anything and get in more trouble. McCoy's attitude was the cherry on top of my sweaty day, and he rattled me. "Fine."

"I was being nice."

"Yup." I stooped, forgetting how low my loose tank top hung when I bent over. I was supposed to be changed by now. McCoy grabbed the base of the handles and I barely needed to use any power to toss the push mower onto the tailgate. He pushed the mower all the way in.

Well. I wouldn't be impressed by his strength. Or the way his biceps still bulged while his arms were hanging lax. But I was only human. It burned that he didn't seem to like me. I'd made it my goal to be likable. "I need to get this back to my brother. Can I meet you back here?"

"If you want to leave the keys, I can get what I need. We can do a walk-through tomorrow, and you can tell me more about what you're planning."

"It's an old place. I only have one set of keys." I'd had weeks to make more, but I liked being the only one with access for a while. It slipped my mind the project manager would need to come and go as needed.

A muscle jumped in the corner of his jaw. "I can run to town and get a copy made. There's a place, right?"

"Carlton makes keys."

He waited a moment, then gave me a *hello?* look. "Who and where's that?"

"It's the only hardware store downtown. You can't miss it."

"Sure." His tone said I should've pulled it up on my GPS for him. "You can stop by the motel later and pick the originals up."

I hated to ditch him when he knew nothing but the general idea of what I wanted, but his engineer would need all the information and perform an inspection before we knew what I could even do. Meanwhile, I had to move out of my bedroom and find a new ride. "Yeah, that'll work. What time?"

"Anytime this evening." He started walking away.

I was tempted to rush after him, but no. I was in charge —and he was rude. Maybe not full-on rude, but curt. Definitely not charismatic. "What room?"

"You can't miss it."

I stifled an indignant gasp. What a dick.

* * *

McCoy

I hated to admit Isla was right. I couldn't miss the hardware store. It was the lone hardware store downtown, which was only a few blocks long. And it was the only place to get a few tools other than the farm and tractor supply and the auto parts store.

I'd been crankier than I meant to be but damn that girl. It was hard to tell my brain she wasn't on the menu. Not only was she paying my salary, she was young. And too much like Hannah.

But when she was wearing shorts that showed off her long legs and was all rumpled and gritty, she was . . . approachable. Attainable. She had smelled like a freshly cut lawn, but underneath, I'd gotten the whiff of the berries-and-cream smell that left me awake half the damn night.

I'd almost run away. And then she'd bent over. Sports bras weren't usually so sexy. Her tits had been encompassed in immobile fabric, but I'd seen enough—round, creamy globes that would be more than a handful and hints of tan lines I wanted to explore—with my tongue.

I lifted that lawn mower with so much force I could've tossed it over the roof of the pickup, but I'd been desperate to get the task done without sporting an erection in Isla's face.

Carlton hummed as his key-making machine whirred. He stared down his nose, concentrating on the task. "The old foundry, you say?" He'd made small talk, and he was only the second person in town I'd really talked to other than Karla. And Isla, but she was a job. Carlton was also surprised to hear about Isla's project. "I never thought that place would sell. Bernie—the owner—previous owner as it were—used to come in and . . ." He shook his head and chuffed. The grinding stopped and he took out the key, blew on it, and rubbed his fingers along the edge. "He didn't know what he was doing, but you didn't hear it from me."

His quick grin crinkled the dark skin at the corners of his eyes. I suspected Carlton had guided Bernie as much as possible before the man accepted he was out of his depth and put the foundry up for sale again. The building wasn't a DIY, but if rumors were true, Isla had oil money.

"Glad he didn't tamper too much before giving the place up."

"Everything still pretty original?" Carlton started on the key for the bathrooms. The last key would be for the dead bolts. Bernie had gone after clearance locks, apparently, and didn't bother to have them all keyed the same.

"The windows have all been replaced over the years." Hail or vandalism were the likely causes. "Patches on the roof, but that's about it."

Carlton glanced over his glasses at me. "She keeping the wood and brick?"

"God, I hope so." The place had character. Losing any of its architectural history would be tragic. Isla was young, but after what the motel owner said, she could've afforded a new build. She had to see the beauty in the place and wish to preserve it.

He chuckled and handed the keys over before waving for me to follow him to the register. "I'm limited here. Most builders get their supplies from the bigger towns, but if you need anything and you've got some time, I can order it in."

"Good to know." Making connections in the communities my jobs were in had saved my ass many times before. I didn't have to ooze personality, just be professional. Until Nashville. The city hadn't cared who the hell I was once Hannah put her face in front of the cameras. "I'm sure I'll be seeing you again."

When I stepped outside, I was working the keys onto the plain silver ring Carlton had given me. A man approached from my side, and I moved closer to my truck so he could go around me.

"You're the project manager for the old foundry?" he asked.

I looked up, tucking the keys into my pocket. The voice was as hard as the guy's expression. He had dirty-blond hair with gray at the temples, prominent frown lines, and a scowl that seemed to be his default expression.

I was the stranger in town, and word about the renovation was spreading. People were naturally curious, so I kept it polite. "That's me."

His gaze flicked to the work truck. "What's the estimate on the project?"

That wasn't a question I was expecting, and it was one I didn't have the answer to until we knew what the building could handle and what we'd need to add. "I can't divulge the specifics. You'll have to talk to—"

"My daughter." His lips thinned. "Isla's my daughter."

My talk with Karla filtered through my head. *And Cameron. Isla and Stetson's dad. Cameron and Naomi. Hopefully you can steer clear of them.*

Too late for that. "Nice to meet you." I stuck my hand out. I hadn't researched the Barrons of Coal Haven after my talk with Karla, the motel owner. I'd decided to dive into emails to the *A* and *E* team, but I'd do some searching when I returned to the motel. "McCoy Cunningham."

His expression didn't lighten as he shook my hand with a strong, unyielding grip. "Cameron. Barron." The last part was tacked on like he didn't usually have to introduce himself. "Isla's young. She's never done anything like this. I'd appreciate it if you talked to me before your people arrive, and we'll go over the plans. I want to check out the—"

"Isla's my contact." I wasn't getting mixed up in any drama. Been there, lost everything because of it. Isla could put a leash on her dad. If she couldn't, then she should sell the foundry because the rest of the business would chew her up. "She's the owner."

"And I want to make sure she doesn't get taken advantage of." His volume was quieter, but the edge to his voice was finely honed.

"Look up McDaniel Contractors. We have an excellent reputation. But most of all, talk to your daughter." *If she doesn't talk to you, maybe ask yourself why.* I'd done my time with controlling fathers. I stepped off the curb and stopped at the driver's side door. "Nice talking to you."

I got in and backed out. Cameron's glare was hot enough to melt my tires, but I drove away like I didn't have a care in the world. Not all my connections in this town were going to be good ones. But I was used to that anyway.

Three

ISLA

The dull roar that was Rattler's helped me forget I'd moved my belongings out of my parents' house while they were at work. I'd used up my bravery this morning. Now, I was as empty as my old closet and as scattered as the clothing piles in the cabin.

Lyric was sitting across from me, rolling her shoulders as she took a sip of water. Her restless gaze drifted around the full restaurant.

"You don't have to stay. I told you this was my treat anyway." We'd just finished eating, but the bill hadn't arrived yet.

"No, that's fine." She shook her head and the purple ends of her ponytail swung. "I'll pump when I get home. I left a bottle in the fridge for Stetson. The boobs can wait a little longer."

Lyric had sent a million messages when Stetson told her what had happened. I refused to let her help me move out.

Her peace with my parents was tenuous, and I wasn't putting her in the middle.

After I dumped my stuff in the cabin, I dropped the Range Rover off and asked Stetson to pick me up. Then Lyric and I went car shopping based on my brother's recommendations. I was the ambivalent new owner of a used red Silverado.

She poked at the screen of her phone. "Here are the places for rent in town. What do you think?"

I scrolled through the openings. Several apartments. A couple of houses and some rooms in basements. I ruled out the rooms in basements. Too much like what I'd been kicked out of. I wanted my own space. "I guess at the Alpine. There are four different apartment buildings in the complex. I can give Rudy a call tomorrow."

Rudy also worked at the credit union in town. My parents didn't bank there, but Rudy's daughter was a year older than me, and she'd made a point of ignoring me while growing up. I hoped her dad was more professional.

"Want me to go with?" Lyric offered.

I'd taken her away from her family too much over this. "No, that's okay. I'll set up appointments after I meet with McCoy."

"When's that?"

"I don't know. I have to get my keys from him tonight."

Her gaze was cautious. "Tonight? From the motel?"

"Yeah."

"Is he trustworthy?"

"With what this project is going to cost, he'd better be."

"That's not how it works."

I wrinkled my nose. "You're so cynical."

"Have you decided on a name yet?" Lyric looked over my shoulder and broke into a smile. "Hey!"

A blonde stopped by the booth. Aspen Whitfield, a

teacher at the elementary school, grinned at us, dressed down—for Aspen, anyway—in a handkerchief dress and strappy white sandals. "You two up to trouble?"

"You know it," Lyric said. "Want to have a drink with us? We're not here for much longer." She lifted her water. "We're not really drinking either."

"Nah, I ordered a pizza." She pushed a lock of hair behind her ear. "I heard some big news." She eyed me, smiling. "You're a new business owner?"

Sudden shyness took over. I went from harboring my plans like state secrets to the whole town knowing, and I didn't know how. My parents wouldn't tell anyone. "Uh, not yet. But soon. I own a building."

Excitement lit her pale, ale-colored eyes. "A brewery and event center? That'll go over so well here."

Her excitement was refreshing. Aspen wasn't from Coal Haven. She hadn't grown up with me. We weren't close, but there was nothing but confidence in her voice. I needed the bolster.

"Oh, yeah," Lyric said, snapping her fingers. "You've got a name?"

I wasn't ready to share that now any more than I was this morning. I liked the name I came up with but putting it out there in the world? It'd be real. It'd be open to critique. It'd be ridiculed. I couldn't do it. "Still working on it."

Lyric's smile was encouraging, as if she knew I had decided but was too insecure with Aspen around. I didn't know if I would've told Lyric. She was concerned about what had happened between me and my parents, and she was too serious of a person to be thrilled for me without also being worried about the scale of the project.

The server swung by with the bill.

Aspen glanced at the bar where her pizza was waiting by the till. "Can't wait to hear more. Either of y'all want to get together, hit me up." A hint of loneliness lingered in her expression.

I knew how she felt. I'd met Aspen through Lyric. She hung out with Lyric and Kennedy, the woman married to Liam, the half brother I wasn't allowed to talk to. But Kennedy was a new mom. Lyric was married and a new mom. And they each socialized with Liam and Kennedy's neighbor Lainey, who's married to my cousin Archer. And since Archer had upset Dad, I wasn't supposed to talk to him either.

Liam and Archer were family, and I'd never really said a word to them. Liam had once tried to sell his welding creations at the farmers' market, and Dad had driven him off. Now Liam's work was sold at a store in town and in high demand. I had admired it through the window.

Stetson and Liam were getting to know each other, but Liam was a few years older than me. We had nothing in common, and we couldn't count Dad in that equation since Dad hadn't parented his illegitimate son a day in his life.

My family had been in Coal Haven for generations, but because of family bullshit, I hadn't talked to my cousins in a long time. I'd see Nora once in a while, but she was friendly with Kennedy and Lainey and younger than all of us. This was my hometown, and my circle was shrinking. Not because I wanted it to.

"I have your number." And I'd make sure to use it.

Aspen left to grab her pizza. I paid and walked Lyric to her car. Then I got in my new, used ride and drove to the motel. McCoy's room was easy enough to find. His pickup was parked right in front of room 5.

Butterflies launched in my belly. Ridiculous. I was picking up keys, not a date.

I knocked on the door and waited, twisting my fingers in front of me. The door whipped open, and I was hit in the face with the woodsy citrus smell of him. Even worse, he was shirtless, and it was like I faced a wall of washboard abs. He had one hand propped on the doorjamb and the other on the doorknob. The muscles of his shoulders bunched and his hair was hanging over his face with a slight bump in the strands from his hat head.

"I . . ." Words were lost.

He was potent as a cranky grump at the foundry, with all of his clothes on and the brim of his hat shading his features. But the sun was still high in the sky, the strongest it'd shine all year, and the strength of the powerful rays snuck around me and hit his flesh.

"The keys, right?" He pushed away to grab a set off the table.

My gaze caught on the flex of his arms as he flipped through each key as if to make sure they were all accounted for. I swallowed hard and forced myself to look away, but he blocked the doorway, and I had to physically shift to get him out of my direct line of sight.

My movement made me seem nosy, but I got a better view into the small, square room. There was a queen-sized bed with a simple white duvet. A medium-sized flat-screen TV on a dresser connected to a desk and a side table.

My interest rose when I noticed the lineup of beer on the larger table. A can with a red label and wild artwork caught my eye. "The raspberry sour is one of my favorites, but honestly, you have to try it from the tap if you're ever in Fargo."

He handed the keys over, and I automatically lifted my hand, palm up. He dropped the set without touching me. "Isn't Fargo on the border?"

"Yes, over three hours away, but it's so worth it. That place has a seasonal pumpkin spice latte beer."

He propped a hand on his hip, his expression dubious. "That sounds horrendous."

"It's not bad." I was transported back to the taste on my tongue. "Like, the first flavor you're hit with is all pumpkin spice, but when you expect to get hit with the latte flavor, it's faint, like watered-down coffee. Or beered down? But then it floats into a fruity pumpkiny shandy. It's like two drinks in one, and they hit at different times, but I don't know . . . It's interesting. Good, but I don't think I'd pick it over another flavor."

He stared at me for a moment.

Awkwardness took over. I was used to silent contemplation or blatant criticism from my parents. I could tell what they were thinking. *How do we save Isla from herself?* I couldn't tell from McCoy, but he had a lineup of beer and I liked to talk beer, so I rambled. "The apricot apple cider is one of my favorites—also better from the tap, but a glass bottle is a close second. It's from a brewery in Minnesota, not North Dakota, though."

The corner of his mouth tipped up. "Is that a drawback?"

Was beer the way to this man's heart? I didn't care about his heart—I *didn't*—but I'd like us to be on friendlier terms. "No, but the local scene has blown up, so it's been fun trying all those."

"'Local' meaning?"

"In the state."

His expression flickered in a way that raised my defenses. I'd seen people give me that *There goes Isla. Isn't she cute prattling on about something she doesn't understand?* But he actually continued the conversation. "I was surprised by the choices, and the liquor store has a make-your-own six-pack option, so I grabbed a dozen to try over the weekend."

I peeked at his options again. "It's my favorite pastime. I

usually grab a ton of samples in Bismarck and Fargo when I go."

"Are you in either place often?"

I nodded. "Fargo has a couple of breweries. Bismarck has some. Every major town in the state has a brewery, really. And there's one over the border in Montana—Wibaux."

"I hate to break it to you, Isla. The towns here aren't that major." There was wryness in his tone, but with all the big energy industries around Coal Haven that drew outsiders to the area for work, I was used to the attitude that we were too small to know what the real world was like.

"They are to us. A large population doesn't always equal quality."

"It usually equals more food. I picked up the beer, but the deli in the grocery store was closed. Gas station pizza isn't in the running for many food awards." He wasn't in a rush to put a shirt on, but maybe since he wasn't eating and relaxing with a drink, he decided to be casual.

Did he forget I was stopping by? Or didn't he see me as a girl who'd be interested or that he cared who would be interested? I'd never know the answer. No reason to dwell on it.

"Rattler's kitchen is open until eleven." The longer I stood in his doorway, the less I wanted to leave. Had anyone driven by and recognized me standing in front of a half-dressed man in the local motel? I had a new vehicle, so probably not. But I didn't care. I was seeing a nicer side of McCoy, and I wanted to make sure we had a good vibe between us. That was all.

"Rattler's?" He glanced down the main highway that ran through town. "That's the place across the road?"

"Yes. The food's really good, and you can order to go. They don't deliver." No shirt, no shoes, no service. But it'd be a shame to cover up that magnificent chest.

He scrubbed a hand over his face. "I might just become their best customer while I'm here."

Same. Cooking for one in my brother's cabin felt too much like I was moving in. "I just came from there."

His gaze landed on my new ride with the dealer plates. "No Range Rover?"

"I'm, uh, looking for a new place and thought a pickup would make more sense. I can move my stuff and won't have to borrow my brother's pickup to do lawn care."

Understanding lit his stout-colored eyes as if he realized what I was driving earlier wasn't mine. As if it made sense I wasn't driving an expensive pickup with pricey lawn care equipment when I had an old building too. "Why don't you hire out?"

"I will. Eventually." Once the landscaping was in and I was a thriving business owner. Until then, I had more time than duties. Which was why I was still standing in front of his room well after I'd gotten my keys. "So, anyway. Try Rattler's. The chefs are the owners. They're good guys. It's a great place."

"Sure."

Was the guy purposely hard to read? Maybe he maintained a tight line between work and friendship, and I was firmly on the work side. I had no reason to be on the other side. It wasn't like we had much in common. "Okay. Well, see you tomorrow? I'll be there around nine."

The earlier, the better. I had to apartment hunt.

"See you then, Isla."

The way my name rumbled from his lips lingered with me as I turned away.

* * *

McCoy

. . .

The Silverado was parked in front of the foundry by the time I arrived. She was early, and I should be more irritated than I was. I liked to get to a job before everyone, prepare myself for the day, and then be forced to chat. At my old place, I would lose myself in the steady work of cleaning tanks and checking temperatures.

I hadn't wanted the office work. I hadn't given a fuck about supplies and shipments. As long as the shelves were lined with malt, hops, and fruit purees, that was all I needed. I hadn't even minded being stationed on the production line when we were short-staffed. The hustle, combined with the monotony, was moving meditation and a hell of a lot kinder to my body than the construction work I'd done in my teens and through my twenties.

But the excitement on Isla's face when she talked beer last night had stayed with me. Working in a brewery, drinking had taken on a new role. It was work, but it was also art. I had fallen out of tasting and sampling others' craft beer for no reason other than to enjoy what hit my tongue. Last night, when I'd opened the lager, I wasn't comparing the drink to what I made, what my top sellers were, or thinking about changes I could make to improve. I hadn't thought about what my stepdad would've said about the drink. I'd just enjoyed a damn beer. Isla's thrill for the craft had been strong enough to last until this morning.

When I walked to the front door that was propped open, hope surfaced. Would I get to witness her get excited all over again? Would she let the pride she felt for the local beer scene radiate out again?

I shouldn't fucking care.

I slipped through the doorway, scowling and letting my eyes adjust. Her lilting voice drifted out from one of the side rooms I thought would make an excellent barrel room if she was interested in barrel aging.

"Hi, Rudy. I saw you have some one- and two-bedroom apartments open. Can I set up a time later today to look at them?"

I walked into the middle of the open bay that used to house train engines. At one time, two lines ran through the place. Engines would be repaired from parts casts on-site and exhaust funneled out via a large chimney in the corner that was gone and the hole in the roof boarded over. Timber soared overhead. I had spent a solid ten minutes staring at the ceiling when I'd first entered yesterday.

Movement caught my eye. Isla's back was to me in the side room. She wore loose khaki cargo pants and a short white shirt. Her shoulders were hunched. "I'm sorry, what? There were four units advertised as open." When she spoke again, her tone was flat. "All taken? All of them?" She stiffened. "I fail to see how that's pertinent. You know I'm good for it—" Her back went ramrod straight. "No, I understand *completely*. Thanks, Rudy." She disconnected. "Asshole. Dickwad. Arrogant, selfish—worse than his fucking daughter." She spun and her eyes went wide, her face paling.

Guilt stained my gut. I wasn't sure what I'd overheard, but it'd clearly bothered her. I wasn't a jokester, but I didn't like how upset she seemed. "I don't have a kid, so I know you aren't talking to me."

She lost some of the tension. She held out her phone and opened her mouth, shut it, then sighed like she'd come to a decision. "Have you been around town long enough to hear about my family?"

"Yes."

Her shoulders drooped. "Yeah. So when you have a last name in a small town and your parents are maybe not the most popular people, but they have money, you get the public's aggression taken out on you. When I need to do things, I'm not Isla Barron. I'm Cameron's daughter. Naomi's daughter. I'm a Barron, but I don't have the financial power the rest of the family does. So when I'm looking for an apartment and the landlord works at the credit union your family refuses to put their money in . . ."

"No apartment for Cameron's daughter?"

"They're all suddenly filled." Bitterness dripped from her voice. She dropped her head back and stared at the ceiling like it was a favorite pastime of hers. "I wonder if I should've done this somewhere else."

I caught myself admiring the slender curve of her neck, thinking how I'd trace it with my fingertips . . . Jerking my gaze away, I let my irritation out. Old buildings like this weren't on every highway, and she was fortunate enough not to have to drive herself into the ground to get out from her family's shadow. Mom and I knew exactly what that was like before she divorced my dad. He had preferred when we were as miserable as him. So getting defeated after being told no? "Because of one guy?" I snarled.

She took her attention off the overhead beams. Her gaze was solemn, too aged for a twenty-five-year-old. She was unaffected by my tone. "There'll be more. What if no one books events because of me?"

"Get a manager."

She recoiled like she couldn't imagine handing the work off to someone else. Did she think she'd be doing it all?

I'd known I couldn't run everything when I opened my brewery. My problem had been who I'd handed the tasks off to. "You're the owner. You can be as involved as you want. But ultimately . . ." I pinched the bridge of my nose like I could dam off old memories. She was young, and she seemed sheltered. Against my better judgment, I offered wisdom and hoped it didn't bite me in the ass like it had before. "All business owners wonder if their baby is going to fail. If they'll open their doors to nothing. No customers, no interest, or worse—ridicule. And you know what? Sometimes that happens. And you shut your doors, or you figure it out."

Or you turn over the PR to your wife and everyone loves her and forgets you and your lack of charm. Then she takes all the credit, and you're left with nothing.

She nodded, her gaze turning resolute. "Right. You're right. Sorry. I didn't mean to have a pity party." She tucked the phone into the side pocket of her cargo pants. "It was the shock of it more than anything. I should've expected it, really."

While grateful she perked up right away instead of soaking in the attention I was giving her, I was caught by the last part of what she'd said. Why the hell would she expect a guy to be an asshole to her?

"Anyway." She clapped her hands. "Where should we start? My grand ideas? Your thoughts on what's possible?"

"How 'bout a name?"

She froze like I was asking her to trade her firstborn.

"What are you going to call this place?" I prompted.

"Oh." An adorable blush crested her cheeks. Again, I should have been irritated. If she was this hesitant over naming her business, then what walls would I bump against later? But as she caught her bottom lip between her teeth, the last feeling coursing through my body was irritation. Curls of lust traveled through my body. Was this my penance for my self-imposed dry spell? "Reservoir Barrel."

Surprised she answered, I worked the name over.

She must've taken my silence as a criticism. "Or maybe The Reservoir. Or maybe that could be the event side of the house. That way, when people ask, Where are you having the reception? customers can say, The Reservoir. Catchy, I hope. And then the brewery side will be trendier with Reservoir Barrel. Reservoir's a nod to the oil history around Coal Haven and in my family without being obnoxious, and barrel fits with both oil and beer. So . . ." She nodded and her gaze darted nervously around the place.

Reservoir Barrel. Goddammit, it was trendy. I could envision the branding that would fit both the brewery and a chic event venue. She could incorporate barrel into all her product names. Emblazoned on a label, it'd look cool as fuck. Of course, she was a fucking genius about it. What was it like to go through life and have everything be easy?

She peered at me. "You think it's okay?"

"It's not my place," I growled, knowing there was no reason for me to be pissy. "You're the boss."

Straightening, she pushed her long hair back and unconsciously started running her fingers through the strands. Were they as silky as they looked? How would they feel gliding over a bare chest?

She caught my eye and blanched. Christ, I hoped my deranged lust wasn't shining in my eyes. I prided myself on being professional. It'd been branded into me as solid as my dad's disappointing tone.

"So, where should we start?" Her head was tilted as she braided her long hair over her shoulder. I tore my gaze away from the way her slender fingers worked over the parts.

"How about you find a place to live?" Because I needed a minute. The brick building was still cool from the lower temperatures in the night, but heat was creeping under my collar, threatening to keep going below my belt. I wasn't always the quickest learner, but I had enough experience in the two days since I'd met Isla. My dick didn't behave around her.

For the last year, the thought of sex made my blood run cold right before the hot fury of what my ex had done hit.

The emotions were strong enough to make me settle for a few cold showers and a steady hatred of the opposite sex.

Until a ray of sunshine got mouthy with me on her own property.

"That can wait," she said, oblivious to the way I was internally combusting. "I have my brother's cabin."

"Does it have AC?" Why did I care? Maybe because next week the temperature was supposed to reach ninety and I was worried about her. I should have been far away from thoughts about her physical comfort.

"Yes," she said absentmindedly and turned her attention back to business like I should've fucking done. "I want a taproom brewery with limited distribution. Ideally, I'd like to plan for room to grow." She finished her braid and left it hanging over her shoulder. Spreading her arms out, she turned in a circle. "I'd like the brewing tanks to be at the center. The focus. The taps would run that way with the serving tanks behind a partition." She pointed toward the far window. "With a bar across from them. The production line can be on the other side, concealed by the off-sale coolers and swag shop."

She spun. "Tables and chairs. Maybe a seating nook like a coffee shop has. The room I was just in would make a good barrel room. I won't start with barrel-aging beer, but I can rent the room out as a meeting room until I incorporate it."

"I thought the same about that space."

She beamed, and I wanted to groan. I recognized that look. I'd felt it enough in my life, and after running across her dad yesterday, I understood. She was probably the kid who'd wanted to make her parents proud. And he seemed like a guy who made it impossible. So when she got validation, she bloomed like a wildflower in the middle of an open field.

"And the event center part?" I prompted, suppressing the guilt from being gruff with her.

"The room on the other side of where the bathrooms will be. Do you think we can get a minimum of four stalls in each?"

"We'll see what Lorraine and Halle have to say. They're the engineer and architect who'll be working on this." I wandered to the open area she mentioned. The stale smell of grease from the building's previous function hung in the air. Perhaps it had been a parts room at one time. "It won't hold much more than seventy-five people."

"I thought it was the best way to bring in revenue for an area that wouldn't be otherwise utilized."

"No food?"

She shook her head. "Rattler's does some smaller catering orders. Bismarck's close enough for larger orders, but I don't want to staff a full-service restaurant. I want to be really good at one or two things. Beer and intimate gatherings too large for a house but too small for a big venue."

Smart. This time her natural sense of business didn't annoy the shit out of me. I didn't tell her that, though. She needed to be confident in herself, not hang on my agreement.

"The second level in the corner would be the offices," she said with a hint of question in her voice.

The second level was above where the bathrooms would be and the same offices the railroad crew had worked out of when the foundry was open. "I figured as much. I got basic measurements to give Lorraine and Halle an idea of what they have to work with. Until then, what about the look?"

"I'd like to keep as much of the exposed original material as possible." She pointed to the ceiling. "If we can't keep those beams, I'm going to cry." The way her eyes twinkled went straight to my gut. The excitement. The optimistic apprehension. I'd had the same feeling when I first walked into my completed brewery years ago.

"Lorraine will tell us more specifically what we're facing with the building's age and how it's weathered, but her favorite jobs are the restorations. She'll do what she can."

"Good. I'd also like to play off the silver of the brewing tanks. Ironwork in the stools and chairs. Wood slabs for table and bar tops. Epoxy resin tables. A wrought iron railing around the tanks and production area." She ran her lower lip through her teeth. "I'd like to go with a simple, sealed concrete floor to match the natural materials everywhere else."

I nodded, relieved she wanted to preserve as much of the building as possible. She held history in her hands but also savvy design. Exposed brick and pipes were the current trend and hadn't burned out as fast as others. If anything, the overall look took a pause before periodically roaring back. "The biggest concerns, other than structural integrity, are water, electrical, ventilation, and drainage, but I think those last two will be the least of your worries. The reason why this place was built makes it possible for us to adapt. It's big, open, and meant to handle ungodly heavy equipment. While waiting for the team to come out and tell us what we've got, I can start meeting with local officials about the water and electrical capabilities."

A thrill burned under my skin I hadn't felt in years. Not since I'd built Nailer's and told my stepdad I'd take his beer recipes and sell them nationally. Going from nothing to something always pumped my adrenaline, and this time, it wasn't my space to lose. I could take an empty building, make it into a thriving brewery and event center, and walk away.

Isla nodded. "I was expecting those two areas to be the

biggest gamble—getting adequate water and electricity this far from town."

"Sylvia doesn't gamble. We'll tell you what's possible and what's not."

I expected pushback, but she appeared relieved except for her twisting hands. "Um, about the iron furniture . . ."

"Okay?" That step was so far down the line I wasn't sure why she wasn't more concerned about custom ordering windows, doors, and loading bay doors.

"I have a . . . I'd like to add a personal touch to some of the stools and chairs."

I crossed my arms, and her gaze dipped to my biceps before brushing across my chest and up to my eyes, leaving a streak of heat wherever she looked. "And?" I was being cranky again.

"There's a local welder who uses old metal—stools, lamps, firepits—to make new items." Her pink lips turned into a wry twist. "Stools, lamps, and firepits, among others, but really modern and cool."

"That's no problem. The sooner I can talk to them about their availability, the better, just give me the contact info." I'd be getting ahead of the project, but there was nothing but the motel room for me, and I'd had enough of being idle over the last year.

"I should probably go with you—if he'll talk to me." She clasped her hands together and her knuckles turned white.

More drama in this town? "Why wouldn't he?"

She pursed her lips for a moment. "I guess you've heard some of my dirty laundry. And I'm sure someone will tell you about Liam if they haven't already."

My hackles rose. Who the fuck was Liam? And why didn't she want to talk about him? "Who?"

"Liam Barron?"

I relaxed. A Barron, not that I had any business being salty about her mentioning a guy. I ran through the names Karla rattled off at the motel. No Liam. "A relative?"

"He's my brother—a half brother. He works full-time and has small kids. If he's willing to do anything, he'll need a lot of lead time."

Willing? The encounter with her dad came to mind. I wasn't getting in the middle of that or anything else. "Am I walking into a family thing? 'Cause I gotta tell ya, sunbeam, I'd rather stay far away from that."

She winced and thankfully didn't seem to notice the pet name that slipped out. What had I been thinking? "I would, too, and that's the problem. I've stayed away too long. We weren't raised together. He's, uh, a touchy subject with my mom."

I'd gathered from his last name that Liam was Cameron's son and not from Isla's mother. I ticked up a brow.

She rolled her eyes. "You'll probably hear it all anyway if you spend any time in town. Dad had an affair with his assistant, she got pregnant, he refused to leave Mom, she had Liam and kept chasing Dad. One day, he told her he was finished with her, she was an embarrassment and crazy to think he'd leave his wife and son for her, and she drove off and slammed into a grain truck."

"Shit."

"Yep. Liam was raised in town by his mom's parents, and Stetson and I were forbidden to have anything to do with him." She hugged herself. "I listened. Both Stetson and I did. But lately, well, Stetson and Liam are talking, and I'm sick of the divide in the family—who can invite who because Liam will be there or because I'll be there or my parents."

And contracting work from Liam was her olive branch.

"Maybe you should just go, find out if he's even willing to think about it."

"It'd probably be best if you're there. So he knows I'm serious. I've never really talked to him. I have two nephews and a niece I've only seen around."

What was it like being surrounded by family? The only constant in my life was Mom. But then I'd experienced enough conflict with my dad. Liam had to be somewhat mellow if he was talking to part of the family, but just in case, I wanted to be clear about what Isla was prepared for. "What if he runs you out?"

Hurt seeped into her eyes, making the blue darker, like denim compared to the yellow. "It's what I deserve, really. But he and my brother are getting along. I have to at least try, and his creations are stunning. They'd fit the look I have in mind. Really."

I'd left Tennessee to get away from my own drama. I didn't want to step into someone else's, but the way she owned her behavior got to me. If Hannah had said something as simple as *I'm sorry,* I'd have been able to deal with what she did a little better. That Isla even wanted to try made the visit like catnip. I had to see how it went.

"All right. When do we go?"

Four

ISLA

I hadn't expected this part of my building plan to go this quickly. My stomach roiled, and my hands were clenched around the steering wheel. Less than a day after I asked McCoy to go with me, I was driving to Liam's place. McCoy watched out the window in the passenger seat.

I had known better than to just arrive at Liam's and say, "Surprise! Am I forgiven? You seem like a cool person. Can we work together?"

Instead, I'd messaged Kennedy. We used to talk when Derek was alive and she was at family functions. I missed chatting with her. She was older than me, and when we were younger, that had made more of a difference. Like I was too young for her to relate to, and I was too in awe of the sweet girl my cousin had married.

Now she was actually a sister-in-law, and she'd steered clear of me since Liam and Dad had a run-in at the farmers' market. The one night I hadn't been there the entire time, but what would I have done? My involvement might've made a bigger scene and my parents might've booted me out of the market. I didn't have much going on, but getting fired by my parents would be humiliating.

When I messaged Kennedy, she'd talked to Liam and told me I could contact him. I had told Liam I wanted to talk to him about Pewter Creations and the old foundry and that I'd be bringing my project manager. Was that better than a transparent "Hey, I'm a dick and I'm sorry" message?

I inhaled a shaky breath. My hair was in a bun, but I should've left it down to cover any blotchiness from my nerves. I wanted to pull into a field approach, turn around, and go back to hide in the future barrel-aging room. When I brought this up yesterday, I hadn't thought it'd progress so quickly, but Liam's last day off was today, and he'd said I could come over. I hadn't wanted to open up communication and then tell him to wait for months until I had a better idea about the timeline.

To distract myself, I pointed to the land on the horizon. "That's my uncle Bruce's place."

"And who are Bruce's kids again?"

I smiled. He'd been getting the rundown like I'd thought. "Evander, who hardly comes back to Coal Haven. He's the oldest of the cousins. And Derek, who passed away a few years ago."

"Shit, I heard about that. I'm sorry."

"Yeah, it was a shock. Liam was his best friend." I wondered how Liam had handled Derek's death. He'd been all but blocked from the funeral. It was Dad's one great concession. Bruce and Willow wouldn't have been able to handle the hurt banning Liam would've caused Kennedy, so everyone had pretended Liam wasn't there, and when the service was done, he'd quietly slipped away. "Liam's wife, Kennedy, is Derek's widow."

McCoy jerked his head toward me. "Jesus, what am I walking into?"

I laughed, catching a snort just in time. Some of my anxiety drained away. "It wasn't sordid, I promise. Uncle Bruce has gotten over it, and I think he and Liam are getting kind of close."

He shook his head and stared back out the window. We passed a field with leafy green corn popping up in rows. Cattle dotted another pasture. Liam rented his pastures to Bruce for cattle and haying. What was McCoy seeing? Did he think it was plain? It wasn't the mountains of Colorado or Tennessee. I knew McCoy had lived in more than one state, unlike me, who'd been born and raised in Coal Haven. I let outsiders' snide comments about my home roll off my back, but it'd bother me if my project manager—if McCoy —didn't respect the area that would be incorporated into my business.

I turned into the driveway and steadily blew out a breath. A large, rectangular shop was across the circular end of the drive from the old-style, two-story farmhouse. I'd driven by this place my whole life and had never been this close.

The house had new black shutters and a recent paint job. The porch was freshly stained a cedar color and looked sturdier than most old porches. As for the yard, it'd been tamed over the years but never as neatly manicured as it was now. This wasn't all Kennedy's doing. I'd heard Liam got a job closer to town and had a more regular schedule.

Two boys darted out of the big open garage door of the shop. My nephews, but it felt wrong to claim the connection when I had nothing to do with them. Would I be able to change our relationship? Being an aunt to Rina was new and exciting, but in reality, I'd been an aunt since I graduated high school. The boys lived in Williston for the first couple years of their lives until Liam got full custody and moved them to Coal Haven. Not knowing much about them had filled me with less guilt than when they weren't living in the same town.

I parked by the shop. Liam said we could meet where he did his welding. He didn't ban me from the house, but the distance was probably intentional.

The kids hovered by the entrance as I parked and hopped out. My pink shorts rode up and I pulled them down. I should've worn something different. What was good for a work meeting that would include possible reconciliation? I was here as a future client but also as a sister. Kennedy appeared behind them with little Ginny on a hip. I'd seen them around, but Ginny grew by leaps and bounds every time.

Kennedy grinned. "Hey, Isla." Ginny waved a chubby arm.

Kennedy's easiness helped dilute some of the acid in my stomach. As I was making introductions, the boys crowded us, and Liam walked out of the shop. His resemblance to Dad was always the most startling thing about him, from his built but lanky frame to the shock of brown hair a few shades darker than Dad's, but it was his eyes. Just as shrewd but warmer, like a tickle of humor was always held in reserve. Dad definitely didn't have that.

"Liam," I said, my throat tightening.

"Isla," he said, his gaze wary.

Before I could do formal introductions, one of the boys pushed in. "Are you my aunt?"

"Owen," Kennedy said, humor in her warning tone. "Didn't we talk about this?"

"But she's Uncle Stetson's sister?" the other boy asked. That must be Eli.

"I am his sister," I said, grateful they were interested in

who I was. "So, yes, I'm your aunt, and I've been doing a really poor job of it. But I heard you're amazing nephews."

Owen grinned, and Eli stuffed the toe of his little cowboy boot into the concrete pad.

Liam's gaze warmed when he glanced at the boys. "Boys, Kenny needs help with refreshments. Can you help her?"

"I'll race you!" Owen took off. While I had the chance, I cataloged the differences between them so I wouldn't confuse the two. I'd known who they were since they were born and moved to Coal Haven to stay with Liam's grandma while he worked in the oil fields, but other than their names, I wasn't sure who was who until now. Owen had dirty-blond hair, while Eli's was a few shades lighter than Liam's.

Kennedy smiled again and hitched Ginny up. My one-year-old niece had Kennedy's brunette hair. "I hope you two don't mind getting bombarded with lemonade and cookies. When we told them we were getting company, they insisted on entertaining."

I glanced at McCoy. His jaw was permanently tense, and the half scowl hadn't left his expression. This wasn't his family, and it likely interfered with the work he had to do, but I couldn't refuse. "It's no problem."

She exchanged a supportive glance with Liam before walking to the house.

Liam hooked his thumbs in his jeans but didn't invite us farther inside. "So what's this about, Isla?"

"I have a little more freedom than I did before." I didn't expect to dive into the long-lived conflict in front of McCoy, but I was also used to everyone knowing our business—or thinking they knew. As awkward as it was, embarrassing even, it was also nice to clear the air for myself. "I've admired your work since you started selling at Haven Furnishings, and I'd love to feature some of your work in Reservoir

Barrel. That's what I'm calling the brewery and events center."

Two people now knew the name, and they were the last people I thought would know, which lent confidence to where there'd been uncertainty before. Funny how my life was shifting so quickly.

Liam's doubtful expression grew harder. "Cameron's going to shit coal bricks, and your mom is going to back him up one hundred percent. They're not going to like it, and they're going to interfere. I can't afford to play games."

I didn't want Liam or his family to experience backlash because of me. "I can handle them."

"Really?" His gaze flicked to McCoy as he paused like he was deciding whether to speak or not. "Because you haven't when it comes to me. In fact, it seemed like you supported their wishes."

"I honestly didn't know what to think, Liam." I didn't agree with my parents, and blaming fear seemed like a dick move, but it was the truth. "I grew up hearing it all and tried to make my own decisions. I wish I could say I was stronger, savvier, but I wasn't. I had to wait until I got the trust fund to buy my way out from under them."

"I heard you got kicked out." His gaze strayed to my pickup. "And they took your vehicle too."

Shame heated my cheeks. Who else had heard? Or had everyone seen me in a new vehicle, driving toward the lake where our family had some cabins? The humiliation grew more acute with McCoy's attention on me. I should've come by myself. This talk was too personal, and now McCoy was seeing how childish I really was. That professional Isla wasn't real, and the hot mess he walked up on while mowing the lawn was the girl he was working with.

I should've known that for Liam, we couldn't do business without clearing the air. He was protecting himself and his assets from my family—his family—because we'd been nothing but unfair and even cruel to him. I might have been a follower and not an instigator, but I'd been an adult long enough to have acted differently.

"I did get kicked out," I admitted, my face burning. "I bided my time until the money cleared my account and I could finish the paperwork on the sale, and they called me on it. But money buys a lot of freedom, and I mean to use it."

The corners of Liam's jaw flexed. "I wouldn't know."

"I know," I said quietly, mentally kicking myself for bringing it up. My cousins and I all got oil trusts. Evander hadn't touched his as far as I knew. When he died, Derek's went to Bruce, and Uncle Bruce left it as dormant as Evander had his. The only one left was Nora. Archer and his brother, Ansen, were left out since their dad had been estranged for decades. Liam wasn't deemed a real Barron. There'd been a lot of bullshit parameters on who got a trust fund and who didn't. "I'm sorry. For everything."

He lifted a shoulder. "I never wanted a cent from them." He rubbed the back of his neck. "Working with me is only going to cause problems for you."

"Only with Mom and Dad, and so many things cause problems with them."

The corner of Liam's mouth kicked up. "That's a given." He looked at McCoy. "Didn't mean to drag you into the family mess but figured you might as well know what you're up against. You'll probably have your own run-in with Cameron."

McCoy hesitated a moment before answering. "Already have, but the heads-up is appreciated."

"You did?" I blurted. I should've talked to him later, but I was nothing if not on brand with witnesses to family BS.

Why didn't he mention he'd talked to Dad? How bad was it? Would I ever quit being embarrassed?

"He wanted me to go through him." McCoy shrugged. "He's worried you're going to get taken advantage of. I get it, but I was also insulted. Sylvia takes the company's reputation seriously, as do I with my work."

"He might get worse if you're doing business with me," Liam warned, like he was giving me one last opportunity to back out.

I shook my head. "I want your pieces in my brewery. I want to get to know my brother and his family. *My* family. End of story."

Liam's gaze jumped between me and McCoy as if this was his last opening to decline my offer. "Lemme hear what you're thinking, and I'll tell you what I can do, if anything. But if I'm able to work with you, I'll make sure everything goes through a lawyer."

"I think that's smart," I said, not offended and nearly giddy at the prospect. My old life could unravel as long as I could build a new one as surely as I was constructing my brewery.

* * *

McCoy

Isla was finishing up her discussion with Liam as we wandered out of the shop into air that was muggier than when we'd arrived.

The meeting ended better than it had started. I wasn't for drama, but at the same time, I hung on every damn word. I was no different than my mom before Dad left us, and I used to come home from school to get filled in on all the dirt with daytime soaps. Then Dad would come home and berate her as he dumped all of the papers from his construction business into her lap to deal with.

Isla's dad had reminded me of him. And her timidity reminded me of my mom when I was younger, before Dad had left us. Then Sylvia had met Fergus McDaniel, and she'd transformed. Mom was the strongest person I knew, making it extra shameful to slink home to Denver after what happened in Tennessee.

Maybe that was why I stayed. Isla was emerging stronger than ever, and I didn't want to miss the show. Maybe I needed to see it happen for someone even if it wasn't me. Or maybe it was nothing more than my refusal to let my mom down after moping on her couch for months.

Plus, I had nothing else to do. There was that.

"McCoy. Hey, McCoy." Owen jumped up and down in front of me. "Do you like horses?"

The boys had brandished their lemonade and cookies like they were classically trained pastry chefs. I wasn't around a lot of kids and usually ignored them. I was an only child and didn't grow up surrounded by siblings and cousins like Isla. Home had been quiet, isolated. Until Dad would get home after work, then it was just angry and isolated.

The hopeful shine in Owen's eyes dug down into me like a furry creature going straight for my heart. Not too long ago, I thought I'd have kids of my own by now. Instead, I had signed divorce papers and no real address.

"Yeah, I like horses as much as the next guy."

Eli bumped his brother, trying to get closer. "We're going to get a horse."

Kennedy rubbed the top of his head. "A pony. I can't imagine the trouble you two would get into with a full-sized horse. Probably the same as your dad."

Eli screwed his face up. "But Dad said we could get a horse."

"A pony," she stressed.

"Still a horse," Owen grumbled. "Aunt Isla, hey. Do you like horses?"

She turned from Liam with a radiant grin. Her usually quiet demeanor vanished when the boys hounded her with questions. "Um, *yeah*, I love horses. I used to show them."

"Really?" they both asked together.

"Oh, yeah. Horse shows all weekend in the summer."

"Do you have any horses now?" Owen asked.

Her smile faltered. If her parents kicked her out, she had nothing. Money was a bonus, and it probably helped, but I couldn't imagine Sylvia yanking everything away just because I started making my own decisions. I wouldn't have been successful in the business I'd been in for a little while without her and Fergus's support.

"No, none of my own," Isla said. "But maybe when I get my own place, I'll look at getting one." She squatted down. The boys were old enough to be taller than her at that level. "But you know, I started on a pony too. Her name was Whiskers."

"That's a cat's name," Owen said, completely unimpressed.

Isla chuckled. "She liked to nip at cats' tails. I thought I was a genius when I named her." She rose. "Thanks for the goodies. That was the best lemonade I've ever tasted."

We said our goodbyes and loaded up. It was nice to be the passenger. I could admire the countryside better than when I'd driven to Coal Haven from Denver. I needed the calm after the year I had.

"That went better than I thought," she murmured as she turned onto the main highway to head toward town.

"His work is good." We'd not only seen what he was

working on and the level of discarded scrap metal he made into art, but he had meticulous records and photos of everything he made and sold. "It'll go well with the aesthetic you have planned."

She nodded, and we drove in silence for several minutes. With the furtive way her gaze drifted toward me, I knew she wanted to ask about the run-in with her dad, but I wasn't offering the information up. The AC blasted in my face, and country music drifted from the speakers while I fed off her anticipatory energy like an asshole.

"What did my dad say to you?" There it was. "Why didn't you tell me?"

I kept my gaze on the dark clouds in the sky. A blue swath that had been a dark hint when we'd left town for Liam's was now an imminent storm. "I try to stay in my lane, and your family is not my lane. I told him everything had to go through you because it does. Your name's on the checks."

"That's embarrassing," she muttered.

"It was a first for me." Other than my own dad swaggering onto my jobsites when I'd left home and started working for Fergus's construction company after he and Mom married. My dad would loudly boast I didn't know what I was doing in front of Fergus's clients. Then later, when I'd dabbled in brewing, he'd declared my finished beer horse piss. I'd named one of my lines Horse Piss, and it was my biggest-selling ale. Shortly after, Dad passed away. Sometimes it felt like he died because giving me shit had been keeping him going.

And now Horse Piss was Hannah's biggest seller.

Fuck. I rubbed a hand down my face.

Isla ducked her head to look out the windshield to the sky above us. "Maybe I should name the place Family Drama."

"Won't book a lot of weddings with that name. Save it for naming your beer. That's what I did."

She giggled and looked at me. "What do you brew?"

"Nothing anymore." I blew out a breath. I didn't talk about Hannah. When Mom had asked, I told her the bare minimum. No one else needed to weigh in on all the shit I should've done, how I should've protected myself. Things they would've told me if I'd talked to them in the first place.

But Mom hadn't liked Hannah, so I had left her out of the relationship and had avoided her opinions. Nashville was far enough from Denver that Mom couldn't easily come visit. But Mom had been married to my dad. She'd learned from the best what a fucked-up marriage was like. When she'd gotten remarried to Fergus, she'd done it right—prenup and everything.

And here I was, with almost nothing to my name and using old skills my loser dad had taught me to get by—only because Mom had thrown me a bone and given me something to do.

So maybe that was what got me to talk about what had happened. Not discussing my life with anyone hadn't changed a thing. "I had my own brewery, and I lost it in the divorce."

Her eyes widened. She looked at me for a heartbeat and then back to the road. "All of it?"

"All of it." The building, the business, the recipes, everything. She was embarrassed about her dad trying to interfere, but it was nothing compared to what I'd let slip through my fingers from negligence. "I built that place from the ground up. Mastered my technique. Made excellent recipes. Built a relationship with all the distributors and local microbreweries. Then I got married, and she wanted in. She learned the craft side, but since she preferred the office work, I happily stuck to brewing and let her do the books."

"She stole it?"

"No, it all belongs to the brewery, and I had to sell my half of the company or face working with her for the rest of the company's life or mine, whichever died first. And since she was the face and voice of the brewery, I quickly learned that no one wanted to deal with me. We were married for four years, and it was like they'd forgotten they'd started with me." Hannah held all the conniving cards and it was my fault. "By then, I didn't trust her not to tank the place and take me down with it while she'd built herself a nice little life raft." It wouldn't have been the worst of her betrayal, but I was raw from saying the rest out loud.

Raw, but oddly a little lighter.

"Dang. That's awful." She scrunched her nose. "I suppose you think I'm just a little girl playing around."

My opinion was slowly changing. She was inexperienced. Naive. But she had a drive I hadn't found alluring until I'd gotten a glimpse inside her private life.

"That depends." The first few fat drops of rain hit the windshield. "Are you going to hire some hard workers and then take credit for everything?"

Her mouth dropped open. "Absolutely not. I plan to be involved in every part of the process until I'm the head brewer."

"You don't want to be the head. That's the ordering, the planning. It's where you step away from the fun—unless ordering malt is thrilling to you." It hadn't been to me, and I'd paid for it.

She flipped the windshield wipers on. The rain grew heavier, lightning flashed to the right of the pickup, and a peal of thunder echoed across the sky.

"It just might be." She pulled into the parking lot of the

foundry. "But I've done some home brewing, and I enjoy the process. Admittedly, my batches are small, but I've been tinkering with spices and different sweeteners."

I grunted, wishing I could return her enthusiasm. When I sold the brewery, my passion went with it. But it was reassuring to hear she had some experience with the brewing process and, more importantly, all the cleaning and sanitizing that went with it. There was a time not long ago when she could've gotten me started with shoptalk and I would've gone all day, only to pick up where I left off the next day. It was what had made people want to intern with me. I wasn't the life of the party, but I knew my shit. Too bad I was terrible at choosing people to work with.

She wiggled in her seat like she couldn't keep her excitement contained. "This is the perfect chance to see what it's like inside during a storm."

What the hell was she talking about? "It's a century old, and it's been fine this long."

"I know." Eagerness made the yellow shine in her eyes. "I love storms, and there hasn't been a banger since I closed on the place."

I chuckled because I didn't know what else to do. The sky was wicked. Dark, but with a shine thanks to the daylight behind the clouds. The rain hammered the windows and pickup frame, hinting that it was going to get worse. "I think you should get this new truck into a garage."

She shrugged and parked so my door was by my work truck. I could get out and get into it without getting soaked. "I don't have a garage." She paused with her hand on the door handle. "Thanks for coming out with me today. And sorry if it got awkward, but it was important Liam knew I was serious about working with him, and I don't think he would've bought it without you along."

I was caught in the beams of her gaze. The light and life

inside this girl humbled me. Being next to her and the energy she exuded made me question when I became the crotchety old guy who yelled at kids on his lawn. "No problem."

She grinned, jingled her keys, and ran out the door toward the entrance of the foundry.

I knew I should leave. I had emails from the architect. Mom wanted an update. I had to come up with local businesses we could work with and pore through dry pages of state legislation regarding alcohol production and distribution. I could recite the federal policies in my sleep. I had plenty of other things to do.

"Fuck," I growled and charged out of the pickup. I slammed the door shut behind me. Rain pelted my face. My shirt was immediately drenched, but I didn't get into the work truck. I ran, splashing through puddles that had already formed in the downpour.

The sky lit up, and I sprinted faster. Thunder cracked through the air. I ripped the door open and stumbled into the cool shadows of the building.

Isla was spinning around in the middle, looking at the roof. She glanced at me, surprise lifting her brows. Unfortunately, I wasn't the only drenched one. Just like my shirt was plastered to my chest, so was hers, molding over her tits and hugging her stomach. A span of skin was visible above the waistband of her pink shorts, which were also wet and clinging to her skin. The material had ridden up and stayed like it was glued in place, giving me an excellent peep show of the globes of her ass.

Heat flooded my body, chasing away the worst of the chill.

"You don't have to stay," she said and continued to wander, studying the walls and floor.

Rain hammered the roof and windows. The sound that

resonated through the place would get tempered once we filled it with brewing tanks, a bar, and a few interior walls. For now, the noise acted like a cocoon. It was just us two.

"Driving in this would be shit anyway," I said roughly.

A smile spread across her face, and she radiated like the damn sun in the darkness. "Isn't this awesome?" She circled again. "This place is *mine*. I talked to my brother today. I have *two* brothers." She pressed her fingers to her lips and stared at me. "That's the first time I've admitted that. God, I am an awful human."

"It's not the first time you admitted it. Maybe it's the first time you said it out loud like a declaration."

The horrified look faded. "True. It feels good to finally speak about it." She shook out the bun in her hair and started finger-combing the damp strands. She wandered toward the future barrel room.

Light flashed through the windows, and every few seconds there was a ping against the glass.

I followed Isla. The berries-and-cream scent of her shampoo was like the yellow brick road leading to her. She was a walking summer day. "I'd stay away from the windows. I think it's hailing."

The pings grew in number and frequency. My vehicle was a work truck. Hail would be nothing but a nuisance. Hers was used, but new. A pain-in-the-ass insurance claim.

Isla feathered her fingers around the hem of her soaked shirt. A tremble shook her body. If I got closer, would I see if goose bumps erupted over her skin? "I guess that'll be the real test. The old owner replaced the windows a few years ago, but we haven't had sizable hail since."

Her tremble was stronger. I was soaked, but her impromptu wet T-shirt contest was keeping me plenty warm. In no world should I know her bra had two clasps and lacy trim around the cups.

"Brr," she said, like she was getting self-conscious about her shivering. "Maybe I should run back to the pickup and turn the heat on."

The hail was too steady, pinging off the building like chips were flying off the brick and we'd be left with a pock-marked foundry. It was fine, but the sound was against a hard material, not her soft skin. "I think the hail's getting heavier."

Just as I said it, the noise died down to only rain. Lightning continued to flash, and thunder rocked the sky around us.

Her jaw was starting to vibrate. She crossed her arms and not too soon. The poke of her hard nipples through the fabric of her shirt made it hard to tell the caveman part of my brain she was miserable and not turned on.

There were no blankets. The only thing warm in this place was me.

"This was a bad idea," she said, her gaze brushing across the high windows. "I should've gone straight back to the cabin. Then maybe you'd be in your dry motel room by now."

"Don't." I crossed to her, and against my best judgment but seeing no other solution, I wrapped my arms around her slim shoulders. She stiffened, her gaze jerking up to mine. "Don't take responsibility for others' actions. I chose to follow you."

"What are you doing?" she whispered, stiff as a board but still trembling.

"Trying to keep you from getting hypothermia on a summer day." A more noble attempt than concentrating on the dampness of her clothing so my hot blood would stay far away from my dick.

"Is that possible?"

"I don't know, but you're cold and we can't go outside yet."

She finally relaxed, melting in my hold. She touched her forehead to my shoulder, and goddammit, I liked the way she felt in my arms. Her arms were still crossed, creating a sort of barricade between us.

Her shivering had decreased, but my discomfort was rising. My body recognized a sexy woman was pressed against me, and muscle memory took over. I'd stayed away from women as soon as I'd heard the full extent of Hannah's betrayal. A quick jack-off in the shower had become a task—like brushing my teeth and shaving. But with this woman, who couldn't hide the press of her chest despite her crossed arms, masturbating wasn't enough. Desire slid through my veins like a full-bodied stout—smooth and satisfying, leaving a demand for more.

"Shit." I hadn't meant for that to slip out.

Isla looked up, and thanks to her height, our lips were far too close. And thanks to my unwanted attraction, I dipped my head. Because I couldn't go one more second without knowing if she tasted as sweet as she looked.

Five

ISLA

His soft mouth was at odds with his hard, smoldering body, and it was enough of a contrast to keep me from pulling away. Shock resonated through me, but it was dulled, like the storm outside when I was safe inside these walls. I wanted more.

God, it'd been too long since I'd been kissed.

His hold tightened, but I managed to unfold my arms and press my hands against his broad, warm chest. Was there anywhere on this man that wasn't hard? Other than his lips? Lips that were usually in a thin line. A mouth that was normally formed into a permanent scowl was now molded against mine. And when his hot tongue flicked across my lips, I was helpless not to open up to him.

He tasted sweet, thanks to the cookies and lemonade we'd had at Liam's. Another conflict. McCoy was a rigid man. I wouldn't have been surprised if his kiss had been steely like a galvanized nail, but the only unyielding part about him was his body—and the hard ridge pressing against my hips.

Impressive.

The wrongness of this situation was settling in—I had hired him. Things could get weird. I adored his mother and wanted her to respect me, but here I was with my tongue down her son's throat.

And my god, was I loving it. A whimper escaped me, and chill was the last thing I felt. My body flushed with warmth like I had my very own propane heater connected to my veins.

He growled and spun us. My back hit a cool wall, but I didn't care. His hands slid down my sides and grabbed my ass and *yes*. His grip was unrelenting and demanding. He made me feel irresistible.

I fisted my hands in his shirt. I'd rip it off to get a view of his amazing abs, but I didn't want to break the kiss. The man knew what he was doing. He brushed his tongue along mine like he was showing me what he could do somewhere else on my body. And that place was going wild. My belly was tight, the energy coiled so tightly in my core a steady throb beat between my thighs.

The thuds and tinks against the building grew deafening again. We were getting another round of hail, and it nailed the place worse than it had before.

Any alarm at the change in storm severity was wiped away when his blistering fingertips hit the flesh of my butt and rubbed. I'd never thought of my ass as my shining qual-ity. But the way he massaged the globes, his fingers caressing and squeezing it changed the way I felt about my individual body parts. He was making my ass feel great. He made *me* feel amazing. This big, hard man who hadn't cracked much of a smile since I'd met him all of three days ago, and he was all over me.

And then he stooped and lifted me. I automatically wrapped my legs around him, the damp, cool material of his jeans digging into my thighs, but god, the big ridge behind the fly of his jeans pressing into just the right place—

The shatter of glass cut right through my lust. I gasped and ripped my mouth off his, my head cracking against the stone wall. "Ow."

He dropped me like a boiling kettle and took three rushed steps back. His chest was heaving, and the horrified way he looked at me slammed my emotional doors open, letting the cold rush back in. Without his heat, a shiver racked my body.

More glass shattered. Grateful for the excuse to escape his dismay, I rushed into the main area. A baseball-sized chunk of hail sat at the base of one of the walls. Rain spat inside onto the floor and dribbled down the walls from a busted window.

"Oh, no!" I rushed to the piece of ice, but a strong hand around my elbow pulled me to a stop.

"Don't. It's still hailing." He ripped his hand off me and pushed it through his hair. The wet strands stuck up in rows between where his fingers had been. "Fuck, Isla. That was . . ."

I hung on his hanging sentence. Spectacular? The best kiss of my life? Unforgettable? Would I be able to hear him over the clatter?

"A big fucking mistake."

I reared back like he'd slapped me. That was loud and clear. The fact I agreed didn't matter. Deep down, I wanted to be irresistible. Deep down, I wanted to be special to someone. Deep down, I wanted to be wanted.

He wasn't looking at me. His glare was on the broken window, his hands loose on his hips. The hard set of his jaw was as firm as his stance, his feet apart and his lines strong.

I did what I did best—pretended everything was fine and that I wasn't the unwanted girl no one knew what to do with. I clapped my hands. "Okay. So I'm over it." He jerked his gaze toward me, but I ignored him. "The window will be fine, and the storm's moving through."

The hail had stopped, and the rain was a steady fall but not a downpour like earlier.

"We need to cover it, or you'll get birds or bats in here." He spoke almost clinically.

"I don't know what we have for bats, but the birds can be little assholes. Kingbirds used to chase me when I mowed between our tree rows. I'll run to town and see if Lyric's mom has some cardboard at the store I can use until I can get some plywood." I chattered when I was nervous, but I was grateful to have something besides the kiss to figure out.

"Who?"

"My best friend. And sister-in-law. Her mom owns the thrift store in town." I started for the door. I was in danger of rambling, and I needed time to gather my thoughts. To nurse my hurt feelings before I came off as an immature little princess. "I can handle it. You can go."

"I have some cardboard and duct tape in the back seat of the pickup. I'll take care of it. Go home and . . . get warmed up." His awkwardness was another knife wound in my ego.

"Thanks. Yup. You too." I took the out he gave me. Without looking at him, I pushed through the door.

The rain pelting my face was a nice wake-up. What was I thinking? I shouldn't have let him try to warm me. I should've been strong enough to push away instead of being so damn needy.

I could control my physical desire. It wasn't like I'd done more than superficial dating since I'd moved back to Coal Haven, but the emotional emptiness, the yearning to be someone's person, was hard to deny.

So I wouldn't try. I'd have to get it through my head and douse the fire in my body. I might want to find someone who got me, who wasn't stuck with me, but it wouldn't be McCoy Cunningham.

He'd made that clear.

MCCOY

Two days after the make-out session that made closing my eyes a nightmare—an erotic one I didn't want to wake from —I was leaning against the front of my pickup, facing Reservoir Barrel. I had the phone to my ear and my eyes squeezed shut.

"Mom, you don't have to come down. It's fine." Then she wouldn't sense the coolness and distance between me and Isla. Two days of being ignored. Nothing but curt messages updating me on when she'd be mowing again and giving contacts to the city offices I'd need to meet with.

There was no reason she had to accompany me to any of the meetings I had yet to set up, but I wanted her there. She knew the town. She had more charm than me. I didn't ooze sunshine like her. People either didn't have a problem with me or they never wanted to talk to me again. Coal Haven was too small for me to find another contact.

The urge to do this place right and make it better than

Isla's dream had nothing to do with wanting to make her dreams possible. With wanting to hear that little moan she made when I stroked my tongue along hers—

"Lorraine and Halle are delayed," Mom continued, "and I know Isla's going to be disappointed. I want to personally check in with her after you talk to her about a change order."

"But I'm here."

"McCoy, don't take this the wrong way, but you weren't the most charming person before Hannah ripped through your life like a Category 5."

I used to think the way my ex bulldozed through my life was part of the attraction. She was a go-getter; she knew what she wanted. Too bad she'd wanted everything that was mine.

"Mom—"

"My travel plans are final. I talked to Karla at the motel and have a room."

"It's not what you're used to."

She tsked. "Don't think I've gone soft in my old age. The success of the company doesn't mean I forgot how I used to live."

The first part of my life had been a lot more like the motel. Small, without many amenities. My stepfather had a stable job and more money than Dad had, and Mom had used the opportunity to open her own business. And she'd killed it. The years of TV dinners with a cold middle because our microwave was as shitty as the rest of the appliances were behind her. Meanwhile, I'd come full circle.

And I knew better than to argue with Mom when her mind was made up. This trip wasn't about kissing up to a client after the project hit a snag. She liked Isla, and she wanted to meet her in person.

"When are you coming?" I asked.

"I'll be there on Monday."

"I'll let her know." I hung up and watched the big fluffy clouds float by. The crew's delay and Mom's visit gave me an excuse to contact Isla. I'd have more to say than, *Do you hate me now?* Or, *Wasn't that kiss fucking amazing?*

I called her and it rang. I hung up before I got her cheery voice mail—again.

There wasn't much more I could do here. I hopped in my truck and drove back to the motel. In the room, I stared at my laptop full of businesses and subcontractors we could work with. I'd used the printer in the front office so I wouldn't have to crouch over the screen with Isla to discuss who we'd get bids from after Lorraine and Halle told us what we'd need.

I tried Isla again. No answer.

Fuck. Was she ignoring me? I wouldn't blame her. A girl probably didn't like being told that kissing her was a big fucking mistake, but I'd never been smooth around women. I hadn't needed to be. I hadn't wanted to be. That was why I thought Hannah was the answer to stop the endless cycle of empty dates. She'd put up with my quiet moods and my lack of interest in anything outside of construction and brewing. It'd been because she was self-centered, but I hadn't known that then.

Didn't explain why I wanted to talk to Isla. Why I wanted to see her face light up. How I hung on the expressions that flitted through her bright eyes. She was an open book I'd never tire of reading.

Fuck it. I'd find her.

I was out the door before I realized I had no goddamn clue where to look. Movement in the front office caught my eye, and an idea formed. Perfect.

I strode through the entrance. Karla glanced up and smiled. "How's it going today, McCoy?"

"Good. Listen, I hate to ask, but I need to talk to Isla about some changes to the schedule. She's not answering, and it's not an emergency, but I thought I could stop by."

"You need directions to her parents' place?"

Time to abuse small-town helpfulness. "Actually, she's staying at her brother's cabin. What are the chances you know where that is?"

Twenty minutes later, I was turning off the highway and onto a dirt road that led to the cabin Karla had given me directions to. I'd also been told how far away the cabin Isla's parents owned was from Isla's brother's, and how often it was lent out to family friends, and who owned the neighboring properties around Lake Sakakawea.

The roof of the place rose above the leafy trees and an expanse of blue water was the backdrop. Short bluffs making up the shore on the other side were visible. I turned into the drive and was met with a line of cars. People milled closer to the water.

Shit. She had company. The thought hadn't crossed my mind. I lost track of days, barely registering it was the weekend only because city offices were closed.

How bad would it look if I backed the hell out? I didn't sign up for socializing, and while the meet and greet with Liam and his family was interesting and, dare I admit—enjoyable—I wasn't an expected guest. I wouldn't acknowledge the part of me that was rubbed raw by the lack of an invite that I would have no business getting.

Isla's blonde hair glinted in the sunlight as she walked out of the cabin with a drink in her hand. A light blue glazed the edges of her long strands. I nearly rear-ended another pickup staring at her.

Christ, she was in a bikini. Shiny like it was made of mother-of-pearl, a little triangle covered each tit, leaving a swath of bare abdomen before the string of the tiny little bottoms started.

I parked in the lineup of vehicles and got out with the papers I had printed. *Don't stare. Don't fucking stare.* I couldn't sport an erection in broad daylight after that kiss. But keeping my gaze off her was an impossible task as she walked toward me.

"McCoy. Is everything okay?"

"Yeah, uh," I said, scratching the back of my neck, my voice cracking like a teen's. "This can wait. I didn't realize you had company."

"It's only Stetson and Lyric, and my cousin Nora was able to stop by." She didn't ask how I knew where to find her. She was probably used to everyone knowing where she could be. "Should we go inside?"

I glanced toward the shore. A big man with a baby on his chest sat in a camp chair and watched me from a dock. Two women in bathing suits were chatting as they waded in knee-deep water. "I don't want to interrupt."

"No worries. You're here. Might as well tell me what you need to." Her tone was cautious. Was she afraid I was putting in my notice?

I wouldn't let Mom down like that. Her faith in me had gotten me back into the game of life more often than not. It was she and Fergus who'd shown me I was more than a guy who could pound a nail. He was gone, but the need to make him proud didn't die with him.

Before I could reject her offer again, she asked, "Want a beer? Nora brought back some Spotted Cow from a trip to Wisconsin."

Shit, I liked Spotted Cow, and I rarely got to have it. "Sure."

Her smile was sunny, making it easier to keep my eyes above the delectable dip her belly button made. "Come on in." She turned toward the others and called, "Hey! I'm gonna be inside talking to McCoy for a minute."

They waved. I waved. Nice and uncomfortable. I followed Isla in and stared at the slope of her butt the whole way, hoping her brother was too far away to see me.

She waved to a stool at the island. My boots hit heavy on the wooden floor and I sat, taking a moment to study my surroundings. Log walls and wood interior. Making it easy to care for. The AC I had asked about the other day pumped from a small window unit, and a dormant fireplace took up the middle of the main room.

Sliding a beer in front of me, she pulled a stool around to the other side of the island so she was sitting in the kitchen while I was technically in the main room. "What's up?" She shivered and my gaze caught on the goose bumps dotting her skin. "Hold on."

She disappeared into the lone bedroom for a few moments. I didn't mean to look over and catch her shrugging into a T-shirt or bending over to step into a pair of beige linen shorts. Before she turned around, I was studying the top of the island. I couldn't fault her for not wanting to be cold around me again. I'd fucked the last time up.

When she returned and sat, I said, "I wanted to go over the different subcontractors we can get bids from, but we can wait until you don't have company. I tried calling first." As if that'd make up for me crashing a family gathering.

What were those like?

She pushed her hair back. "It was an impromptu lake day. I feel bad taking up their cabin in the summer." She reached to the edge of the counter where it connected to the wall and tapped on her phone. "I left it inside."

I started in on work before my body got any ideas about the coconut hint to her berries-and-cream scent. Did she have sunblock on? Was it the spray or did she rub it in on the exposed satiny skin—*fuck*.

I cleared my throat. "Sylvia called. There's some bad news—Lorraine and Halle are delayed. There have been some problems finishing the last project. I can still do the footwork to get the federal brewing permit, your state liquor license, and the brewer's bond. I can also start at the city offices about local permits and licenses and meet with the wastewater contact."

"Okay, but how delayed?"

This was why I wanted to tell her in person. "Two months."

Her mouth formed an *O*. She took a drink, dismay in her eyes. The wrinkle in her brow didn't leave. She didn't like the news and seeing her struggle to remain nonplussed left me feeling like shit. Two months could be an eternity when you were building your dream. "Okay. I mean, it's not like I had a hard date for the grand opening, and we have plenty of other things to do."

I nodded, striving to be as professionally aloof as her. Construction often came with delays, and we were working in two parts—the restoration and the brewery. But the longer it took, the longer the wait to be profitable. An empty building didn't make money, and Isla was putting everything into it. Sure, she had a place to land if things went to shit, but I knew from experience it wasn't the easiest hit to recover from.

But there was nothing to be done. Time for the next part. "I'll also get a change order ready for us to sign, and Sylvia is planning to visit. She's arriving in a couple of days."

A smile spread across her face, and delight lit her eyes. "Really? That's awesome. I can't wait to meet her."

Pleased more than I expected to be, I opened my beer

and took a long pull. Why did I like her excitement about seeing my mom so much? "She's staying at the motel."

Her smile fell. "Oh. I mean, it's nice enough, but it's probably not what she's used to."

I'd had the same worries, but Mom had reminded me of too much I tried to forget. "You'd be surprised."

Her brows lifted like she was waiting for me to continue. Wouldn't happen.

Yet, I spoke anyway. "She's built McDaniel Contractors up, but the company wasn't really lucrative until ten years ago."

"So the motel won't be too much of a downgrade?"

"No. As long as it's zero entry." At Isla's quizzical look, I clarified. "She uses a cane. An old car accident."

The reason Dad left. Through sickness and health only pertained to him. When it had come to Mom, he was gone.

"Oh, I had no idea. I'm sorry. Will she be able to get around the foundry?"

"Reservoir Barrel? Everyone's going to call it the foundry if you do. Gotta start the branding now."

A smile played over her lips. "The Foundry has a nice ring, but yes, Reservoir Barrel."

"She'll be fine."

Isla pulled out the list I'd printed, and I stole a few moments for a forbidden hobby I was quickly becoming addicted to. The spark of yellow in her eyes gave me a glimpse into her opinions on contractors she recognized. We'd discuss all of them, and I couldn't wait to see if she got as animated about businesses as she did beer. I let my gaze wander over her face and the pop of color in her hair. Subtle but cheery, like her. Sunshine in a flawless blue sky.

For once, I didn't want to talk about work. "Blue?"

"Hmm?" She squinted at the printouts like she was looking for the color in the black ink.

"Your hair."

Laughing, she pushed the papers away and grabbed the ends of her hair. She let the strands slide through her fingers. The color wasn't blocky but done in streaks, so it didn't take over. "Lyric came over last night and helped me before she had to get home to feed Rina. I finished the rest. I had my hair colored once before, but . . ." She grimaced and took a drink. "My mom demanded I go back to my natural color. 'No one takes a woman seriously with purple hair.'"

Probably too often true. "It's just hair dye."

"Yes, but it's also a sign I think for myself, and for some reason, that makes me a danger to myself in her eyes."

Her family dynamics weren't unlike what I'd had with my dad. A controlling parent morphed in many ways. "Why would that be dangerous?"

"I don't know. I'm not like my mother. She's hard, and I think she thinks that since I'm not like her, I need her to run my life. Same with my dad. But I refuse to believe I have to be a bitch to get things done."

I'd also seen Mom get walked over by being compliant. "Mom would say that women get labeled as bitchy whereas a guy would be called a good businessman."

Her smile was delighted. "You said 'Mom.'"

"We're not talking about work."

"Well, my mother would agree. And the last thing I want to do is call my mom a bitch. She's tough, but she can also be insensitive and blunt to a fault in order to get her way. And your mom's right. My dad is exactly the same, and he's a CEO."

The door opened, and a blast of hot air swirled in. One of the two women from the water came in holding the baby. I figured she must be Lyric. "We're going to head out. Rina's afternoon nap is coming up, and I think she'd sleep better in a crib."

Stetson stepped into the house behind his wife and blocked the doorway. "And that means we get two or three hours to ourselves."

"Oh, god, don't traumatize me," Isla joked.

The other girl, who I decided must be Nora, nudged Stetson aside to enter.

Isla swept her hand toward me. "You guys haven't met McCoy yet."

Stetson lifted his chin as a quick greeting. "Liam told me you two were by his place. You're going to work with him?"

"He's going to think about it. He's worried about the scope of what I'm asking," Isla said. Her tone was neutral, but her fingers were twined together. She was nervous about Liam's answer. Working with family could get like that. She didn't have the emotional callouses I'd built up from working with my dad.

"His work is so good," Nora said. "But I can't imagine him having time to take special orders with his work and kids."

Stetson nodded. "It won't be personal if he passes on the opportunity." His gaze flicked to McCoy. "Everything all right?"

"Yeah, except there's a delay," Isla said lightly. "But there's still stuff to do."

"I can't wait to see it all when it's done." Nora arched her hand in a wide wave. "I'm going to leave too. Thanks for inviting me over. I needed a lake break."

She left, and Stetson and Lyric followed.

"I didn't mean to scare everyone away." I should've waited. What the hell had I rushed out here for? Being alone with Isla wasn't a good decision, yet my ass stayed rooted to the stool.

She smiled. "It's not you. Late-night parties aren't really happening like they used to. A lot of naps and early bedtimes these days. My cousin Holden went from having no kids to having five."

Stetson looked younger than me. Holden likely was too. I was supposed to be those guys. Wife. Kids. Thriving business. Instead I was living in a motel room and using my weekends to work.

Isla was young. She should have a life. "The contractors would be better to go over when you have time to really concentrate on them." I pushed away. "I won't take up more of your time."

"I went on a craft beer run yesterday," she blurted. Her cheeks flushed. "I have a fridge full of flavors and brands to sample. Want to join? It's not like I can drink much of each one or I'll be a mess. And . . ." Her brow furrowed, and she peered toward her bedroom like she could see around corners. "I had to dispose of what was fermenting when I moved out, but I have a case that's finished if, um, if you'd like to try it."

She was nervous, and she didn't have an accurate idea of how experienced I really was. Making and selling beer had been my livelihood, and I'd been good at it. Excellent even. Yet I couldn't summon an ounce of interest in it again for myself.

When she'd stopped by the motel, I'd thought about how long it'd been since I enjoyed others' art in the beer world. I had no stakes anymore, and maybe I could admit that I didn't miss the actual brewing like I thought I would. Her offer might've been enough to make me stay, but the chance to sample her own brew clinched it. "Show me what you got."

Her radiant smile told me I'd made the wrong decision, but I couldn't take it back.

* * *

Isla

I sipped from a can of pilsner, letting the flavor sit on my tongue. It was dark out. Before we'd started drinking, I'd asked McCoy if he'd had anything to eat. We had to take care of a meal first.

I'd fired up the grill, and he'd taken over, a trait I was used to and honestly didn't mind. Stetson usually grilled, and I had a penchant for burning burgers and making hot dogs crispy.

After we ate and chatted about the lake area and everything he'd heard about my family's cabins, we took out a couple of the craft beers I'd bought, and we took our time with those. Nursing them, looking up details about the company, and for one, he'd admitted he'd helped install the brewing equipment. McDaniel Contractors had built the place.

I liked learning about him, and now that I was a few drinks in, I finally asked, "Why brewing?"

His throat worked as he swallowed, and I envisioned putting my hand on it and feeling those strong muscles work up and down. "I like beer and construction."

"Did your mom do both? Professionally or for a hobby?"

He shook his head and smacked his lips. Staring at his glass, he said, "Caramel. You can taste it under the honey."

"Honey?" I took a long drink from the can. We'd been splitting the cans and bottles and taking our time. "Mm. Caramel, yes. I don't get the honey."

"My dad." He twirled the glass on the Rattler's coaster I'd set down. "He owned a construction company. Mom did the books. She didn't get into beer until she married my stepdad, Fergus."

"And you?"

"Same. I was older when she remarried, and as much as I wanted to hate him, Fergus wasn't a demeaning asshole like my dad."

I winced, but his admission gave me a lot of insight into him. "Sorry." He shrugged and I was afraid he'd close in on himself. "My dad is a demeaning asshole, but not usually to me. He coddles me—too much. He demeans everyone else. But, like, really skillfully."

"Not my dad. He had no tact, and he built himself up by tearing others down." The add-on of *especially for me and Mom* was unspoken but loud and clear. "Fergus was so excited about tasting his finished beer with me. Then he invested in a brewery and beer hall in Denver, and he and Mom went all the time and the rest is history."

"Is he why you wanted to build your own brewery?"

"Yep." He went to take a drink and shook his glass. Empty. He got up and crossed to the fridge, and I stared at his ass like it was going to tell me my future. His jeans hugged his butt and powerful thighs, letting me see the bunch of his muscles as he bent.

"How about a lager?" He turned with the can in his hand, and I barely got my gaze off his backside in time.

"Ooh, I've had that one before. It's good, but I want to hear what you think."

"Details?" He sat and cracked the can open, emptying half into his glass, then pushing the rest toward me.

I finished off the pilsner while bringing up the web page for where the beer was made. "Italian malt and dry hop." I leaned forward and said in a dramatic whisper, "Creamy foam head."

He sputtered into the glass. "Jesus, Isla."

I giggled and drained the can in a few gulps. My inhibitions were dropping by the second. "Sorry. Was that a mistake?" I asked in too innocent of a voice.

His jaw clenched, and my fingers itched to find out how hard those muscles were. "Isla . . ."

I shook my head and rose to grab another beer. Should I slow down? Yes. Did I want to? No. "Mango pineapple sour." The tartness would force me to slow, and I wasn't having the lager to keep from getting sloppy. I grabbed a fresh glass for him, and when I spun back to the island, his brooding gaze was on me.

"We should talk about the other day."

"You made your feelings loud and clear." I slowly rotated the can to mix the contents and forget about how he called it a mistake. "I get it."

"I said it was a mistake. Not that I didn't like it."

Oh. I wasn't expecting that. Delight swirled in my belly, but it didn't matter. "But we're like . . . coworkers."

"I don't want to fuck this job up, but it's not that." He drained the lager faster than I'd ever finished a drink. "That's good stuff." He took the can from my hand and opened it, pouring himself more than me.

"Are you afraid I'm going to get drunk?"

"Maybe."

"I don't have to drive anywhere. But you're different." I tipped my head toward the futon behind him. "You can always crash here."

"That would just add to my bad decisions, sunbeam."

A giggle burst out of me. I thought I had imagined it the first time he said it. "Sunbeam?"

"You're always sunny—and the swimsuit you're wearing is the color of a sunrise. Don't think I can forget it," he growled.

It was like my shirt and shorts burned off. This was my favorite swimsuit. I wore it when I wanted to minimize my tan lines, and since there'd only been a few people here today, I had thought it was a good choice.

"Then why did you kiss me?" I took a drink and let the sour pucker my lips until the sweet mango pineapple sank in.

"You were close, and I was weak."

He spoke plainly. Was he purposely keeping emotion out of it, or was it that simple—he felt like a kiss, and I was there? I kept drinking, mostly to have something to do. "Okay, but like, you almost threw me across the room. What was that about?"

"I didn't hurt you, did I?"

"It was more like you nearly threw yourself across the room," I amended.

He stared into his light-orange drink. He hadn't tried it. "My divorce was final a few months ago, but we've been separated for over a year. I'm not . . . I'm not looking for anything."

"Neither am I." I'd never been married and therefore had never divorced, but I gathered he didn't want more complications he thought women were responsible for.

He surprised me with a chuckle. "Isla, you're looking for a lot, but you don't know it."

My defensiveness rose. Everyone knew better than me. "What does that mean?"

"Nothing." He glowered into the liquid in his glass.

I yanked the sour away from him and drained it, forcing through the tart hit. I smacked my lips. "It meant something."

The room was starting to spin, and I had most of my share of sour left.

He took the can from me and guzzled it. "You're young. You're hungry. You want to prove yourself. And . . . you want someone. I'm not that guy."

I scowled and pushed off my stool to get another can, never mind how he stripped me bare with his description. "I'm not looking for a relationship."

"Isla, I think you've had enough."

I opened the fridge and let my head fall back, hanging on to my balance so I didn't stagger in front of him. "Ugh, I just moved out of my parents' house. I'm sick of being told what to do. You want to tell me what to think next?" I grabbed a can, any can.

"No, you do just fine there."

I flopped on the stool, a bout of dizziness hitting me. I squinted at the can I'd grabbed from the fridge. "Hard cider. Anyway"—I popped the top—"I'm not looking for a ring or whatever guys are afraid of."

"We're afraid of a lot." He watched me pour half the cider into his first glass. "Especially bright, ambitious, sexy women who can take everything we've worked for without notice."

I paused. He'd lost everything in his divorce, including his business. He was afraid I'd do the same.

Before I could get offended, he said, "I don't have anything but this job. Mom's had my back all my life. I'm not fucking it up."

I couldn't blame him. I constantly let my parents down whether I did anything or not. I'd love to make them proud, just once. "I don't have anything but Reservoir Barrel, so consider me cautious."

"Rumor has it you have oil money. Is it all pumping into Reservoir Barrel?"

Versus investors having a say over what I did and how I operated? Absolutely. "My grandparents left me a trust. A lot of damn money. I need to use it to find a place to live, and whatever's left after this restoration and construction is what I have to live on until the place is making money. If I fail, then what? Let's see, my résumé will have the farmers' market my parents set up for me—and that Dad takes over whenever he fucking feels like it. And then I'd get to add a failed—expensive as hell—business. Will I ever be out on the streets?" I gestured to the cabin around us. "I have family to fall back on, but it's not as if I want to mess around with my project manager and risk losing time or money—or respect."

I sighed and pounded the cider. Only half a can was left and the alcohol was beginning to hit me hard. "Light body, apple blossom finish, and no cough syrup aftertaste. Not bad."

Tension was easing out of the room. Had he been more worried he'd offended me when he said the kiss was a mistake? Or was he worried he'd fall for me and I'd hold my hand out with my ring finger waggling? After living under my parents' rule, I was not interested in settling down.

Did I think McCoy would be good in bed? Oh, hell yes. I'd love to know—but it'd complicate things. I didn't like complicated. I wanted straightforward. I wasn't looking for easy or free.

"I thought you said you had your own brew ready to try." His change of subject sent a shot of adrenaline through my veins. I hadn't thought through who he was when I told him about my batch.

I'd put two and two together from what I'd read about the beer world. Craft beer industry sweetheart Hannah Cunningham and her brewery in Nashville—no mention of McCoy, but the coincidences piled too high. The brewery was named after the owner's construction background. Recipes from the owner's family. A vaguely referenced divorce that left McCoy's name out but made Hannah look like the hero of the beer world.

If McCoy was telling the truth, then her accomplishments were actually his. She'd been a finalist in the largest beer festival in the world. Her IPA—or was it his?—was an award winner. Craft beer publications and social media loved the dark-haired, waifish beauty with a smile as bubbly as the beer she took to festivals. If she was the face and he'd been the talent? My stuff would taste like hoppy water.

I didn't want him within a mile of my home brew. "We don't have to tonight."

His gaze was steady. "Go get it."

I wanted to make barrels of beer and sell it. If I couldn't uncap a bottle for McCoy, how would I open my own place? Resigned, I took an amber bottle out of the fridge. I set it on the island and grabbed a few fresh glasses. When I turned, he had it up to the light, inspecting the sedimentation at the bottom.

He didn't wait for me. Using the bottle opener, he popped the top and took a deep inhale.

"It's an ale. I've been working on this recipe since I first started. I want to perfect the vanilla and cardamom blend, so it's like a treat but not too sweet."

He poured the beer into the fresh glasses. I left mine untouched, barely able to draw a breath as he smelled his cup and then raised it to his lips. He kept his gaze on me as he took a drink and let it sit on his tongue.

I wanted to shout at him, *What do you think?*

His jaw worked. He swallowed and his eyes got a faraway look. "Christ, Isla. That's really good."

Euphoria swept through me. "Seriously?"

"You need to name it. Did you take notes? Exactly what you did so you can scale up?"

I nodded, the ends of my blue-tipped hair flying in the periphery of my vision. "You really think it's that good? I mean, you've won awards." His expression shuttered so quickly I panicked. "I-if that was your beer. Unless she did some, I mean—" God, I was making it worse.

"It was mine," he said quietly, setting the glass down. "I can assume you've studied her during your research? Another female brewer in the industry?"

I nodded, a sense that I'd intruded tightening my chest.

His lips thinned. "I couldn't be bothered with the festivals and the awards, but Hannah thrived on it. Said it was good for business."

"I'm sure it was, but it certainly made her the face of Nailer's Brewery." At the time I was poring over everything Nailer's, I thought I was trying to learn from Hannah Cunningham. I'd been encouraged and enamored by another woman breaking into the scene. The betrayal curling through me had to be nothing like what he experienced.

He rolled his lips in like he was still tasting my beer. "You've been looking me up."

"I knew of her before you. I just thought . . . what everyone thinks, I guess."

"That it was all her?" When I nodded, he took another drink, but he didn't down the glass. He drank like he wanted to savor it. "I taught her everything, and some of the products we distributed were hers. But not the ones she took to festivals. She went on behalf of Nailer's and let everyone think she'd been the brain behind the product."

He'd shared more of himself than I ever thought he would. How many others knew the truth? As tight-lipped as he was, I doubted there were more than me, his mom, and his ex.

Since he was growing more morose as we talked, I changed the subject. "How do you think it'd be with cinnamon instead?"

"Try it, but I think you made the right call with cardamom." He lifted his chin to the fridge. "You got any more?"

Seven

MCCOY

I blinked at the obnoxious sun assaulting me. Squinting, I looked around the room. Where was I? It'd been too common of an occurrence to wake up in a strange place since shit went south with Hannah. Motel rooms blended into hotel rooms and the occasional buddy's couch. But I was in a cabin and had little idea why.

I rolled to a sitting position. The hard frame of the futon dug into my ass. I smacked my lips together, the light flavor of vanilla and hops still strong on my tongue.

Sun filtered through the cabin, and I took a moment to let the heat combat the chill of the whirring AC. How the hell had I ended up in Isla's cabin all night?

Empty cans were scattered on top of the island. The glasses I'd used for tasting were sitting by the sink, but that was the extent of the cleanup we'd done.

I hadn't thought I was that bad off last night until I'd stood. Working around alcohol had made me both cautious of imbibing but aware of how much affected me and how hard. When I was working around booze all day, making it, sampling it, shipping it, I didn't drink for enjoyment. I puzzled out the flavors, determining what caused undertones like oak or marshmallow, but it was mostly sipping.

I rubbed a hand down my face. A slight headache tapped at my temples, but it was likely due to lack of water more than anything.

I rose and rolled my neck and shoulders. Couch surfing wasn't a sport I cared to participate in at my age but seemed to do a lot of lately. In the kitchen, I found another clean glass and downed a few cups of water. There was a small dishwasher. Opening it, I saw it was empty and quietly loaded the dishes from dinner and our tasting, not wanting to create a heavier pound at my temples or wake Isla.

I did a quick wash of her amber bottles, and there were a few more empty than I'd thought. But, damn, her beer had been good. I'd been irritated, but once she showed me her notes, I could see how hard she worked. Her passion. And it'd been hard to ignore the way she lit from the inside out— so I'd had another beer until driving was a bad idea.

A little closet was around the corner from the kitchen. I found the garbage and another bin for recycling. After the counters were clear, I went to the bathroom. The door to Isla's bedroom was closed. She'd need more time to sleep off what she'd drunk.

While I raided her toothpaste, I squinted into the mirror. My hair hung in chunks over my forehead, and a section I must've slept on stuck up in the back. I wasn't a vain guy, but if I couldn't sneak out before Isla woke up, she'd see me in all my rumpled glory. She'd already seen me rude and sulky. I had a little pride.

Giving up, I found a towel and washcloth. After

undressing, I stepped into the shower and let the cold blast my face.

I needed that.

I turned my back to the spray, waiting for the water to warm. The rest of the small square bathroom was visible through the plexiglass. The water heated and became my worst nightmare, kicking up Isla's berries-and-cream scent. When I squirted a dollop of shampoo on my hand, I realized where the scent came from.

I rubbed the shampoo into my hair, and my traitorous mind imagined her naked in the shower. It shouldn't be so easy to envision the sight, but after the revealing swimsuit, I couldn't keep the fantasy from forming. I had wanted to run my tongue over her tan lines, and I'd seen them up close. The urge was stronger.

Letting the spray wash the shampoo out, I reached for the body wash. I had to scrub away the image. Blood was rushing toward my dick like it was late for a midmorning jack-off session in someone else's bathroom. No. No fucking way. The dark privacy of my motel bathroom was bad enough. I wasn't stroking myself to fantasies of Isla in her own fucking bathroom after I told her there was no chance of anything happening between us.

As suds washed down my chest and caressed my ball sac, I groaned. The soft, soapy foam combined with her smell was a special form of erotic torture. The view of her long, golden legs with a gently swaying behind dominated my memories.

Why the fuck had I come here yesterday? How long would I have to stay in the bathroom to get this damn erection to go away?

I bit back another groan and let the water pummel me. I flipped the lever to cold and waited for sweet relief. Unfortunately, my dick was stubborn, like it had a censor for the too-young-for-me girl in the other room.

What should I do?

I squinted down at the obnoxious fucker. Standing tall and proud, beating in rhythm to the pounding water, it wasn't going away.

Letting out a heavy sigh, hoping I didn't waste a shit ton of water, I wrapped my hand around my shaft. The soap had been washed away. My skin wasn't slippery. If I stroked myself like this, I'd chafe in the worst way, but I didn't care. I needed my erection gone. Using Isla's body wash would be expedient but wrong. I'd have nothing but her in my head, as good as if she was in the shower with me.

I pumped, bracing my feet so I could get the job done as efficiently as possible. The triangles of her bikini hammered at my brain. I was a creep. An old fucking douche who couldn't think dignified thoughts of a young woman in the confines of his brain and this small bathroom. I could barely treat her decently in person because of how she affected me.

Another stroke, a tightening of my fist. Yeah, this wouldn't take long.

The door burst open, and Isla's shocked, wide eyes landed on me half a heartbeat before they dropped to the hard-as-a-rock dick in my hand.

"Fuck," sputtered out of my mouth, and I ripped my hand away, sticking my hands in the air like I was in a holdup.

Her hair was a tousled halo around her head, and she was in the same clothing from last night, like she'd just collapsed onto the bed and passed out. Her gaze didn't fly to mine but stuck on my erection like it was a special rock formation and she was a world-renowned geologist. Then she squeaked, her stunned eyes flying to mine.

"Sorry!" She backed out the door and slammed it shut.

"My fucking god." I heaved out a breath and flipped the water off. Blood started reorienting. Apparently, humiliation was effective at making my privates behave.

I toweled off as quickly as possible, giving my flagging erection a wide berth in case a single touch reignited it. Dressing, I cursed myself for my stupidity. I should've left. I should've gone to the motel to shower and clean up. She'd have woken to an empty cabin and a pervert-free shower.

Heaving out a gusty breath, I faced the door. Time to find out what my mom's client thought of her project manager stroking one out in her shower.

* * *

Isla

My face couldn't burn any hotter. I could be roasting a marshmallow from within a firepit and I wouldn't be as singed. I was embarrassed, and oh my god, I was turned on.

The pounding at my temples had ceased as soon as I'd charged in on a vision I'd never witnessed before. Seeing McCoy with his hand around his cock only proved I'd been with boys, college guys whose skills hadn't caught up with their egos. Then there were a few brewery guys who were my age and good enough in bed, but not . . . not that . . .

McCoy had big hands, and it'd been a handful. And the body?

I finished gulping my water and set the glass on the cleared counter, my mind barely registering that he must've picked up the kitchen, and how considerate was that? Instead, my brain was locked on rippled abs. Strong legs that had been straining as hard as his . . . Well. McCoy

Cunningham had a nice body, and that was an understatement.

Pushing my hair out of my face, I leaned against the counter and crossed my legs. I had to pee so damn bad. I needed fresh clothing, but I also wanted to clean up first.

Did I have pillow wrinkles on my cheek?

As if that was the main concern of the morning.

The bathroom door opened. I leaped to the fridge with no plan for what I was looking for. I spotted the individually wrapped meat and cheese containers I'd bought a few days ago. I withdrew from the fridge holding the snacks and a jug of orange juice.

McCoy stopped at the end of the short hallway. His wet hair was pushed back. The planes of his face were concrete, but a brush of pink touched his cheeks. Was he blushing?

"So. Sorry about that." His voice was a raspy rumble.

"Yeah, no. Sorry about barging in. I don't usually keep the door shut and I should've known, but I'm not used to having anyone over." I'd lived with my parents until a week ago, and now I'd had a naked project manager in my shower.

"It was a . . . I didn't want to . . . You know. It's the normal morning shit guys have to deal with."

Oh. Embarrassment stung. Was I expecting him to be hard for me? He'd told me he couldn't be interested last night and that we wouldn't work.

"Anyway," he continued, oblivious to the way he'd devastated me trying to explain the situation. "It was rude, and I should get going."

I couldn't blame him for wanting to flee, but the disappointment his words caused was strong. So was the incessant warning of my bladder. I dumped the food I was holding on the island. "I've gotta pee."

I would've bumped into him in my rush to the bathroom, but he jumped to the side like I had some deadly, contagious skin condition. In the bathroom, I buried my face in my hands. After I was done on the toilet, I shoved my hair out of my face. I might as well shower. He had likely burst out of the cabin and run home, forgetting his work truck.

No, he wouldn't want to come back. He and the truck were probably gone.

I stripped and got into the shower. The tile was unusually cool, but then I recalled his need for cold water and got humiliated all over again. *It's the normal morning shit guys have to deal with.*

Nothing to do with me. And why should it? I got too tipsy while sampling beer for a career I wanted to start, and I had no experience other than dabbling at home and going out to drink beer in the name of research.

He'd had his own place that he built from scratch. Beer that he made and sold and won awards for.

I flipped the water off and squeezed out my hair. His ex was a popular and well-respected brewer. Her Nashville restaurant and brewery was listed as one of the must-visit places in the city. I'd read so many articles touting the quality of her products.

Had it really all been McCoy? Or did he think he was the victim when she did all the work? I didn't get that impression, but I also didn't know much more of him than I knew of Hannah.

Still, when I thought back to all the articles I'd read, Hannah's descriptions had been vague. Her comments lacked specificity, like the person presenting a team project in school that assumed all the responsibility as if they'd done all the work and the rest of the team was left unrecognized. Family recipes that were most likely McCoy's step-dad's. Construction background that was most likely McCoy. Fond memories of home brewing in a basement could've been hers or had come straight from McCoy's experiences.

I got out of the shower and twisted my hair in a towel. I grabbed a bath sheet to wrap around myself. Stepping into the hallway, I stopped. The cabin was quiet, but the sense I wasn't alone seeped in.

To my right, McCoy was sitting on a stool at the island, blinking at me.

I jumped, barking out a yell. "I thought you left!"

He rose, adopting the same pose he had after I'd busted him in the shower. "Shit, I did it again. I didn't mean to. I just wanted to stick around long enough to make sure you were okay, that we were cool."

I clutched the spot where the towel flap was anchored between my breasts. I'd seen him naked. I was mostly covered. Seemed like I got the better end of the bargain. My laughter came out nervous, not nonchalant. "Um, no, it's fine. Let me get dressed. Help yourself to whatever's in the fridge."

"You hungry?"

When I peered over my shoulder on my way to the bedroom, he wasn't looking at me. Had I imagined him asking? His hands were shoved in the pockets of his jeans, and he was staring at the top of the counter.

"Yeah. I might make some eggs before I go."

I pushed into my room, closed the door, and leaned against the cool wood. Rolling my eyes to the ceiling, I marveled over the weirdness of the day, and it had just begun. At least I wasn't naked. Before I dropped the towel, I made sure the door was indeed securely shut. There'd been enough privacy mishaps today.

I dressed in gray shorts with a lace fringe that looked more like a skirt and a blue top with a gauzy white overshirt. Summery with a hint of professional. I had a hard enough time getting taken seriously; I tried to dress the part on Thursdays and Sundays. Market days.

When I rushed into the bathroom to comb out my hair, I didn't see McCoy, but savory scents assaulted my nose. Was . . . Was he still here—and was he cooking?

Twisting my hair into a damp braid because I had more pressing matters to check on—like, was there a sexy man who wasn't interested in me cooking in my kitchen?—I found McCoy at the small cabin stove.

"You're cooking?" I said to his broad back.

"It's the least I can do." His muscles rippled as he pushed eggs around the pan. "I hope you like scrambled."

"All my eggs end up scrambled."

The corner of his mouth was hitched up when he twisted to grab the meat and cheese package. He dumped the contents into the pan. "I got pretty good at them when . . ."

I waited, but he didn't continue. Frustrated with the figurative doors he kept shutting in my face, I decided to risk stepping in a steaming heap. "Nailer's had a restaurant, too, right?"

He flipped the burner off but continued to push the eggs around. "Yep. Still does."

"That sucks."

"Tell me about it." He finally turned, the pan in one hand and the spatula in the other. "Word from the now wise? Keep everything in your name. Make it your business to know what everyone who works for you is up to. When you marry, don't add anyone to any of your accounts, and for fuck's sake, a prenup is critical if you have a business before you tie the knot."

Solid advice, if spoken bitterly. "My mother would trip me walking down the aisle if I didn't have a prenup. She almost disowned my brother because he refused one."

"Why would he refuse it?"

I shrugged. "He's in love, and Lyric has too much pride to take anything of his. Plus, she brought her own assets to the marriage. It was the way my parents broached the subject that made it controversial."

"You won't be the same?"

"No. My parents gave me a good life, but it was always theirs, and I had to live the life they wanted. Do what they wanted, act how they wanted. But thanks to their lessons, whatever's mine will stay abso-fucking-lutely mine."

"I wish I'd learned that."

I knew I was pushing my luck by being blatantly nosy, but I'd also seen this man naked. I wanted to know more about him. "Was it because of your mom?"

His head jerked up. "What about Mom?"

"You saw how she was treated by your dad, and when you met your ex-wife, you didn't want to be like your dad and instead went in the opposite direction. Only you got taken for everything."

He frowned. "Shit, I never thought of it like that. More like when Mom met Fergus and he helped her with the company until she flourished and I admired him, so I tried to be like him."

Because McCoy was a good guy. "Parents, am I right?"

He snorted and doled out the food on separate plates. "Ain't that the truth?" He set the pan by the sink and rounded the island to what I would always consider his spot. I took the stool I'd been sitting on the previous night.

"Where are you going today?" he asked.

I scooped a forkful of cheesy eggs. "The farmers' market. It starts after lunch, but I try to get there early, and I was messaged this morning about location issues." I took a bite and suppressed a moan. Was this guy good at everything? I could cook whatever I wanted, but he'd leveled up simple scrambled eggs. "Becca Hansen is upset that she's been assigned the spot next to Henrick Spiel again."

The expression on McCoy's face while he chewed asked why that was an issue.

Location, location, location wasn't just important in real estate. I'd learned it was quite critical in the farmers' market world. "Henrick refuses to put his offerings on the far side of his booth away from her and sell his canned goods on the table that borders her table. She's an organic producer, and Henrick, in Becca's words, 'uses so much chemical his rhubarb could be used as glow sticks.'"

McCoy was midchew and his mouth quirked. One of his almost smiles.

I continued with the drama I was sick of. "Of course, she didn't talk to me first. She bitched out Henrick, who honestly must have stock in Miracle-Gro and Roundup. I've seen him soaking his gardens before, and he wasn't using water. And then she went to Dad, who told her, basically, that he didn't care, and she could deal with it or not sell at the market."

"Nice." His lips curved like he could picture the fallout without knowing the people involved.

"Yes, you can imagine how well that went over. I would've moved Henrick or talked to him, but now I have to talk Becca down first and find out how divided all the vendors are over the subject." I stabbed a pile of eggs. "I've had five fewer vendor sign-ups this week than last. We're losing people over it." If the market fails, it would be my responsibility. I'd have failed my parents and the town, and I'd lose what trust I'd built in the community. They wouldn't want to become my customers at Reservoir Barrel.

"What is your solution?"

"To be the opposite of Dad. I'll talk to everyone, kiss some ass, then give Becca the spot she wants while finding a decent area for Henrick since he has a dedicated following that come for just his produce."

"Customers who don't care if their squash glow in the dark?"

"Not when his buttercup squash tastes like it's already buttered. I don't care what he uses, it's amazing."

"Are you going to tell everyone to quit going to your dad?"

Didn't I wish that was all it took. "Not in so many words. I keep reassuring them that if they have any issues, they can come to me."

"Sometimes it takes more than that."

His censuring tone grated on my nerves. I wasn't going to charge in like my mom or dad and demand they treat me like the director. It would have the opposite effect, and then there'd be talk that I was just like Mom.

I loved my mom, but I didn't want to be like her. I didn't want to act like her, and the farmers' market was one way to prove I could do business and be nice. "Sometimes being kind and consistent gets the results I need." Someday it would.

He grunted and continued eating. "It got my ex the entire restaurant."

"What do you mean?"

He glanced up like he couldn't believe he'd said it out loud. "I dealt with everything. I was your dad, I guess. The guy who did the hiring and firing. Everyone would cry to Hannah, and she'd tell them what they wanted to hear. I had to make the tough decisions. And when it all blew up, I was left standing alone. People were Team Hannah, and my side was noticeably empty. That was part of the reason why I sold." He lifted a big shoulder. "I was fair and respectful. But I was the tough one, and it got results. I'm not saying you have to throw your weight around, but sometimes bees have to use stingers to defend their honey."

He had a point, but he also hadn't grown up in Coal Haven hearing my parents dress down people and call it a normal Tuesday.

I put my plate by the sink. "Okay, well, I have some rhubarb to rearrange, so just flip the lock on the doorknob when you leave. I can activate the security from my phone."

He glanced up in all the corners like he was suddenly afraid of being watched.

"The cameras are outside." At the door, I grabbed the tote bag that had all my market papers.

"We still need to go over details of what you want and who we should get bids from."

I could meet him in town, but the table in his motel room was right next to a bed and coming off the heels of seeing him stroking himself, that wouldn't work. We could meet at Rattler's, but they were busy in the afternoons on Sundays when the lake was full. Reservoir Barrel didn't have a table.

My idea was lame and sounded like an excuse for him to stick around. "You can just wait here. Or meet me back when I'm done. I don't care." He was putting his plate next to mine when the next words came out of my mouth before I considered them. "Or you can come with, and we can grab some food and come back to go over them. The market is only a couple of hours."

He paused, brushing his hands off. Why had I invited him? Did I seem desperate? Yes, I liked him in the cabin. I enjoyed last night, and despite the awkward mishaps of the morning, I enjoyed having him around. I had market drama to deal with, but maybe he could witness me getting my way with honey instead of salt.

I thought for sure he'd hard pass when he said, "I can't resist glow-in-the-dark rhubarb."

Eight

MCCOY

Watching Isla work the crowd was like being back in Nashville with a twist. She seemed genuinely kind and like she cared about sorting out people's issues. The big difference was that she didn't want her vendors to go over her head to her dad. She preferred to deal with the conflict herself.

Yet I wasn't sure how effective she was. Becca had launched into her complaints as soon as she spotted Isla. For her part, Isla iterated the market was for all types of growers, but she'd move Henrick. Then she sweet-talked Henrick into a prime booth right off the parking lot. She'd caught him just as he arrived and listened to his complaints of Becca and her bossiness and righteousness about her organic fare. She stressed she was concerned about improving his experience and gave him a corner spot where the highest traffic occurred. Henrick was happy, but when I looked back, Becca was glaring at both Isla and Henrick.

The market was an hour from being done, and I chatted with an older woman who had canned eight different pie fillings and had over ten varieties of syrup.

I couldn't shut my creator brain off when it came to finding out what the local fruit selection was and how they could be incorporated into a product. Fergus loved using local produce for new flavors, and I'd tried to emulate him with lines of products at Nailer's. As much as I wanted to distance myself from the thriving company I'd built, I couldn't carve out my old passion as thoroughly as I wanted. Not after Isla revived a part of it last night.

Was my renewed interest in the beer—or her?

"There's rhubarb, of course." Sonya, the syrup maker, leaned closer, her hands going as fast as she talked. She shot a pointed look at Henrick. "I grow my rhubarb close to the house and out of the wind. It gets full sun and naturally grows as big as Henrick's without getting woody."

I chuckled, knowing she was on Team Becca when it came to Henrick's goods. "Good to know."

"I can get good rhubarb most of the summer from my patches because of how I grow them. And there're the buffalo berries." She tapped her fingers on the lids of a row of orange-red syrup. "They can be hit or miss, depending on rain. Chokecherries are often good. I also have grapevines, blueberry bushes, and currant bushes." She dropped her voice. "Don't tell anyone—I have to use some pest control with those and my wild strawberries. And of course, I have my apple, pear, and plum trees. A few varieties do okay in our zone."

She meant, "don't tell Becca," and I wouldn't. Almost feeling like a local, thanks to her confidence in me, I pulled out my wallet. "I need to try the buffalo berry syrup."

"It's straight," she said as she took my money. "Lots of sugar makes it sweet, but I prefer the hint of bitterness, so I don't add another fruit. This is last year's batch. They ripen in the early fall."

It sounded like something I'd be tempted to add to a sour. Mix it with a sweeter fruit like a strawberry and I could have a signature seasonal line.

Only, I wasn't in that business anymore. Maybe I could bring it up to Isla. By this time next year, she could be planning a seasonal sour or even a shandy, and—

What the hell was I doing? I was the project manager. Nothing more.

Isla was in the middle of the portion of the parking lot that was cordoned off for the market. A woman not much older than her was bobbing her head as she spoke and gestured at various booths. First, I thought she was upset at Henrick and his glow-in-the-dark produce, but then she stuffed a finger in the direction of the pie booth. I was tempted to buy the peach pie. Mom used to make them when school started each year, but once she started McDaniel Contractors, her baking grew infrequent.

With a flat hand, the woman indicated a booth full of handmade aprons, dishcloths, and scrubbies. I wandered closer to Isla, my curiosity too strong to ignore.

The stranger planted her hands on her hips, a sign that it was Isla's turn to talk. I was close enough to listen.

"I understand your frustration, but our community is too small to niche down its farmers' market, so we entertain all types of growers and booths. If the vendor produces the item, they're allowed to sell it here."

"Farmers' markets are supposed to be healthy," the woman said. "There's, like, a hundred pies on that table."

There were ten, with a note that said frozen pies were sold too. Good thing I didn't have a deep freeze. I missed pie.

"And she makes those," Isla said patiently. "What are you looking for? I can pair you up with a vendor—"

"*A* vendor. Maybe one? It's a disgrace."

"We're a small community." Isla's smile was understanding, but she wasn't budging.

"Small and ignorant," the woman huffed.

That would've been the end of my patience. I had no problem kicking insulting people out of my business, but Isla must have her tolerance set at a higher bar.

She dug a small piece of paper out of her tote bag. "How about I give you ten market dollars? That might help offset the frustration of not finding what you're looking for. I'd love to introduce you to Becca. She's one of our organic producers, and she's been at the market since the beginning. If anyone has what you're interested in, she'll know who to send you to if she doesn't have it herself."

The lure of free money was enough for the irate customer to follow Isla to Becca's station. The vendor's penciled brows rose higher than the arc she'd drawn in and it was like her animosity against Isla melted away. Her expression changed from astonished to grateful to recognizing a fellow market lover she could commiserate with. Becca was getting a small boost from the market fund even though she'd tried to go over Isla's head and had glowered at Isla since she'd arrived.

Smart, but only time would tell how effective. I'd still have told the customer she was free to not shop there.

Isla turned and found me watching her. She crossed to me, a pained look on her face I had the strongest urge to caress until it disappeared. "You heard all that?"

"What I didn't hear was clear from her body language."

She chuckled, and we wandered farther from the women who seemed to be sudden fast friends. "Becca will take care of her. They share the same sentiments—that we should be more exclusive." Isla shrugged. "Coal Haven has three thousand people, and even with the surrounding communities, we have a hard time getting enough foot traffic to make it worthwhile twice a week. I've been contemplating talking with a few local bands to get more of a draw. I don't know how that'll go over."

"Money always makes the most diehard change their mind."

"I'd have to prove a band would bring the money first." She rolled her eyes. "The in-between might drive me nuts."

"I would tell everyone they can be the director if they don't fucking like it."

"And that's a good way to get the market to shut down," she said sweetly. She crossed her arms but kept walking. I kept pace with her. "Our first market was two people who sat on their tailgate and sold corn and tomatoes. Then we built up and now there are at least ten vendors twice a week." Her pride was clear to hear. "I like to think I had a part in that, but people still say this is an easy job my dad created for me so I could have something to do with my business degree after college." She dropped her voice to a conspiratorial whisper. "It was Mom's idea."

Her honest self-reflection wasn't expected. I laughed and her eyes flared. She looked at me like she hadn't seen me before.

"What?"

She shook her head and looked away. "Nothing."

"No, it's something."

She sighed, and I couldn't tell if the flush on her face was from the heat of the day or something else. "It's the first time I've really seen you smile."

"I smile."

She arched a light brow, and I scowled. "I only met you like a week ago." A familiar man was talking with Becca and the woman who'd complained to Isla. I seized the distraction. Better than acknowledging that I felt more like myself around Isla. "Is that your dad?"

Isla didn't bother to look. "Probably. He shows up, gets in on the gossip, checks up on me, and chases away perfectly valid vendors."

"Oh?" Between what she'd said about him and my quick meeting with Cameron, I could see it.

"I told you how Liam tried to sell some of his stuff here one day, but Dad chased him off. So now we don't get Liam's booth fee, and the furniture store gets all the traffic his welding would've brought. Admittedly, it's mostly online sales, but he could've set up a few times a year."

"Has he gotten back to you?"

She shook her head. We wandered more, and Isla angled toward her father, who was making his way toward us. He spotted us and a dark cloud passed over his face when his gaze landed on me.

"Hi, Dad. Did Mom send you to get more strawberry rhubarb pie filling?"

His headshake was nearly imperceptible. "Did Becca tell you about a customer's complaints?"

"The customer told me herself." Isla glanced around. "Is she still here?"

"Becca said she left after she used her market money. But what she said is pertinent—and she's the customer."

So was what Isla had to say about the subject. I crossed my arms, interested to see how this played out. Isla was intent on doing things her way, but he didn't strike me as a guy who allowed that to happen. I wanted her to have the win when I shouldn't care otherwise.

"She's not really a customer, though," Isla said. "She's in town visiting family, spent the gift certificate I gave her, and left. I'm sure if I checked with Becca, she wouldn't have spent one more cent. You know how some of those city people are when they come here. Live to put us down without offering any support. She never planned to return, just make herself feel better."

Good point.

Cameron spoke, and my gaze was jumping back and forth like I was spectating at a tennis match. "Isla, you've had the same complaint before, and you continue to ignore it. I told Becca we'll look at narrowing the market's focus so it's not as much"—his hard gaze raked the pie and sewing booths—"knickknacks and miscellaneous."

"Nothing here is miscellaneous." She dug in her bag to pull out her clipboard. "In fact, when I do a poll of income, the vendors who regularly bring in the most money are—"

Cameron clicked his tongue against his teeth, and it was like watching Pavlov's dog. Isla immediately quit talking. What the hell?

"You've got to start listening to people with more experience, Isla." Disappointment dripped from his tone. "Especially if you think you can be a business owner yourself."

His belittling tone yanked me out of the spectating position. "She's looking at the data, though. Isn't that what a good business owner does? Evaluate the numbers?"

Isla caught her lower lip between her teeth. I didn't expect gratitude, but her anxiety was a surprise. Was it what I said, or that I challenged her father?

Cameron's eyes narrowed, and the air around us grew still. "You're the project manager, correct?"

"Yes," Isla answered and pretended she didn't know he and I had talked before. "This is McCoy Cunningham, and he's overseeing both the restoration and the brewery construction. McCoy, this is my father, Cameron."

"And the market's involved with that?" His gaze was on

me, ignoring his daughter, and his question was clear. *What the hell are you doing here with her?*

Cognizant I was the guy who'd been naked in her shower and stroking the erection that I got from thinking of her, then the guy who'd seen her in nothing but a towel and fought getting hard while making eggs, I didn't answer.

"He rode with me." Isla wasn't touching the fact I had stayed overnight at her place either. "He's going to be in town for a while, so he might as well see what Coal Haven has to offer."

Cameron's narrow scrutiny settled on me. "McCoy Cunningham? From Nailer's in Nashville?"

The hair on the back of my neck rose. He wasn't admitting to confronting me earlier in front of his daughter, and his tone suggested he knew more about me than that I was the project manager and he wasn't afraid to use it against me.

I struggled to answer like I wasn't worried. "Yes."

"I should say you used to be associated with Nailer's." The words were extra smooth. "The harassment charges make that a little hard, I imagine."

Isla's jaw dropped. Blood roared between my ears. Fucking Hannah and her duplicitous bullshit. I should've taken notes. Cameron seemed to work from the same playbook.

I drew in a slow breath and willed my blood pressure to calm down. I had nothing to hide, and as much as it gutted me to speak about what happened, I wasn't the fucking criminal in the scenario. "That was a misunderstanding on my part. I didn't realize that the company that had bought my half of Nailer's was actually owned by my former friend and employee. I taught him everything he knew and then he used what he knew to hit me at my lowest."

I gave a lazy shrug that was at odds with the raging

emotions inside me. "I also didn't realize that I wouldn't be let into the establishment, after I found out, to ask him, 'what the hell?' A lot of unanswered calls and messages later, I go to the house I bought and paid for and lost in the divorce, only to see his truck parked in the driveway. Finally putting two and two together, I pounded on the door to get answers, and well, since I was the ex-husband and my ex was just a struggling woman trying to get on her feet after her cold, emotionless husband left and dumped all the work on her, I was the bad guy. She and my ex–best friend's statements coincidentally supported the harassment. Also a coincidence? His father's a lawyer, and my ex-friend had gone through law school before he started working with me."

Compassion whirled in Isla's eyes. "That's awful."

It was fucking awful. Humiliating. Gut-wrenching. All the words for being a spectator when my world was ripped apart. All because I'd been too trusting.

"It's his side of the story," Cameron said simply. He turned his pointed focus to her. "You didn't know any of this? Didn't you do your due diligence?"

"Yes," she said tightly. "Thank you for bringing it to my attention."

Why was she thanking him? Doesn't she see that it was part of the plan? Dismantle her credibility and make her question herself?

"Isla," her dad said, urgency in his voice, "you need to talk to people. You can't do this all on your own. That's how you get scammed."

Indecision flickered in Isla's expression. Finally, she lifted her chin. "It sounds like giving someone else all the power is a good way to lose it all, too, and I guess that's what I'm cautious of. If you'll excuse me, I need to talk to McCoy, and also, I'll take another look at the data for the market and see if the customer's complaint has any relevance to how I run things."

Annoyance crossed Cameron's face. His glare landed on me, but I was too busy trying to contain the boiling anger in my veins. She'd put her dad in his place while at the same time placating him about the damn market. Just tell him to butt out already.

"Call me tonight." His request was more of an order.

She nodded and walked toward the end of the lot. I followed, the familiar burn of betrayal and humiliation resurfacing from the past. Isla didn't earn either of those emotions. They were mine to deal with. And someday, that was what I'd have to do.

* * *

Isla

I stopped at the farthest edge of the parking lot, away from the vendors and customers. Dad had gotten into his pickup and left. Had he been here to check up on me, or was he searching for me to drop that little bomb about McCoy's past?

McCoy's expression was stormy and I couldn't blame him, but there was something in it other than anger. He tried to hide it, but the devastation was there. It wasn't hard to imagine restoring Reservoir Barrel into a reputable micro-brewery only to have it yanked out from under me by Dad. It was why I had kept my plans to myself, as if speaking them before I had the money and pen in hand to sign the paperwork would rob me of everything.

But to get screwed over by a spouse and a best friend? McCoy was anything but cold and emotionless. He'd been hurt by those who were supposed to care about him. He was guarded. There was a difference, and someone who cared to look outside of their own interests would see that.

"Look, I can explain the harassment charges better." He loosely propped his hands on his hips and stared at the asphalt. "I'd suspected Hannah of cheating on me. It's why I didn't fight it when she said she wanted a divorce. It's why I moved out, and why I was willing to walk away from Nailer's. I couldn't show up and pretend I was okay that she moved on while we were still together. But to find out that . . ." His jaw worked like he was trying to figure out how not to lose his temper. "They'd planned it. It worked out so neat and tidy for them, there's no other way to explain it. They'd taken time, and they'd planned it. And that's the rub. I'm still fucking raw, and I don't know that I'll ever not be. Hannah ruined me."

Irrational jealousy tore through me. She did not get to ruin him. I wanted him.

I tucked that thought into the recesses of my mind. He wasn't mine to have. He was supposed to be nothing but a project manager to me, not a romantic interest and not even a fling. A guy I was supposed to trust who didn't want to let down his mother, one of the few people who'd been there for him.

"She shouldn't get that type of power." A lesson from my mom. *Don't give them the power, Isla. You have a tender heart, but people will use it to get what they want and you'll be distraught. Don't give them that power.*

"Easy to say when she has everything. My lawyer got the rest fighting the harassment charge."

Ouch. He was still hurting, and there wasn't anything to say that would make it better.

"Did you ever have a chance to talk to her?"

"I wasn't willing to risk a restraining order." The resignation was clear. The hurt in his eyes wasn't something I could whisper away. "My reputation has already been reduced to nothing. I didn't need to trash it."

Good point. His logic made it easier to believe the harassment charge had been purposely trumped up against him. "Okay. Well, I'll have to do my due diligence and talk to Sylvia about it when she arrives, but I don't see it changing business as usual."

I was a little confused about why Sylvia didn't mention McCoy was her son, but I could see she was trying to maintain professionalism. He had harassment charges against him. Even if they'd been dropped and buried, still. A sliver of betrayal lodged in my throat, but maybe I wouldn't have done anything differently had I been in her position.

"I appreciate it." His body was rigid. He clenched his jaw and then said, "Buffalo berry."

"What?" The subject wasn't even a one-eighty of what we'd been discussing. Buffalo berries were in another realm.

He pulled a small bottle out of his back pocket. "When you get started, you should try something with these berries if you can get enough. Even if it's for something you only serve in-house, it'd be unique enough to draw in customers."

Oh. He was giving me advice? Did that mean he believed I could do this? A warm glow settled deep in my belly, different from the usual heat he put there.

We had buffalo berries in several of our pastures. They grew all over the county, but the harvest could be unpredictable. "I'll think about it. They're a bitch to pick, though."

"How so?"

"Thorns. One berry at a time with gloves to keep from getting pricked. It's meditative, and I sometimes go out with Nora in September and October. It'd take hours, maybe even days, to harvest a big enough amount to make syrup for a batch. But it's worth looking at."

"For real, or are you going to look at it like you're going to change what your market offers?"

I planned to do what Dad asked, if just to prove him wrong. "Yes," I said cautiously. "Are you upset I didn't tell Dad to fuck off?"

"The guy tried to undermine my credibility, so yeah, I'm a little upset about how he was handled."

He had every right to be, but couldn't he see the position I was in? "He's my dad."

"And you run a business. You can't thank him for sticking his nose in my private life and demeaning you in front of the contractor you hired, then tell him you'll think about a change you clearly don't agree with and already had handled."

Fatigue swamped me. I'd had a late night, an exciting morning that I wasn't sure was a good thing and a trying afternoon. McCoy didn't realize he was questioning me as much as everyone else in my life. He wanted me to jump as high as he thought I should, just like my parents.

I checked the time. "I have a half hour left, and we still need to eat and go over the plans. Are you good with that, or should we do it another day?"

His pickup was at the cabin, so unless he flagged a stranger down to help him, we were stuck together for a little while yet.

I thought he'd keep pressing the subject, demand I call Dad and tell him to back right off, and we'd be in a standoff, but his tension drained. "Yeah, I could use a bite. Is that diner downtown open on Sundays?" When I nodded, he did the same. "Why don't you tell me what you want, and I can walk there and order for us."

And by the time I was done, I could drive to the diner

and have food waiting. I'd have time to cool down. "Grilled cheese and tomato soup, please."

He ducked his head and started across the lot without looking back.

I was left with a market I didn't want to run and a contractor who thought I lacked backbone. It didn't help I agreed with him, but what was the cost of being tough? I'd turn into the stereotypical Barron in Coal Haven who talked with my money and power?

No, thanks. At the same time, I couldn't see the payoff for the way I ran things. It just seemed like I alienated different people.

* * *

McCoy

The diner door dinged when I walked in. Rows of brown booths lined one wall with a central servers' area, and a long counter filled with black stools stood across from them. Toward the back, the space widened big enough for tables that seated four or six. The place had clearly been around a while but was well cared for with what looked like a fresh coat of paint, updated wall art, and the booths weren't an old brown but a trendy earth tone. Heads turned my way, but I didn't make eye contact, just ducked my head and found an open booth by the big window facing the sidewalk.

The door pinged again while I was looking over the menu. Footsteps and men's voices traveled closer, but I thought nothing of it until two figures towered over me. Looking up, I wanted to groan.

Isla's brother had his hands shoved in the pockets of his

jeans and an old Coal Haven Miners shirt clung to his large frame. Standing next to him was intimidating, but I was sitting. He blocked out the world, and the way the sleeves of his shirt hugged his muscles added to the effect.

The other man resembled Stetson, but he wasn't as tall and had a lankier frame. His dark-blond hair was covered in a white and navy ball cap, while Stetson's hair had a look that he'd had a cap on but took it off and finger-combed the strands into a haphazard pile.

Their expressions weren't hostile, but Stetson's eyes were more evaluating than they had been yesterday.

"We meet again," I said and pushed the menu away. It wasn't like I'd read a word on it anyway.

Stetson's nod was almost imperceptible. "Holden, this is Isla's contractor. McCoy, this is my cousin Holden."

I snapped my fingers. "Nora's brother."

"She mentioned you." Holden slid into the seat across from me and scooted all the way to the window. Stetson got in next to him, and now I had dinner guests.

"Dad just called," Stetson said after he was settled.

Christ. "I can guess what he said."

"Yup, but that's not why we're here, in case you're wondering. Holden and I were grabbing a bite." Stetson nodded at the waitress who appeared with three glasses of water where he'd just been standing.

"Whatcha having today, boys?" She didn't have a tablet. Either she memorized orders, or she'd been waiting on these guys since they were in diapers, and from her age and the fond way the other two looked at her, I could figure out which one.

They ordered. I got a burger and fries and ordered the grilled cheese and soup.

"Isla coming?" Stetson asked.

I nodded. "After the market. I explained the harassment charge. It's between her and Sylvia now."

"And Sylvia is . . .?" Holden shoved a straw in his water.

Since much of my dirty laundry was aired, I went for the truth. "My mom. She owns the company, and since I suddenly had an empty plate, Mom threw me a bone and gave me this job since I'm experienced in both restoration and brewery construction."

"And the charge?" Stetson asked. His dad had likely concentrated on that part of my past.

I told them what I'd said to Isla. The only other time I had talked about what happened was when I'd slunk back to Denver. Now twice today, the story had spilled out, and each time was like I shrugged a load off my shoulders.

"What would your ex say if we asked her the story?" Stetson asked.

I snorted. "Google her. She was happy to tell every publication about how she's striving to move on after the divorce and the harassment. She wishes me the best, but she just wants to move on from"—I threw up air quotes—"'that messy business.'" I took a drink of water and hissed like it was hard liquor. "She won't mention how she was fucking my best friend or that the settlement just happened to be equal to my share of the house she'd had to fork over in the divorce. In fact, you'll have a hard time finding my name anywhere near Nailer's. She's vague when she talks about me, or people might not think she's a martyr."

"Damn," Holden said.

"That's straight-up cold," Stetson said. His expression relaxed. "I'm protective of my sister, but that doesn't mean I don't know what my dad's like. By any chance, did he tell you to go through him and you refused?"

I nodded.

"That's why he dug up your past." He ripped off the

end of his straw and blew the wrapper toward Holden, missing and hitting the window. "My mom probably knows more about you by now than your mom does."

My chuckle surprised me. Was this what it was like for Isla? Everyone knew wherever you went? "I guess I'm an open book. That was the worst of it. The rest will just be me hustling, trying to make a living doing something I don't hate." And I'd ended up giving what I hated over to Hannah, and she'd wielded it against me.

"So are you going to be here for a few months or what?" Holden asked, twisting the straw wrapper Stetson had shot at him. He was conversational, and it'd been too long since I'd just . . . chatted. I was doing a lot of that in Coal Haven.

"I think so." With the crew delayed, I might have to find other options besides the motel. I could return to Denver, continue to rein my bitterness in until I returned with Lorraine and Halle. But staying appealed to me more, and I didn't have the energy to question it. "You guys know of any decent places to rent for a few months?"

Holden nudged Stetson. "What about that love nest you and Lyric had for a while there last winter?"

Stetson's brows drew together. "It might be open, actually. The people who took over our lease were planning to be there for only a few months. I can give you Zelda's number."

If this Zelda had rented to him, maybe she'd be open to Isla. "Let your sister try."

Stetson's gaze sharpened. "Why?"

Ah, hell. I'd stepped in it. Isla kept a lot from her family. After meeting her dad, I could see why. "You'll have to ask her."

Holden's gaze went to the door. "Hey, you can do it right now."

I glanced over my shoulder. Isla smiled at the waitress, and when her gaze landed on us, she faltered before she continued walking toward us. "What are you guys doing here?"

"Lyric's at her mom's," Stetson answered. "Thought I'd give Erin room to smother her grandbaby."

"Same with Emery," Holden said.

"She's at Erin's?" Isla asked in a joking tone. She sat on the edge of the booth like she was afraid of touching me, but she wasn't far enough away to keep her berries-and-cream scent from surrounding me. I adjusted how I sat and concentrated on the coffee smell in the air rather than letting my mind drift to this morning and how intimately I knew her smell.

Stetson snickered. "I don't think all of Holden's kids would fit in her apartment."

Holden chuckled. "She's at Lynnie's with Grady. The older kids are in Arizona with their dad for the next couple of weeks. So, are you having trouble finding a place to rent?"

Isla glanced at me like *really?* and I shrugged.

"Your brother said he might have a place for me to check out since the crew is delayed." And I had no other place to call my own, so I might as well lick my wounds in the middle of nowhere.

"He said I should refer you to Zelda but wouldn't tell us why." Stetson arched a brow like he was asking, *Care to share?*

Isla fiddled with the straw I didn't use. "Yeah, Rudy told me none of the Alpine complexes had openings."

"There are always empty apartments," Stetson said. Disbelief drew his brows together. "He keeps a sign up full-time."

Isla opened the straw and stuck it in my water. "Yep. But not to a Barron, I guess." She took a pull.

Amused, I watched her drink from my glass. I hadn't

touched it yet, but it was so automatic she didn't realize she'd done it.

When I looked up, Holden was watching us, his face impassive. Alarm beat through me. The moment of intimacy I'd been unknowingly enjoying was witnessed. How easily I didn't care if another woman thought what I had was hers.

It's only a glass of water, jackass.

But the warning bell had been rung. I switched my gaze out the window as Stetson reassured Isla she was welcome in the cabin as long as she needed.

"I have a newborn," he said. "Lyric's getting used to full-time work. We don't have any lake plans this year. Maybe next."

"Unless you get her pregnant again," Isla said. I recognized a deflection when I saw one.

Holden snickered. "Stay out of my tack room, and you should be fine."

Stetson shot him a disgruntled glare. "You're never going to let me live that down."

"Nope. You made history, and she's called Rina."

The corner of Stetson's mouth lifted. "Next one will be a little more planned—and I'll make sure to sneak into your barn when we're ready."

Isla stirred the ice in the glass that was no longer mine. "You might have to take a number. That's probably the only place Holden and Emery can get some privacy."

Mirth gleamed in Holden's eyes. "We manage just fine."

Isla shuddered. "TMI. You're going to scare my project manager away."

I should be cringing, but I was fascinated. I didn't come from a big family and I hadn't been raised around a lot of relatives. Isla couldn't turn around without seeing a family member. The easiness between them, the joking, and the butting into lives was what I thought I'd built in Nashville. It'd been a facade—my friendships, my relationship, my network—but this was real.

If Isla was mine, I wouldn't have to worry about her running off with anyone since she was related to everyone.

I gave myself a mental shake. She wasn't mine. What the hell was I thinking? I didn't belong here. I didn't belong anywhere. And I didn't belong with someone as young and optimistic as Isla.

ISLA

I waited nervously inside the entrance of Rattler's. Sylvia was supposed to show up. My excitement hadn't died from last night. After eating at the diner, McCoy and I had gone to the cabin to go over some of the information he compiled. He was very clinical about the process, standing the whole time and cruising through each point, only pausing to make sure I didn't have anything to add to the process. Then he'd left before I could suggest cracking another can of beer for us to try. Before I could offer another one of my finished products.

Point taken.

Waking up in the same cabin, seeing him naked? Meant nothing and I was wrong to think we'd hedged past a professional-only relationship. But then it had been my dad who'd dragged up his private past and aired it in public, even calling my brother. Hell hath no fury like a father scorned.

My phone buzzed. I craned my neck to peer out the

window of the door. No cars were driving in, and no silver-haired woman was walking through the parking lot.

I checked the message. **I can bring the mower by.**

Ugh. I had to buy my own equipment. I couldn't keep borrowing from my brother. Did I have time to do that today? And where would I keep it?

McCoy didn't take Zelda's number, so I gave her a call this morning. She'd said the current tenant mentioned he planned to renew for another six months. I did a drive-by of the other open places in town and none of them would fit my needs, so I switched to house rentals. Stetson might not mind if I stayed in the cabin, but I did. I couldn't be Miss Independent living off him.

I had an appointment later this afternoon to see a house for rent and another look-through set up in the morning.

Sending Stetson a message, I tapped my foot. **No. I may not need it. I'll let you know.**

After I looked at the house, I'd see if the farm implement place would cut a deal with me on a lawn mower. They might even have a trailer I could purchase. I hated to store everything at the cabin, but it grated to keep asking Stetson to borrow his shit when I was also living on his property.

"Oh, dear," a rich voice said. "I certainly hope I haven't kept you waiting."

I spun to find Sylvia with a contrite smile, leaning on a dark cane. She was dressed in head-to-toe black with a white silk shirt. A total power suit, while I was in white linen pants and a turquoise shirt like I was heading to a family picnic afterward.

She leaned on her cane, and her smile widened. "My apologies. I arrived early and didn't think to call you."

Crap. I'd gone from being early to being the one who

was late. "It's no problem. I didn't think to look for you. I'm sorry."

She waved her hand around the restaurant. "I thought since it was a small town and all, I would stand out."

"Rattler's gets a lot of people passing through or who come just to eat here."

"I'm glad I came outside to call you." She turned and I followed. Her cane was rubber tipped and didn't make a sound against the hardwood floor. She walked with a limp, but it didn't slow her pace.

She stood at the corner of a table that held two menus and two glasses of ice water. Hers was half-empty. Chagrined, I sat and she settled in her chair. I should've checked if she was here already.

We sat at the same time. She dug readers out of a dark McDaniel Contractors tote bag. "I'm afraid I didn't have a chance to look at the menu. I might be away from the office, but smartphones have made it almost impossible to actually be away."

"You didn't have to come, but I'm happy to have a chance to meet you in person." I didn't need to look at the menu. I had it memorized by this point.

She peered over her readers, and her expression reminded me of Mom. I hadn't talked to her since I'd left the house. I swallowed a sense of longing. Would Mom and I get around to having lunches like this, or had she iced me out of her life until I returned groveling?

"What do you recommend?" Sylvia asked, diverting my thoughts.

Pleased she asked my opinion, I summoned my years of experience eating at Rattler's. "Everything's good, honestly. The alfredo is popular, but their steaks are so good that my ranching family has no issues eating beef here. The chefs are also just as talented with chicken. I'm having the chicken parmesan, but if you're in the mood for pizza, they make those really well too. I think they wood fire them."

She chuckled like I'd told a fabulous joke. "I'll do a soup and salad."

Oh. She was making conversation, not actually looking for recommendations. Familiar heat crawled up my neck toward my cheeks. This wasn't an interview. If anything, Sylvia should be kissing my ass, but that wasn't how I felt. She was older. Experienced. Someone who did business the way I wanted to—professionally kind but knowledgeable and confident.

"You can't go wrong with that," I said.

She set the menu down and assessed me. "I'm going to ask you to be honest—have there been any problems with McCoy?"

The heat in my face turned to a raging ditch fire. My butt cheeks tingled with the memory of how his hands felt on my ass, just as the perfect image of him naked in my bathroom with his hand wrapped around his cock streamed through my mind. I shouldn't have such a clear picture of what his private parts looked like, but what details weren't stamped into my brain were supplied by imagination to make a crystal clear image.

I had a hard time thinking about him without picturing him in my shower. Without feeling the way he claimed my lips and devoured me.

I called on Mom's impassiveness to help me answer without giving secrets away. "No. Why? Do you have any concerns?"

"He can be . . . curt." She relaxed into a fond smile. "Some might say surly, but it's always been his personality." She was making excuses for him, but his personality had been forged growing up with a toxic parent. "And when I talked to him this morning, he mentioned the incident yesterday."

Ugh. How often did she have to deal with her clients' parents? Embarrassing. "Oh. Yes. We discussed that. I'm afraid my dad can't help but be my dad."

Fondness lit her brown eyes, but it didn't crowd out the concern. "I imagine it's hard for him to see you going from college grad to savvy business owner."

I was a few years out of college. It shouldn't be such a jump. "Yes, exactly." There was one thing that had popped into my mind, but I tried to shut it out.

"You have a question?"

Too many years of trying to be different from Mom had made it difficult for me to hide what I was thinking. I tried not to sound suspicious, but I had to ask if only to be thorough. "I, uh, looked up McCoy before he arrived, but I didn't see much about him."

"Right, that. Well, it's out there." She was dismissive, but I had attempted to do due diligence about who was on this project. His information hadn't been on the company website and sifting through links of people with similar names, last names, or the Army base hadn't been productive. Hannah's awards and recognition had crowded out everything else.

Sylvia knew what she was doing, and I knew I shouldn't doubt her. Taking out his abrupt personality, his experience and knowledge were a benefit. Sylvia hadn't lied about that.

A familiar perfume wafted over me before my mother glanced down and did a double take as she was walking past. She stopped, and a pleased but worried expression took over her face. "Isla?" She waved off the women she'd been lunching with, her coworkers.

It was like I'd summoned her. I hadn't noticed her car in the lot. She must've caught a ride. I doubted she walked the several blocks in a chic and fitted power suit and her Kate Spade pumps. Her gaze went to Sylvia, and the icy mask slammed into place. The brief beat of delight I had at seeing my mom was wiped out by nerves.

I jumped to introductions. "Mom, hi. This is Sylvia McDaniel with McDaniel Contractors. She flew to Coal Haven to meet with me before we got started. Sylvia, this is my mom, Naomi."

"How nice to meet you." Sylvia's smile was wide, and she moved her chair back to stand.

Mom snapped her hand up to keep Sylvia in her seat. "Hello." One word that could draw in a blizzard. "You're the mother of the project manager I've heard about?"

I'd have loved it right then if a trapdoor could open underneath my chair and swallow me up. First, my dad accosted Sylvia's son when he was in Coal Haven to work for me. And now my mother was slinging her attitude around like Sylvia did something wrong.

Sylvia was stunned speechless for only a moment. "Why, yes. McCoy is my son. He started at the company when I did. Worked from the ground up, but he's been in construction since he was old enough to run a table saw."

I didn't care to hear Mom's retort. I pushed back from the table. "Are you here for lunch break? I can walk you out."

Mom's eyes narrowed. She knew what I was doing, but since she was making-a-scene averse when in public, she took a deliberate step back and pivoted on her wide heel. I followed her.

She tossed her blonde, highlighted hair over her shoulder before she pushed out the door. "You didn't need to interrupt your work meeting." Her tone was cool.

We stopped outside under the overhang. "No, it was good to see you." Not a total lie. I was used to seeing her every day, and even though many times being around her was like facing a dance floor of eggshells, I was struck with a sudden sense of missing her.

Her expression didn't buy what I said. "You need to watch out for yourself."

"I've done my research—"

"People like that have more experience than you." She leaned closer, and for once I was grateful for her unwillingness to let the public in on our family's doings. "Did you know that man was her son?"

"McCoy? No, but he told me when he first arrived." After I'd threatened to discuss his attitude with Sylvia.

"And why wait? Family companies are often proud of their family status. Other CEOs would've touted the connection as a boon."

She had a point. "Mom, I trust her. I did a lot of footwork before I hired her."

Her expression softened, but the underlying look of *you sweet summer child* was still there. "That might be, but she's also an expert at image—her company's image. So maybe ask yourself why she wasn't up front with you. If the first excuse you come up with is that it probably slipped her mind, try again. Do you think your father would've hidden the fact that Stetson was his son if he'd followed in his footsteps?"

Dad would've been infinitely hard on Stetson if my brother had made it to the C-suite of the refinery, but Dad wouldn't hesitate to drop our last name if he had.

No. This was Mom being her normal self. Undermining me. She didn't understand the situation. McCoy hadn't planned to be jobless when I'd hired Sylvia months ago, and he wasn't airing his dirty laundry. Of all people, my mom and dad should respect that.

"I've got it under control, Mom."

Her face was full of doubt, but she stood more relaxed. "Are you still at Stetson's place?"

"Until I find a house to rent."

"Shelly said her in-laws are thinking about selling but would like to rent first."

Shelly was the receptionist in the city offices. Mom had known her for years, and I'd gotten to know Shelly and had seen her around town. Her in-laws were good people with a cute house by the golf course. Yet I couldn't get kicked out and then have my mom find a place for me to stay. Not after she and Dad had confronted Sylvia and McCoy the way they had.

I kicked my chin up. "Like I said, I've got it all taken care of."

Mom's sigh was sharp. Disappointment traveled through her eyes. "All right, then. I guess I'll let you get back to your meeting."

"She's a nice person." I hadn't meant it as a dig, but that was the way it came out.

Mom stiffened and hurt flickered in her expression. "I'm sure she is." She marched through the parking lot, and I was left standing outside like a lost little girl. I waited to see if she had a ride, but yes, there was the Range Rover parked in the corner opposite where I had parked.

With a sigh, I brushed my hands over my summery outfit, a stark contrast to what Sylvia and Mom were wearing. I'd better get back to my guest. Since I claimed I had everything taken care of, it was time to prove it.

* * *

McCoy

. . .

I held the door open to the diner. Mom went inside. When I entered, the waitress from the other day swept past us.

"Mornin', McCoy," she said, giving me the same welcoming look she'd aimed at the Barrons. "Only the two of you today?"

"Yep, just me and my mom." Dammit, I'd meant to say Sylvia, but it wasn't like the town didn't know I was a nepotism baby, and now they probably knew I had faced harassment charges. Or not. The Barrons were as salty about their personal business being out there as I was. No one in the diner looked at me differently, only shooting mildly curious glances toward Mom.

"I'll be there in a sec." The waitress rushed toward the kitchen.

Mom picked a booth and spun on her cane to get in and wedged it under the tabletop. "My flight is on time so far, and it's an hour to Dickinson. What a cute little town. People were saying it's really grown since the last oil boom."

I wanted more of Mom's insight about Isla, not about a fucking town. All she'd told me after meeting Isla yesterday was that she was a sweet girl with a good head on her shoulders. Then Mom had wanted to rest after traveling.

"I haven't been there," I said, skipping the menu since I always ate the same thing for breakfast when I went out.

"You should." She put her readers on, pored over the menu, then sighed and put her glasses away. "I've been talking to Lorraine. The project in the Springs has run into more snags."

"Surely she can come out here and at least get us started?" Without Lorraine's inspection we were at a standstill planning-wise. I could only go so far without knowing what the building could handle.

"What about Deagan? He's good." A new engineer grad, but Mom wouldn't have hired him if he wasn't competent. Two months wasn't an inconsiderable amount of time. Isla shouldn't be at a halt before the first date set in her contract.

"He's not licensed in North Dakota. Lorraine is. She graduated from one of the universities here. Send Deagan to the Springs."

She gave me a flat look. "It's the Orlans, and I can't send them the new guy."

One of her longest clients, Dev Orlan had built his first brewery in Denver, giving Mom her big break. She'd gotten other clients, he'd grown, and now he was expanding into another city. And he'd likely build more. Mom didn't want to upset him, even if it meant holding up other crews and generating change orders.

But while she catered to Dev, Isla was sitting rudderless in the middle of a lake, going nowhere and making no money. "You're toeing the line of an inexcusable delay."

"She understands. We talked about it yesterday." She folded her hands and gave me a pointed stare. Discussion over. "I met her mother."

"What was that like?"

"A little on the chilly side, but I can see why her mother's worried about Isla."

The abrasiveness of her comment wasn't expected. Hadn't I warned Isla about the very reason Mom was worried? Isla couldn't be too nice. She should stand up for herself more instead of playing placating politician. She'd get eaten alive.

Yet, she'd been the director of the market for a few years and it'd done nothing but grow. She had a comprehensive business plan and a clear vision for her company.

"So," Mom said, intruding on my thoughts, "how long are you going to stay here?"

I'd thought about leaving less than I'd thought about

staying. I had nowhere else to go. "I can put the room on my card and pay for gas out of my personal account." I wasn't going to be sucking up Isla's dime when I wasn't working. I knew what it was like to have someone milk everything you worked for.

I knew Isla had gotten a trust, and I doubted she'd had much for jobs in high school or through college. She was using the money for herself, but in a way that'd benefit the community.

"Is this simple place growing on you?" she asked innocently, but I knew my mother better. She was prying without being obvious.

"No one knows me here." Except for Isla's family. Karla. Carlton saw me at the gas station yesterday and chatted with me for a few minutes. There was the waitress here. What was her name—Oh, yeah. Jocelyn. She probably knew my story like everyone else I came across. Yet none of them treated me differently. If anything, they opened up more and I didn't mind. I'd buffered myself so much toward the end with Nailer's I didn't realize I missed the connections.

"It's not Denver, that's for sure. Or Nashville."

"No, it's not." Two points in favor of Coal Haven.

"But it's not exactly moving on in life."

"I've got enough to hold me over for a while."

Her look was knowing. I had enough to tide me over and not much more. Legal bills were a bitch, the settlement had hurt, and before that, I'd thrown everything into growing Nailer's, sacrificing my retirement. I had wrongly assumed I had time.

Jocelyn swung by with glasses of water. We put in our order. It was the same—ironically, a Denver omelet with hash browns. Mom used to make them before Dad left, and then after she'd married Fergus, we could afford to go out to eat.

"Say you stay here until the project's done and decide to put down some roots. Then what?"

"I'm not putting down roots. There's nothing for me here." When Reservoir Barrel was done, then I was done, and I had the time in between to figure out what the hell I was going to do and where I'd go do it.

"There are plenty of new construction needs, and the state's growing. People are only going to keep flocking here." She settled her elbows on the table and leaned on them. "You can start again."

"I don't have the means." It didn't matter what I wanted to build, I wasn't drawn to any one thing. Did I want to brew and sell beer again? No, honestly. I enjoyed craft beer. I enjoyed witnessing Isla's enthusiasm, but to do it all over again? Nope. And the restaurant side? Absolutely not. It was a fucking headache. The idea of building something lit a fire in my veins, but I didn't know what would make me want to stick around after the last nail was sunk.

"You've gotten investors before. You've raised the capital."

"When Fergus was alive and had connections. Before I had a harassment charge against me from the guy who bought my part of Nailer's."

"That was settled."

"Which made me look guilty as fuck." Along with draining my savings.

"Everyone knows how that works. Everyone will see Hannah was after the money—which we damn well know she was."

"Or they will think I wanted to shut everyone up as fast as possible." I shook my head. "Look how I was outed in Coal Haven. Next time, the person looking to hire me might know the right places to look for the real dirt." Isla hadn't, and Mom hadn't offered the information. Uneasiness robbed some of my appetite. Technically, Mom had been professional, but the sense of wrongness didn't leave.

"So you're going to stay here and wait out the delay?"

I rolled a shoulder. I didn't have long enough to justify finding my own place, and it's not like I was going to start a company that directly competed with my mom's.

"Is it her?" Mom asked quietly.

"Her who?"

She gave me a *don't be dense* look. "Is Isla the reason you're not leaving?"

"That'd be inappropriate." How I managed to sound scornful when the image of her in a towel burned through my head, I didn't know.

Her eyes narrowed briefly, but she must have thought Isla wouldn't go for a washed-up guy like me or that I wasn't interested. The girl enthralled me, but that was my problem. For whatever reason Mom backed off, I didn't care.

"Why don't you open a brewery here?" she asked.

My resistance to the idea remained unwavering, and the last place I would build a brewery was on top of Isla's dream. "And compete with her? That'd be a dick move."

"Coy." I shook my head, but she held a finger up to quiet me. "Since when have you worried about whether the competition can survive?"

I had to think for a moment, forming my words, so I was saying more than *I can't do that to Isla*. It was insulting to her on so many levels, for one, to even be pondering the issue. But also because I had to have a better reason than not wanting to hurt the feelings of a pretty girl. People hadn't been concerned when they tore my world down, and I refused to let opportunities pass because my heart had gone too soft for me to notice.

"In Nashville, I worked hard to build a network." I wasn't the friendliest guy, so my contacts had been built on a love of the craft and mutual respect. "We supported each other, even though we were competition because the more people we could get out to drink beer and socialize, the more customers we all had. That's not what you're talking about."

She sat back, a satisfied gleam in her eye. "Okay."

"Were you testing me?"

"After the divorce and the ensuing mess, I wasn't sure how much of my son was left. But you're still there. I have faith in you, and it's why I thought you were the best person for the job."

Our food was delivered. I nodded to Jocelyn.

Mom cut into her steaming omelet, but I waited, unsure what to think. The little boy inside me preened from her praise, but just because she still thought highly of me didn't mean I wanted to sit around Coal Haven with fuck all to do. "Now all you need to do is get the other right people on the job."

She rolled her eyes. "Delays are normal, Coy. You know that. Isla understands."

Isla didn't know Mom wasn't juggling multiple accounts, she was prioritizing one over hers and manipulating Isla's naive nature. The basis of Mom's advertising was all the states McDaniel Contractors could work in, yet here we were, dead in the water.

I didn't agree with it, but Mom had met with Isla yesterday, and I trusted her business savvy over mine. At this point, everyone who hadn't been run out by a spouse or a trusted best friend was doing better than me. But just in case, I would stick around Coal Haven and figure out something to do with my life.

Ten

ISLA

Four weeks had gone by since Sylvia was in town and I'd bought a damn house. Mom had sent me the info for her coworker's in-laws to contact them about the rental. At the same time, I'd been checking out a rental home with demolished front steps leading from the raised yard to the sidewalk, a pervasive musty smell from the perpetually wet basement, and a landlord I worried would either install a secret camera or who'd decide he could enter at whatever time of day he wanted. I decided not to rent after that. I wasn't pumping money into other people's wallets for a subpar living space.

I just closed on a fairly inexpensive, run-down, ranch-style home with three bedrooms, one bathroom, and an unfinished basement. I hadn't watched enough HGTV to think I could flip anything, but whatever I did would increase the value, and since I was waiting on McDaniel

Contractors to begin the physical stages of the restoration, I was at a standstill.

I had to do something with my time, yet there weren't a lot of jobs I could work. Anyone I interviewed with would know about the foundry plans and suspect I would ditch another job as soon as the last fermenting tank was installed. Which I would. This house would be another revenue stream.

The inspector hadn't found major structural problems, and I didn't plan on removing walls or ripping out and installing new cabinets. I was a party of one who wondered if she'd jumped in way over her head. Funny how a little house under two hundred thousand dollars could create more anxiety than a restoration and brewery construction that'd be in the seven figures.

But I wasn't living at the foundry. I'd hired experts for that project. I hadn't done more than some painting in my life. The odd times I helped Dad fix random things around the house and on the ranch were infrequent. He'd taught Stetson everything and preferred not to repeat himself with me and endure my clumsy attempts.

A message buzzed on my phone. My pulse kicked up when I saw McCoy's name. After his mom had left, he'd driven back to Denver to get more clothing, muttering that he'd return to the motel, and he didn't want to mess with rental leases. I hadn't counted the days he was gone or anything—eight—but when he'd returned to town, he hadn't done more than message me to let me know he was back and in room five again.

Over two weeks had gone by, and I hadn't seen him. Each time I mowed at Reservoir Barrel, I'd hoped to catch him. Then, when I hadn't, I'd told myself it was for the best. What did I have to talk to him about?

I need your signature for some of the permits.

McCoy's message meant we had to see each other face-to-face.

Biting my lower lip, I held back a smile. I was only looking forward to seeing McCoy because I was lonely. I'd pulled the same stunt with the house and kept the purchase to myself. Mom and Dad would likely have *opinions*, but I wasn't ready to deal with them. Lyric and I had planned to go out once a couple weeks ago, but Rina had been sick, so Lyric had to cancel. Then she and Stetson went out of town for a weekend, and after that, she'd been catching up at work and taking some overtime to cover her coworkers' vacations.

Liam hadn't gotten back to me yet about working together, and the rest of my cousins and their spouses were busy with their families. Even Nora was taking summer school classes for her graduate degree, and Aspen had gone back to Kansas City a few times for family emergencies. So I'd spent the long nights alone at the cabin, sitting on the dock and writing out my plans.

McCoy might as well be the first to know. A nice parallel to announcing the name of Reservoir Barrel. The engineer would be here soon enough, and McCoy and I would be working together more. He should know where to find me if I didn't answer like last time. I'd no longer be in a bikini at the cabin but elbow deep in repainting the peeling Masonite siding. Or replacing a door. Or more things I'd never really done.

I shot him the address, grateful I was wearing a camisole top and linen shorts instead of sweaty clothing for the yard-work I planned to do later. I should have gone inside, but instead I waited. No need to overwhelm myself and slam my brain with WHY DID YOU THINK YOU COULD DO THIS questions until after I signed.

He pulled up in the same white work pickup and got out. He squinted at the house, and I drank him in. He was in standard McCoy wear—faded T-shirt with a logo that appeared to be a beer place in Nashville but not Nailer's. I doubted he owned a thing with his old place's emblem on it. His worn jeans with athletic shoes capped off his rugged, workingman casual appearance. Something I was apparently quite into.

"No blue?"

It took a second to realize what he meant. I touched the ends of my hair. "It's faded. I haven't decided on another color." Without Mom's disapproval, I wasn't as interested in a rebellion.

"This the place you're renting?" he asked and pushed his hair back. Whatever he'd done in Denver didn't include a trim.

"I, uh, bought it, actually."

Only a slight lift to his brows preceded his nod, and he stopped next to me, his arms crossed. "You moved in?"

I didn't have much to move. "Not yet. I just closed this morning." I jingled the keys. My nerves were making the same sound. I wanted to be excited, but I had to live here. If I failed with my home, what would that say about me? "Since I've got some downtime, I thought I could fix it up and see what I can sell it for. Or maybe rent it out. We have enough families coming through town that work at one of the plants and want a place to stay while looking for a house."

"You're getting into real estate now?"

I couldn't tell from his tone if that was good or bad. The only thing I could concentrate on was how nice it was to be next to him again with his woodsy citrus scent that I could wrap around me. "I guess I am."

"Well, give me a tour."

I hadn't even been inside yet since it was officially mine. "You're my first guest."

Amusement crinkled the corners of his eyes. "Did you do this secretly too?"

"I told Stetson and Lyric." I didn't, but I'd message them after McCoy left. McCoy had met my dad. I shouldn't have been afraid to admit I did the sale totally on my own too. He'd probably understand more than anyone, but facing a house I knew nothing about owning, I'd kept it to myself.

"Isla, you're determined to do your own thing."

I started for the door, growing more insecure with each step. Once he saw the inside, he'd think I was a little girl who thought a quick paint job would earn an extra six figures on the sale. "Do you think it's a bad idea?"

"You're living here while you work?" When I nodded, he said, "No. It's a smart plan if you've got the money to do it. If nothing else, you'll have a place to live."

I unlocked the door and took a deep breath. His confirmation helped more than I cared to admit. "I have new doorknobs and dead bolts in the pickup. I was going to do that first and then haul my stuff from the cabin." I hadn't loaded the pickup. As if I didn't want to jinx the sale or alert my family I'd done something that looked impulsive with a lot of money, I'd carried on with life as normal.

Inside, the stale air didn't decrease my worries. Old, matted carpet stretched from wall to wall. Wallpaper on one side of the living room promised to be a bitch to remove but didn't have the disco look of the wallpaper in the bathroom or the stains of what hung in the kitchen. The bedrooms were all wallpaper. There was wallpaper everywhere.

I stepped aside so McCoy could enter. "An older couple owned it for years. The husband passed away a while ago, and the wife wasn't able to keep up with updates and repairs. Her kids finally talked her into moving closer to them in Sioux Falls. I think it's mostly cosmetic updates though."

"That's good." He wandered through the living room and tapped on the wall between it and the kitchen. "No dining room?"

"No, more like an elongated kitchen. I figured I'd use the space for my fermenting bottles while I'm here. I won't need a big dining room." It wasn't like I would have large groups over while my house was mid upgrade. And I needed the stove to boil the wort for home brewing.

He straddled the entry into the kitchen and peered back and forth. I knew what his next question would be. "You gonna open it up?"

"The wall is load bearing." The wife of one of the Rattler's owners was my real estate agent. Tenielle had passed on the house to flip herself since she was currently working on a place on the other side of town. She'd shared her ideas with me, and maybe since I was paying her to be my agent, getting her advice hit differently. It had felt like we were colleagues. She'd been my age when she'd started renovating on her own, and she'd faced her own challenges of being taken seriously.

"You can open it." He knocked on the door frame behind him. "Build this wall out and move the appliances to the adjacent wall. It'd really brighten it up."

"Yes, but then I'd have to hire someone. The point was to minimize my expenses. I was going to do everything myself unless absolutely necessary."

"If you want to get the most money from a resale, you'd want to open this wall."

Easy for him, maybe. How many walls had he removed? If I had to pay someone for their time and for the work, I might lose any resale value, but he was being open and wasn't condescending. He spoke as if I could do it or figure out how to have it done. The realization made me glad he was the first one I told. "I'd have to do some market research. How much will it cost versus how much added to the sale."

His amber gaze was made brighter by the sun streaming through the picture window I wasn't sure I could transform into a bay window by myself. I hadn't intended to become a renovator, but I couldn't sit on my money without trying to grow it.

"Got it," he said. "What's the basement like?"

"The stairs are through the kitchen."

Downstairs, he wandered like a boy who'd found a neat cave. The concrete walls radiated coolness. It was clean and dry, and that had been my biggest concern buying an old house. Other than a few hairline cracks that had been in the walls longer than I was old, the basement was in really good shape.

"Please tell me you're at least going to finish the basement?" He stared like he was a master artist facing a canvas that was blessed by his muse. I saw excitement, like the final result was streaming across his vision.

"I definitely can't do that myself, but it's all part of what I need to evaluate."

Without the big windows, his gaze was darker, fathomless, and with a loud but unspoken, *What the hell do you plan to do here, then?*

"I knew when I saw the house I likely wouldn't lose money on the resale, and since I'm not leaving Coal Haven, I have the time to wait for a seller's market. Any little upgrade I can make myself will only add to the profit margin. I haven't demolished walls or built them, so I'm concentrating on easier improvements."

His nod was matter of fact, but his gaze was distant, like

his mind had already wandered out of the room. "Is there functioning plumbing down here?"

"There's a laundry room, and they left the washer and dryer. There's nothing else in there but a counter."

His gaze sharpened. "Is there a utility sink?"

"Yeah. Why?"

He shook his head and went in search of the laundry room, wearing an amused expression. Stopping in the middle of the room that smelled faintly like fabric softener, he held his arms out and gave me a questioning look.

"I'm lost." But his optimism lightened the anxiety that had been coursing through me.

His arms flopped down, but a smile played along his lips. "Isla. You're killing me. Don't you see it?"

"No," I said with a laugh, utterly unaware of what he was getting at.

"This is your prep room. You have all the space to move and fill jugs, and you can even use the floor drain for spills."

"But there's no stove."

"You're just boiling wort. You don't need a hood or an oven. Get a countertop stove. A hot plate might even work." Could it be that simple? He answered as if I spoke out loud. "You don't need a commercial kitchen, just a place you can keep clean."

I spun in a slow circle, mapping out the process in my mind. I could totally see it. I'd be able to do a hobby I enjoyed, something I knew how to do when I was armpit deep in shit I'd never tried before—stripping wallpaper, replacing carpet, and installing a new sink and toilet.

"I'm going to haul my brewing equipment first. I don't care that I have nowhere to sit." I started giggling and did a little dance. "Oh my god, McCoy. Do you realize how frustrated I've been for the last month? My dreams are at a standstill, but I can get a batch done in time to celebrate the engineer finally arriving in Coal Haven."

His grin faltered and a shadow passed over his face, but he wasn't the one causing the delay. "Yeah, the wait sucks."

"So bad." My light mood refused to die. "I bet I can even find something portable to cook with in town since so many campers come through. I just need time to move my stuff over. Want to help me start a batch this weekend?"

The offer slipped out, but after our tasting, I wanted to see his experience in action during the simplest home brew. What were his tips? Any tricks he'd picked up over time? Was he still gruff while he worked, or did he loosen up—did the despondent undertones in his eyes disappear when he was doing something he loved?

My questions didn't have a chance to get answered. His expression hardened with fewer lines than the basement walls. "No."

My initial hurt turned to worry. Had I insulted him? He'd run a huge place with distribution to three other states. Why would he want to play around in a basement with me? "O-okay. I'll hit you up for taste testing, then."

"I have those papers I need you to sign." He darted around me, and his heavy footsteps sounded on the stairs.

The papers. The reason he came. Not to fuck around with me. Not to ask me how I'd been the last few weeks. And not to talk to me about what being back in Denver was like.

He'd made sure I knew what our relationship was, and for a split second I'd forgotten. I wouldn't make the same mistake again.

* * *

A bonus of having no real job was that I could go to the grocery store during the off-hours. The drawback was that it was summer and teachers could also be doing their shopping at the same time. Same with ranchers. Teachers like Kennedy and ranchers like my cousin Archer's wife, Laney.

I had stopped to peruse spices for my brew since I now had to stock up on my own and heard familiar voices chatting around the corner.

"That sounds amazing," Laney said. "What time?"

"You can come over whenever, but Liam thought he'd be starting the grill around five. That way the kids can eat and run around."

"Perfect. Want me to bring anything?"

"Whatever you want to drink and maybe a dessert? Holden and Emery are bringing all the kids."

"Duly warned." Laney laughed. "Enough sweets to feed a child army. How about Stetson?"

"Oh, yes. Lyric just got back to me and said they could make it. And I'm sure Nora will swing by. She loves playing with the kids."

At Stetson and Lyric's names, my heart plummeted. I was happy for them, but that would be everyone. But me.

"Awesome." Laney's enthusiasm scraped across my hurt feelings, rough as sandpaper. She and Kennedy never used to get along. Laney hadn't even gone to Derek's funeral. I didn't know her circumstances, but she was now Kennedy's best friend and part of the family. And I wasn't sure I was. "I can't wait. These Barron summer bashes are going to be epic."

They were finishing up. I couldn't have them catching me eavesdropping. I hustled in the other direction, hoping I'd career around the corner and be tucked safely in the next aisle before they were done talking.

A gathering of my brother and all the cousins. I checked my phone like I'd missed an invite. Nope. Nothing.

The back of my throat burned, but I refused to let tears gather. How could a grocery trip to fill my first-ever kitchen with my stuff turn into the worst day of the summer? I hadn't been this devastated when my parents kicked me out.

I wrapped up my shopping trip. I had my food and the items I needed to make my wort and start a batch fermenting. In the self-checkout, I had stuffed my debit card in the reader like it owed me money when Kennedy's voice broke in.

"Hi, Isla."

I adopted a smile that shouldn't reveal I'd heard all the party plans and was trying not to cry. "Hey, Kennedy." I had never left the store with more than a shopping basket. Kennedy's cart was full of cereal, fruits and vegetables, and enough snack food to feed the twins for a year. How long did a cartful like that last her? Or was a lot of it for the party?

She stopped at the end of the aisle. "Oh, hey, you know what, we're having a get-together tomorrow night. Just some grilling and lawn games. You want to join us?"

My emphatic *yes* stuck in my throat. I wanted to go, and if I hadn't overheard them talking, I would've said yes. Had she seen me fleeing the baking aisle? Was this a guilt invite? Or hadn't she given me a second thought until she saw me and realized her oversight? Neither answer helped me.

What was a Barron without their pride? "Um, tomorrow night? Sorry, I'm still getting settled into my new house."

She grinned, and there was nothing but true excitement shining in her soft, brown eyes. "That's amazing. Congrats. What place did you buy?"

Her sincerity aided my attempt to sound natural, like

the last month of being a party of one wasn't bothering me. "The Millers used to live there? It's by the park, tucked into the trees at the very end."

"Oh, okay. I know the place. That's great. Congratulations."

"Thanks."

She gave me a little wave and pushed her cart toward another checkout. I grabbed my bag and beelined out of the store. In my car, I stared out the windshield. Did I do the right thing? What if the party was last minute? What if they hadn't thought of me because I wasn't one of their usual invites, but when she saw me, she remembered that I had visited? I had talked to my nephews and my brother, and I wanted to get to know them more.

My phone buzzed and I jumped. Checking it, Liam's name flashed across the screen.

Had Kennedy already told him she'd run into me and she thought Liam should do the asking? Should I have said I'd go? "Hello?"

"Isla, hey. I wanted to give you a quick call and talk about the work you wanted done."

Using my best grown-up professional voice, I still ended up nodding as if he could see me. "Yes."

"I'm sorry, I can't. I've got too much going on, and I'm still working with Hattie, which fits me better. I appreciate your interest."

He appreciated my interest, said in a detached, professional tone. I'd wanted my brother's work in my place to somehow symbolize a relationship we didn't have, and he only saw it as interest. "Oh, okay. No, I understand."

"With the kids and the job—and I work in scrap. You'd want a consistent look for it all. Sometimes, I can get stools in and change them, so they're a matching set, but that's sporadic and based on what I can source from garage sales and thrift stores. Anything I'd do would probably stand out from your other work."

I'd planned the aesthetic to fit the difference. The picture was so clear in my head, and now it was dissolving. "No, I get it. I just thought since you've taken custom work . . ."

"Small projects—and they ask for an idea, and I come up with a spin on it. You're asking for more than I can do. I'm sorry, Isla."

I could do professional detachment too. "Thanks for letting me know."

"Best of luck on the brewery. How's it going?"

It wasn't. "You know, it's moving along. A few snags here and there." My standard answer for the last month when I wanted to shout *Not a damn thing's happening.* I was prepared for delays—it was why I'd hired a company instead of being a project manager myself, but Reservoir Barrel shouldn't even be at the stage to start having delays.

"Glad it's going well. Hey, I mean it. Thanks for pitching me the idea."

My reply came out wooden. "You're welcome."

"Kennedy's going to be home soon. I'd better go."

His wife was across the parking lot, clueless I was talking to Liam. Had she known he would be calling to turn me down?

After he hung up, I sat in my pickup. It was the middle of July, and the cab was hot. A trickle of sweat rolled down between my boobs, but I didn't turn the engine on until Kennedy loaded her groceries and drove away.

My family had founded the town. I'd been born and raised in Coal Haven, but growing up, I'd felt like I was on the outskirts. There was conflict around Liam, issues between my parents and others, and I hadn't found a place that was my own.

No big surprise I was building on that very spot. Only it sat as empty and alone as I was.

Sucking in a breath, I closed my eyes. I still had my oil money. The building purchase hadn't cost as much as one would've expected. The previous owner had wanted to unload it. Since no work had been done, I'd paid nothing but McCoy's time and the initial up-front fees that showed I was serious. I'd already proven I had the money before I could sign the agreement with McDaniel Contractors.

I had a house. A little more of a dent in the funds I'd left unallocated for the construction. Both purchases showed that I was in charge of my life. So, maybe I should go out tonight.

My thumb was poised over the screen to message Lyric. She was working and . . . I didn't feel like talking to her right now. She had a family party to get ready for.

I was happy for my friend. She'd grown up as alone as me. But I was also standing in the rearview mirror of her life.

This time, tears misted over my eyes. I sniffled. It wasn't like I could talk to Lyric about what was bothering me. It felt pathetic enough to think it. And maybe a little like she was getting to take my spot in the family gatherings.

Who could I call?

McCoy had practically run out of the house when I'd asked him to basically boil water with me, so he was out. Between the way McCoy booked it out of my house, what I'd overheard in the store, and Liam's call, I wanted to go home and bury my face in my pillow . . . on the plastic inflatable bed I'd purchased until I could buy some real furniture. I didn't want to move a frame and mattresses around while I painted and replaced carpet, but the inflatable mattress made it feel temporary.

Going home would not make me feel better. Who wasn't related to me who might actually want to hang out?

Aspen popped into my mind. Before I could talk myself out of it, I messaged her. **Want to meet at Rattler's for supper and then brew some beer like we're on an 1890s homestead?**

Her reply was instant, bolstering my mood. **Dang! I can't. Another trip to KC.**

Of course. Everyone had their life. **Sorry. Hope everything's OK.**

Me too. Thanks for the invite though.

Sighing, I tossed my phone onto the passenger seat next to my groceries. Well, that sucked.

I had my spices, and I had a house. Time to make beer and have a good cry.

Eleven

MCCOY

I entered the diner and the smell of coffee wafted over me. Nodding toward Jocelyn where she was ringing up a customer, I headed to an open booth. A few of the guys I'd seen in here other mornings tipped their heads toward me. I hadn't done more than make passing comments about the weather or some shit when they walked past where I was sitting, but the familiarity was there.

Jocelyn brought a water. "Same?"

"Yes, ma'am." Smiling, she bustled off.

I was officially a regular. I hadn't ventured to Rattler's by myself. Too much chance of running into Isla.

She hadn't asked me on a date. She hadn't come on to me. She'd been thrilled about the hobby, and she'd invited me along for the fun since it had also been my passion. I still hadn't figured out if I'd run from the brewing—or Isla.

The way she'd danced and clapped her hands. A guy would think I'd gifted her a priceless heirloom instead of pointing out the possibilities of a basement with a sink and countertops. She'd been so damn happy, and for a second, I had taken credit. For several moments, I had enjoyed pointing it out to her and seeing her reaction, watching the delight register on her face. Her gratitude.

Osmosis had been in full effect. Her happiness had become mine, and I'd known what it meant to feel certain about one good thing instead of facing a future of what the hell did I get myself into?

And I'd left. I couldn't figure out why, other than I didn't want to get embroiled in the process. I didn't want her to look at me like I could teach her what I knew while I was secretly panicking with questions like, *When is she going to use this against me? How can she take what I've told her and steal everything out from under me?* And the worst question—*When is she going to realize I'd only drag her down?*

A tall man with dark hair walked by the window. He waved to someone on the street as he passed. A second later, the door opened. I forgot about him until Liam walked by the window and tipped the brim of his cap toward me.

Next thing I knew, he was by the booth with the other man. "Morning, McCoy."

"Liam," I greeted.

"This is Archer Barron, Isla's cousin." As I shook the man's hand, Liam asked, "How'd Isla take my response?"

"What response?"

Confusion flashed in his eyes. He looked around. "Mind if we join you?"

I shook my head. "Having Barrons appear on the other side of the booth seems to be a thing here."

Archer chuckled. "You get used to it."

I couldn't imagine. In Nashville, when I saw people I knew in public, it was Hannah they'd wanted to talk to. In

Denver, people steered clear of my dad. Mom and Fergus were workaholics who'd made contacts, not actual friends.

I glanced at Liam, silently urging him to continue.

"I had to pass," he said. "It's too big of a project. I had to wait for my work schedule to come out for the rest of the year and next year will be the same and I just couldn't commit."

Understandable. Isla was likely disappointed, but she hadn't said anything in the week since I'd bolted after she signed the documents. "She hasn't mentioned it. We're in a bit of a forced waiting phase for a delay."

He frowned. "Really? When Kennedy and I talked to Isla, she said it was going fine." Then he curled his hands around the brim of his cap and chuckled. "Never mind. It's not like she's going to tell us her business."

"It's not personal. She's aware of how she's viewed in town."

Liam and Archer exchanged a look. "How?" Liam asked.

It was clear to me, and I wasn't from Coal Haven. "If Reservoir Barrel is a raging success, what will people think? Honest—what will they think?"

Archer was the one who answered. "That it was her parents' doin'."

Liam shrugged as if to say, *Well, isn't it?*

I waited for Jocelyn to drop off the guys' waters and get their orders—which she already knew. "And if it's a failure, what will they think? Same brutal honesty."

Liam stared out the window, but he answered. "They'd claim that of course it failed. Isla's a sheltered girl who doesn't know anything. So when anyone asks, she's going to say 'fine' no matter what."

"Exactly. But when she approached you, it was because she admired your work. I don't know the history between you two"—my gaze flicked to Archer—"you three, but you weren't a charity project."

"I didn't think I was." He pressed his lips together. "Okay, maybe a little. Wonder if that's why she didn't come over last Saturday night."

"What was last Saturday?" Other than a boring night watching TV. I'd even contemplated buying a fishing pole and going to the lake. I didn't like fishing. It'd been just another father–son activity where Dad yelled, claimed I was doing it all wrong, and stomped to the truck with a huff threatening to leave me there. Fergus didn't fish; he worked and made beer. So I worked and made beer. But Isla wasn't me. What else did she have going on?

"Kennedy and I planned a quick family grill night. She said she invited Isla, but Isla had plans in her new house."

The house needed plenty of work, but I couldn't see Isla turning down the invite. She'd put herself out there to ask Liam to work with her. But if he turned her down, how would she feel?

Jocelyn dropped my plate in front of me, loaded with a steaming omelet I couldn't be bothered with. Alarm bells in my brain went off about Isla. I was just the person to recognize isolating oneself. Wasn't that exactly what I was doing in Coal Haven?

"Delaney worried Isla overheard her and Kennedy talking about it and thought maybe she made an excuse not to come," Archer said. "Like it would've felt too awkward after that."

I didn't recognize the name and struggled to connect the dots of who married who. "Who's Delaney?"

"My wife," he answered.

"Laney," Liam said at the same time.

"She had a quick chat with Kennedy in the store the other day and saw Isla haulin' tail away from them." Archer continued. "Then Kennedy told her that Isla turned down the invite."

It burned to feel like you meant nothing to people you wanted to be important in your life. Didn't mean it was my business. Also didn't mean I couldn't quit wondering if she was okay, but she wanted these guys to think she was. "Isla's got plans for her plans, so she might legitimately have been busy."

Archer leaned back when Jocelyn appeared with piping-hot plates full of food. When she charged off, he ignored his meal. "If everything's on pause, why are you still in town?"

Liam's mouth twisted in a wry grin. "What we mean to say is—we heard about Nashville."

Goddamn, word really did spread like a forest fire around here. "And you're worried I'm here to harass Isla?"

Liam's grin still hinted of irony. "I, of all people, know that what lands in people's ears isn't necessarily what happened. But I have to admit that I would've loved to be a fly on your pants leg when Cameron confronted you."

Archer chuckled quietly. "You don't strike me as the usual guy Cameron thinks he can bowl over."

This coming from Cameron's relatives. One of them was his son, for fuck's sake. No wonder Isla was at times so timid I thought she'd dart across the lawn and hide in a bush and at others unwavering to the point of breaking. She had too much of her parents in her to fight nature versus nurture.

"He was justified in being concerned about his daughter, but he has a shit way of dealing with it." I stabbed a fork through a pile of hash browns.

"From what I've seen," Archer said, "that should be his motto. 'Shit way of dealing with my problems.'"

"That tracks," Liam said. "I'm sure I take first place as his biggest problem."

Archer dug into his food. "Who are we if our parents don't fuck us up a little?"

"It's when your wife and best friend are finished fucking you up that there's a problem." If I could've lit those words on fire as they left my mouth, I would've. No one could've heard them if they were smoke. Why the hell was I telling near strangers my business?

Liam paused with a grimace. "I married my best friend's wife, but it isn't what it sounds like."

"Isla promised it isn't as sordid as it comes off," I said.

"It isn't," Archer said, "but Delaney didn't tell her family that we married. She didn't even tell them about me."

Isla wasn't the only one keeping life changes close to her chest.

Liam nodded. "Not one word and she'd been back for over a year."

"A year and a half," Archer growled.

"Afraid I don't know this story." Was it bad that I wanted to? To see how other people's lives fell apart and were pieced back together?

Archer put his fork down like he had to gear up for the tale. "She moved to Texas for college and had heard of me. So, when my company hosted a job fair, she showed up to be nosy, and I hit on her hard. We eloped since our family situations were less than ideal at the time. But I was a workaholic ass and she left."

Liam let out a mournful sigh. "I wish I coulda seen her parents' faces when you showed up, announced your last name, and said you were her husband."

"They matched hers." Archer's grin stayed in place, but understanding simmered in his eyes. "Sorry 'bout the shit you're going through."

"Aw, it's nothing." A lie, but it didn't burn like it used to. Especially with two people who sided with me without waiting to find out Hannah's side of the story. Just easy acceptance that shit happened and I was still McCoy. "Wife had an affair with my best friend. I'd taught them both everything they knew about the industry, but I preferred to stay behind the tanks. Everyone was used to dealing with them, so when the shit hit the fan, it seemed best to bow out. I just didn't know he was the one who'd bought me out."

Archer winced. "He went through a company?"

"Formed just to get what I had."

"So he has it all while you're in North Dakota helping a young woman build basically what you lost?" Liam asked.

"Sometimes it felt like it was never mine." Where had that come from? Nailer's had been mine from conception to construction to production and distribution. I'd worked my ass off. I'd done what my dad said I couldn't do. Fergus had been damn proud of me. If he'd still been alive, he'd have been distraught, and my humiliation would've filled the goddamn universe.

Archer nodded. "It can be like that when we're doing it for the wrong reasons. I thought I had everything I wanted until I moved here. All I had left was to make partner in the firm I worked for. Turned out I wanted exactly what I'd been running from. Life is crazy like that sometimes."

My situation was nothing like Archer's. I didn't want what I'd grown up with. It was a special kind of purgatory being stuck on Groundhog's Day. Except Dad had owned his own business. Then Mom had her own business. I was back to being nothing but an employee, and I wasn't going to fuck this up for Mom.

Liam and Archer peppered me with questions about Nashville, and as the meal went on, I relaxed. The only reason I left before they were ready was because the nagging concern for Isla wouldn't diminish.

* * *

Isla's pickup was parked on the street in front of her house. The trailer with the mower was neatly backed onto the concrete pad in front of the garage. I hated to be impressed and my first inclination was to wonder who did it for her. Just because she was a girl didn't mean she couldn't back a trailer, but there was a level of skill and experience that went along with the task. But she'd said she showed horses when she was younger, so she'd likely backed a trailer several times.

Dad had ripped me two new assholes when I'd been learning to back tool trailers at home and at the jobsite.

I jogged to the door. Country music filtered out. I knocked and waited. Had she heard me?

I tried the doorbell, but either the house had excellent insulation, or the buzzer didn't work. I knocked again. No answer.

Was she doing okay? What if she was downstairs? I should call first, but I didn't want to be told she was fine like I was anyone else. Instead, I tried the doorknob. She'd replaced that since I was here last. Good. Small wins when it felt like everything was falling around her were important. Even better, the house wasn't locked. I'd be worried, but I doubted many Coal Haven residents kept their houses locked twenty-four seven.

When I stepped in, I couldn't stop the "whoa" that left my mouth. The wall with the wallpaper in the living room was shredded like a couple of mountain lions had wandered through the house and took the pattern as a personal insult. A gallon of paint was tucked into the corner of the room, but it'd be a while before the wall was ready for paint.

I stopped at the entrance to the kitchen. A Bluetooth speaker sat by the sink. The cupboard doors were open.

Shelf liners for the cupboards were wadded in a mass on the counter. Nice design though. It'd brighten the insides.

Continuing down the hall, I peered into the bathroom and recoiled. What the hell happened? Was Isla okay? And where the hell was she?

There was water pooled on the floor, and the toilet was two feet from where it should be. The sink and counter were full of tools. But the wallpaper had come off easier than the living room. The little space was already more cheerful and less discotheque.

"Isla?" As I stepped back to peek in her bedroom, the carpet squished underfoot. There was no active water leak. She must've gotten the water shut off but not until the leak had migrated out the door. I'd have cussed a blue streak. That shit happened all the time, experienced or not, but she was a noob at remodeling.

Where was she?

Her bedroom was empty except for an inflatable mattress and small plastic bins for dressers and end tables. The spare room and the room that'd be good to either convert to a pantry or an office were also empty.

She wasn't upstairs. I stuffed a hand through my hair. Did she get hurt? Had someone picked her up and taken her to the ER? I had to find her. I went through the kitchen, the damp bottoms of my shoes squeaking slightly. A light was on in the basement. Hopeful I'd find her alive and well, I took the stairs down and went straight for the laundry room.

A giant jug of beer was fermenting in one corner, a four-gallon pot was on a tabletop stove plugged into the wall, and Isla was sitting cross-legged on the counter next to it with her head buried in her hands. Her hair was gathered in a messy ponytail, the faint blue ends like a dying sparkler, and an amber bottle of her homemade brew was open at her knee.

Her phone was on the counter next to her. Country tunes drifted into the basement, but the sound was muffled.

Relieved to find her intact, the knot loosened between my shoulders. "Isla."

She popped her head up and blinked. She might've been crying earlier, but her face was dry, if blotchy. "Shit." She swiped her hands over her cheeks. "McCoy. Is there something wrong? Do you have news on the *A* and *E* team?"

She was trying to pretend like she was fine, even ignoring how I walked in without an invite, and I wished I had a better update for her, but I didn't. I stopped in front of her, my hands propped on the edge of the counter. There was no heat coming from the stove, and when I glanced over, there was no water in the pot.

Malt and hops were piled on the other side. She'd been planning to start another batch but, for some reason, had ended up here.

"What's going on?" This close, I could inhale the berries and cream I missed like my last breath. This close, I could touch her skin and quit wondering if all that bare flesh I saw when she got out of the shower was as satiny as it looked. This close, I could lean in like I did last time and plant my lips on hers. It'd been weeks since I tasted her, and it wasn't just the dry spell talking.

Isla Barron was something. I hadn't been able to ignore her like I had every other woman since my divorce.

"I messed up." She sniffed, and her shoulders hunched. "So many times."

"Hey." I lifted her chin with two of my fingers. When I took my hand off her, I rested it on her knee. Big mistake, but I couldn't move now that I was touching her after so long. "We all fuck up. I'm guessing the bathroom?"

Her scornful chuckle was accompanied by an eye roll.

"That wasn't even the beginning. I got the bathroom wall-paper off so easily I thought the living room wouldn't be an issue. I think I tore half the wall off with the pieces I actually got removed."

"Wallpaper can be a bitch."

"So the next day, I tried to line the cabinets with contact paper."

"Contact paper can be a bitch."

She huffed again. "And then the huge crack in the toilet bowl started leaking now that it was being used again. So I bought a new toilet, watched a few videos, and well, the plumbing hasn't been messed with in a while."

"Old plumbing can be a bitch."

She scowled at me but continued. "I have no idea what I'm doing, so I came down here to make some wort and get a quick batch started, you know, for a morale boost, and didn't even think that shutting the water off would make it impossible to make a batch of beer." She held her hands out. "Who wouldn't realize they can't use the water when they were the one who shut it off?"

"Didn't you just shut off the water in the bathroom?"

"They leaked too. Old valves."

"Old valves can be a—"

She pressed two fingers to my lips. "I swear to God, McCoy, if you keep saying that, I'm going to . . ." A defeated sigh left her. She slid her fingers down my lips to my neck, leaving a blazing trail where she touched.

"What are you going to do?" I murmured.

Her gaze flicked from my collar to my face. "Shut you up."

"How?" I infused enough challenge to make sure she'd rise to meet it. Because I was desperate to know.

The defiance was there. The need to prove herself, but she was guarded. "I don't want it to be a mistake."

Ah, hell. "It'd be a big fucking mistake, sunbeam, but I can't seem to quit thinking about how I want to kiss you again."

"A mutually agreed-on mistake?" Her fingers curled around my neck. She pulled me toward her.

I had no problem closing the distance until my lips landed on hers. She tasted sweet, like the beer she'd been drinking. The spicy cardamom flavor grew stronger as I licked into her mouth.

She groaned, and that was the moment it was clear a kiss wasn't going to be enough. I moved the bottle of beer farther away and tugged her closer to the edge so I could properly invade the depths of her mouth.

Without breaking contact, she unfolded her legs and put one on either side of me. I could pull her flush against me, but I needed room to touch her. To roll her old shirt up, get frustrated that it kept falling down, and rip it over her head.

It was worth the separation. The tits I couldn't quit imagining were right in front of me, cupped by a simple white bra.

Pink dusted her cheeks and her lips were plump from our kiss. I needed a moment to think, to keep from falling on her like a starving animal. I grabbed the beer and drained half of what was left while keeping my gaze on her.

I swallowed, her eyes fixated on my throat. "Do you still think it's good?"

"I think you're going to taste better." I set the bottle down and focused back on her not-bare-enough breasts.

Rimming a finger under the band of her bra, I took in the situation. There was no going back. I needed more with Isla. The project was at a standstill, and that bothered her. But she and I weren't paused—we'd have to be moving forward for that, and we weren't. I'd tabled our progress as soon as the hail busted the window, and I was hating myself for it.

Reaching behind her, I unhooked her bra, marveling that I hadn't forgotten everything about women's clothing when I'd been purging my life of females for the last year.

I wanted her. I wanted something that was mine, and that was the problem. She couldn't be. So maybe that was why I was okay with giving in—just a little. We wouldn't go all the way in the basement of her new house. I could have a sample while making her feel better.

That was a little superficial, but as I slipped the bra from her arms and dropped it on the counter, I didn't fucking care. Her chest rose and fell with her breaths, and the movement of her pink, pearled nipples was mesmerizing.

"Fuck me, Isla." I didn't wait for her response. I cupped a handful of her warm flesh. The way she shivered under my touch was the perfect tease before I licked over a tight nipple.

A moan left her, and I massaged her other breast while flicking the tip with my tongue. Her little jerk, followed by a tremble, encouraged me to indulge in a little fantasy. Releasing her breast, I picked up the bottle of beer.

Her dazed eyes were filling with questions until I stopped with the mouth of the bottle hovering inches over her chest. "You know what I think would go well with this flavor?"

Her response was barely a whisper. "No?"

A tiny tip of the bottle and some liquid dribbled out. I ducked to catch the trail of beer as it slid between her breasts. Licking every drop, I groaned. The slight sweetness of the drink on her skin was the best I'd ever tasted. She'd created the flavor and it was her. "I like the way you taste."

Her lips were parted and need raged in her eyes. "I'm never going to look at that beer the same again."

The rest of the beer could wait. I trailed my fingers through the glistening path my tongue left and went farther down.

Was I doing this? Some quick making out between two adults was easier to move on from when I hadn't been inside her. I might not have been planning to go all the way, but I was going to get into Isla today.

Her waistband was elastic, thank fuck. I tunneled over her lower abdomen and hit her hot, wet center. Heaven. That was what paradise felt like. She bunched her fists in my shirt, tugging me closer while arching her back to give me more room.

I sucked a nipple into my mouth again when I tapped on her swollen clit. Satisfaction spiraled through me. This girl had been as needy as me.

Releasing her pearled flesh, I licked my lips. Someday, I'd taste where my hand was. "Did you stroke yourself in the shower like I did that day?"

Her eyes were hooded. She panted against my hand, but she met my gaze. "No, but I have since then."

Fuck. "Were you thinking about me like I was thinking about you?"

She let out a soft keen. "Yes." Her gaze flickered. "You were thinking about me that day?"

"Naked in your shower? Surrounded by your smell?" I added pressure to her clit with my thumb and tunneled my fingers through her slit to her opening. "Fuck yeah, I was thinking about you." She rocked into my hand, and I thrust a finger inside, loving the way her eyelids fluttered. "I wanted to know what you looked like under that tiny swimsuit."

I dropped my head, capturing her other tight nipple in my mouth. She raked her hand through my hair, fisting and tugging in time with the roll of her hips. Christ, she was a feast. I kept up the pressure but released her. Her lips were parted and her head rolled. Drunk with desire. I was what she was getting intoxicated on.

"McCoy?"

"Yeah?"

"I can't get the picture of your cock out of my head."

Jesus. "You'll get to see it soon enough." This was about her.

"I want to see you now. I want to see your fist around it again." She had to release one hand to brace herself on the counter. She rode my finger, wildly abandoning her inhibitions—something I didn't think she did with many people.

My focus was on her, but her wet nipples bounced in front of my face, and goddamn, I was never going to let that image escape my brain. "Let yourself go."

"McCoy." The breathless way she said my name made me impatient to witness her finish.

"Come for me. Now." I threaded another finger into her.

Her head dropped back, and a long moan left her. Heat washed over my hand, and I watched her. Fucking spectacular. She fell apart for me, and once wasn't enough.

I licked across a nipple, and Isla's entire body shuddered. Her orgasm continued, and I let her ride it out while I tasted what I could. When she went limp, I gathered her to me, hating the loss of her sweltering flesh around me. If I indulged in a second of imagining what that climax would feel like around my dick, I'd come in my pants.

She laid her head on my shoulder and murmured, "If you were trying to make me feel better, job well done."

I chuckled softly. "That was only a thought when it came to the timing. I've been trying to keep from seeing if you'd let me in your pants since I saw you."

"Even when you thought I was a spoiled college girl?"

"Especially then. The last thing I needed was to become an old pervert."

She traced light circles on my back, as igniting as they were soothing. "You're not that much older than me."

"Sometimes it feels like decades, sunbeam."

"Quit being so grumpy, and it might not." She shifted enough to meet my gaze. "Is it my turn to put my mouth on you?"

I groaned, but I yanked the logic out before it got buried. I couldn't maintain the walls I'd built around myself with her. If anything, the way she responded to me, the way she asked—so close to begging—put us on equal footing. Made me think that the sensation of getting swallowed up by quicksand when she was around was more of an illusion. "Soon, sunny. We need to get that bathroom fixed, and the hardware store's closing soon."

The defeat resurfaced in her gaze. "You shouldn't have to rescue me."

"Do you think I've done everything in my life by myself? I'm a loner, but even I know I can't do everything on my own."

"I wanted to prove—"

"That you're suddenly an expert in fifty-year-old plumbing?"

She sighed, but a ghost of a smile played over her lips. "Point taken."

Satisfied she was in a good place, I helped her stand. Her legs were shaky, and she had to lean against the counter for a second. When she saw what must've been a smug expression, she laughed and an adorable snort escaped. And it hit me—I was the happiest I'd been in a while, including the years before my marriage imploded.

Twelve

ISLA

I might not have done the repairs myself, but that didn't stop pride from expanding inside of me until I thought I might explode. "I can't believe we got that done. And I hope to never replace a toilet again. Gross."

McCoy grinned from where he was leaning against the door frame, his arms folded across his chest. It'd been hard to concentrate on the work we were doing. Only the fact that we were working with dirty plumbing kept the proximity of the small bathroom from being a sexual experience. Instead, it was cramped, sweaty, and I learned how many swear words McCoy knew.

"Motherfucking cocksucker" was one of his favorites.

The water was back on and nothing was leaking. I thought I'd have to pay for a plumber to replace the older piping, but McCoy had rescued me from that too. *Dad was a cheap bastard, and he refused to pay a professional if he could do it himself.* While we were at it, we'd done the kitchen sink too.

"I don't know about you, but I need a shower."

I looked down at myself. I was wearing the shirt McCoy had stripped off me earlier and the same shorts, but after working in a bathroom, I needed a shower. "It just so happens, I have running water if you'd like to wash up here."

He pushed off the door frame. "I need fresh clothes, and we need dinner. Your stomach has been complaining for the last couple of hours."

I'd eaten breakfast, but the half a beer I'd had before McCoy arrived hadn't lasted long. Definitely got burned off during the powerful orgasm I hadn't expected.

One time. Once with only one hand and McCoy had obliterated all my past experiences. I craved him. I wanted him naked in my shower. He could wear nothing but a towel.

Unfortunately, I had little more food in the house than I had men's clothing, which was none. "I owe you. I'll clean up and pick up something from Rattler's and bring it over."

I waited with my breath suspended. Had I just asked him out? Bringing food to his motel room wasn't a fancy date, and after earlier, we both knew what we wanted to happen in his motel room.

His gaze turned smoldering. "Is it because there's an actual bed in my motel room?"

"Maybe." I sounded like I'd run a mile, breathless and waiting to be told to sprint to Northern Lights, room 5.

"Burger and fries. I'm not a fancy guy." He strode down the hall toward the door. "And bring any of that sunshine beer you have left. I'm getting addicted to the stuff, dammit."

I stayed in the hall, or I'd run after him and beg to join

him in the shower. He shot me a promising look before he pushed out the door. I fanned my face and danced back into the bathroom.

While the water was heating up, I ordered the food. Then took the fastest shower of my life. My body thrummed. After having had such an intense orgasm, I was ready for another round. Or two. Maybe three. God, the broody energy rolling off McCoy said he was good for it.

At Rattler's, I trotted inside and made my way to the bar.

Lyric appeared at my shoulder. "Hey, girl. Where've you been?"

Genuine delight coursed through me. I smiled. "Hey! I've been at my new house."

She frowned like I'd hurt her feelings. "You didn't call me to help you move in."

"I know, mama, but I didn't have much and you're busy." It wasn't like I was included in everything in her life. We'd been so close for so long, and now there was distance.

Lyric's eyes flickered like a dying light bulb. "I had a baby, but I'm still me."

"I know."

She tilted her head, her gaze serious. "Do you?"

Frowning, I was about to reply when the bartender leaned over the table. "Got your order here, Isla."

I handed over my card and turned back to Lyric. "I don't want to be a bother. You're busy with your family and work."

"Life is busier," she agreed, but her lips formed a troubled line. "I just feel like you're avoiding me."

I didn't want to feel like a bother to my best friend. "I've got stuff going on too."

"I wouldn't know."

Drawing back, I processed her statement. She was acting

like I was the one who wasn't available. We still messaged—not as much or for as long and mostly about Rina, but it wasn't like I didn't have time for her like she didn't have for me. "I have the house and the foundry—Reservoir Barrel."

My gaze strayed to the round table in the back where Stetson used to hang out in his single days. He would attract all his buddies and all the single women. He was back there now, but the view was different. Kids rounded the table. Holden's wife, Emery, was handing their baby boy, Grady, to Holden so she could help her youngest with her food. A baby carrier was in a sling holder next to my brother and the empty chair by Stetson was where Lyric had been sitting.

"Here ya go." The bartender slid a bag with two to-go containers across the bar top to me and gave me back my card. Having my hands full took the sting off being a spectator to another family gathering.

Lyric eyed the two to-go boxes. "Company?"

"I'm meeting with my project manager." I couldn't hold her gaze, not while a flush spread from my core upward just thinking about McCoy.

"The hot one?" she asked flatly.

"The same guy it's always been." The defensiveness in my tone gave me away. Lyric knew me. She'd be able to tell I felt more than professional toward McCoy. I wanted him to be anything but professional.

"Isla, are you sure it's a good idea—"

"I'll let you get back to your family. Tell my brother and the others I said hi." I gave her a tight smile, grabbed my food, and rushed out.

The backs of my eyes stung like tears wanted to appear, but I wouldn't let them. Lyric sounded hurt, but it wasn't like our friendship was a one-way street. She was busy and I understood, but I wasn't going to feel guilty about not updating her on everything.

What would she tell my brother? I doubted she'd inform my parents of issues I didn't want them to know, but I missed having that one person I could talk to. The person who was a fortress. Nothing she told me got past my lips and vice versa. And now? It was just different. I refused to feel like the bad guy for accepting that.

The encounter shouldn't have bothered me that much, but I stewed during the short drive to the motel. Parking beside McCoy's truck, I took a calming breath. The hurt and conflicted feelings in my chest would stay in the pickup. I wanted to explore the tension between McCoy and me, and the outside world could just . . . move on like it was doing. Without me.

I was about to knock on the door when he opened it, his phone tucked between his shoulder and ear. He was dressed in the same grungy clothes. "Got it. No, I know. It's critical. Remember what I said, though." I edged around him, and he shut the door behind me. "Just . . . think about it, okay?"

He hung up and tossed the phone on the small table. "Sorry. I had to make a quick stop, and Sylvia called when I walked into the room. I haven't had a chance to shower yet."

"Better hurry or I'll dive into your burger too."

"Be back in a minute."

I set our food out. Doled out the silverware. Despite my best efforts, I couldn't forget Rattler's. Why did that bother me so much? I wasn't the one pulling away from people. I was the one who didn't get invited to meals out with family. Who was an afterthought invite to a gathering every sibling and cousin I had in the county went to. My parents hadn't been speaking to me either. Aunt Kira never talked to me if she could help it, and Uncle Bruce and Aunt Willow probably avoided me like they'd started doing with Mom and Dad.

I crunched the bag in my hands. Emotion smoldered,

clogging my lungs until I thought I'd combust. Lyric's chiding tone cut through my haze. She hadn't finished her question, but I knew what she was asking.

Did I think it was a good idea to mess around with McCoy? There was no other reason for me to meet with him when we'd done all we could do on Reservoir Barrel until we knew what was possible.

I stared at the closed bathroom door. We were two adults. We'd been wanting to get together since we'd met, and we'd worked together just fine. We could be mature about it all. Maybe he was the distraction I needed.

I stepped back from the table and stripped my shirt off, tossing it on the bed. Next off was my bra. I toed out of my slip-on shoes and tossed my shorts and underwear onto my other clothing.

At the bathroom door, I knocked. I wasn't brave enough to charge in. What if he locked it?

"Yeah?" came his cautious reply, like he thought something was wrong.

"I want an appetizer."

Just like when I'd asked him to come over, I held my breath.

"Door's open," he said gruffly.

When I pushed in, he was behind the plain beige but opaque shower curtain and the water was still running.

I pulled the curtain back.

There he was. His cock was growing and suds slid down his body, getting washed away by the spray. "Get in here. If you're going to stare like that, I get to look too."

I crowded in the tub with him and he stared, his gaze raking over my breasts and stopping at the juncture between my legs. Water peppered me, but he blocked most of the spray. Goose bumps erupted over my body, and my nipples were harder and tighter than they'd ever been.

When he moved, it was to gently lift my hand and bring it to his erection. "Feel what you do to me."

I stroked his hard length, tightening my hand as I went. So much power under my fingers. It went to my head as much as the heat pooled between my legs. Carefully, I lowered to my knees.

"Fuck, Isla, you don't need to—"

I lifted my gaze to his. He towered over me like a water god I was worshiping. I put my lips at the head of his cock and it twitched.

A small grunt left him. "You're killing me."

I licked over the tip. The faint flavor of soap was washed away by the water pouring over his shoulders and down his abs. My hair was plastered to my face and back, but I didn't let it slow me down. I sucked him in as far as I could handle.

He brushed the soaking strands of hair off my face. "I'm going to come every time I picture you kneeling at my feet in the shower. Hell, I don't think I'm going to be able to shower without jacking off again. *Fuck.*"

I didn't lick along his length and hum to quiet him, but he wouldn't be talking if he was being driven out of his mind. I pumped along his cock, and he began moving with me.

The water went from warm to cool. His flesh pulsed in my mouth, and I alternated between closing my eyes and gazing up at him. Each time I opened my eyes, his angles were harsher. He was straining to last longer than he wanted to. I was in charge, in control, if only for this moment.

The range of his hips shortened. He was getting closer. I put everything I had into the blow job, taking him farther with each bob of my head.

"Fuck, Isla. Oh god, oh fuck. I'm going to—"

He was warning me off, but I wanted to taste all of him.

The guy who had captured my thoughts since I'd seen him. The man I wanted to figure out.

With a long growl, he climaxed. I caught every drop, nearly choking myself, which made his hips buck harder. When he was finished, I sat back on my heels with a satisfied grin.

He pressed one hand against the wall and sagged. "You look pretty proud of yourself."

"I am." Dominating him from my knees was just what I needed.

His eyes narrowed, and he flipped the water off behind him. He jerked open the curtain and grabbed a towel. He toweled me off quickly before running it over himself.

I was in the process of standing when he stepped out and yanked me toward him.

"What are you—" The world spun and I was looking at the floor and the long strands of damp hair hanging by my face. He'd tossed me over his shoulder. "McCoy!"

"Time for me to show you what I can do." He marched toward the bed. My ass was in the air, and I caught the view of us in the mirror. My naked body draped over him and held by a strong arm with thick biceps. My butt cheeks were right next to his head and my boobs jumped with each step. Not exactly a centerfold-worthy picture.

Insecurity chased away my pride. "McCoy, you have to put me d—"

He lightly spanked my ass and I squealed, the sound covering the smack of my flesh. I'd . . . never been spanked before. It wasn't like he'd done it hard enough to sting, but it was that moment any feminism I possessed drained out of my body. I'd let this man do whatever he wanted to me.

He ripped the top blankets off and tossed me in the middle of the bed. I bounced, barked a startled cry, then he had my ankles wrapped in his hard grip. My knees were bent and my legs spread before I could orient myself.

"McCoy."

He paused, wedging his shoulders between my thighs. "Do you want me to stop?"

"God, no." My heart pounded from the caveman carry, but it wasn't fear. Pure exhilaration and delight for what was to come flooded my body with lust. "Sorry I interrupted."

His quick grin was almost menacing. He delved into my folds, and I collapsed back, immediately arching as his tongue hit my already sensitive clit. His wet hair was cool against my legs and shivers erupted from the evaporated water, but inside I was melting—and he was licking me up.

"You're good at that," I panted. I couldn't interpret his answering rumble.

I didn't have a ton of experience, and not with the regular sex that happened in a long relationship. I'd gotten bored with guys as quickly as they'd lost interest in me. But all of them had been close to my age, and none of them had the talent and straightforwardness of McCoy.

I fisted the sheets and rode his face. When he put that wicked finger back into me, I almost came undone, but the pleasure was ridiculously high and I didn't want it to end. When the restoration was done, the brewery built, would McCoy go back to Denver? Would we cease being a thing? What was this?

All questions were wiped from my mind. He rose to his knees and devoured me. A muffled voice in my mind reminded me we were in a motel, and people could be on either side. I frantically grabbed a pillow and stuffed it over my face.

My moans and my yells were dulled as I came hard. McCoy was ruthless, coaxing every last bit out of me until I was shaking and had nearly suffocated myself in the fabric.

I tossed the pillow off, and he surged over me. His gaze soaked up my body. He traced a finger along my hip bones. "I've been dying to see all of your tan lines."

A wavering giggle left me. "I have a few." I feathered my fingers over his arms. "So do you." I cocked a brow at his hip bones. The line of pale flesh didn't hold my attention long. "Are you hard again?"

"Sunny, I was never soft." He rolled next to me and reached for the nightstand and pulled out a box of condoms. "This was the stop I had to make."

"You didn't have any?" I didn't know why I was surprised, but McCoy was a guy who could get laid any time he wanted. His looks and the don't-mess-with-me aura around him were enticing. They'd drawn me in, but it was the peeks underneath it all that had hooked me. He was generous and thoughtful through his actions. And he was crazy about me.

"No. I've been trying to decrease the amount of trouble in my life." He flipped the box open, grabbed a packet, and tossed the box aside. "I was right about you, for the record."

"How so?"

"I knew you were going to cause issues as soon as I saw you." He nudged me to roll to my other side. "It's why I was so pissy when I learned who you were. Attractive and so damn sweet under that dose of salt you gave me, I knew I could suck on you all damn day."

The big head of his cock slicked through my wetness and prodded my entrance. He'd gotten me off twice today, but the idea of being filled with him, with the bulk I'd held in my hand and had in my mouth? I scooted my ass over to give him better access.

"Is that why you're so cranky?"

"No, I'm just generally a dick." He thrust inside, and my god, he was big. I gripped the sheet to keep from getting pounded off the bed, but I didn't need to worry. He had a hold of me. And wasn't that the real reason I was drawn to McCoy? He had me, and he did it in a way that made me feel important to someone.

* * *

McCoy

Isla was greedy. Her warm, wet body took me all the way in and demanded I punch back in as soon as possible. I wanted to take her in every position I could. Would I get the chance?

Grunting, I kicked my hips and plunged into her. "How can you feel so fucking good?" I didn't recall being this desperate for every morsel of any other partner. This frantic need to experience everything she offered in case she closed herself off from me. This much lust and desire pumping through my veins until I thought there'd never be a time I wasn't hard and thinking of Isla.

She was bracing herself against the bed, her fists in the mattress. I couldn't get the purchase I needed, so I withdrew, my erection hating me, and flipped her to all fours.

Rising to my knees, I slammed my hands on either side of her lush hips. "Stick your ass in the air."

She did, and I pumped. I kept pumping, losing myself in the rhythm, the hot velvet of her body, and the way she gripped and rippled around my dick.

"I think . . ." She bowed her back, her hands on the headboard. "I think I'm going to come again."

The sheer disbelief in her voice was the challenge I needed. Damn right she was going to come again. The thought of getting her off three times today and blowing her damn mind while I blew out her back was enough to shove me toward my peak.

But not yet.

I folded over her, reached around, and found her clit. A needy whimper left her and I answered, only resting my finger on her swollen bud. With my other hand, I spread her legs farther apart, keeping her as open to me as possible.

Her climax hit, and she buried her face in the sheet to muffle the sound. I did what I could to quiet myself as I slammed into my climax like a bowling ball taking out a thousand pins.

I clenched my teeth and let out a long "fuck" as I poured everything I had into her. I'd gone from no sex to getting off twice in a shamefully quick amount of time, but that was fine. After what we'd done, how we'd exploded together—that shit doesn't happen every day.

I collapsed next to Isla and tucked her close to me. I'd have to get rid of the condom and we'd both need to clean up again, but I couldn't bring myself to move.

Holding her unearthed a deep yearning inside of me. I could lie with her like this every day. What would it be like to wake up to her? What would it be like to shower with her? To devour her before we sat down to dinner?

Where'd those thoughts come from?

Been there, done that, had nothing to fucking show for it. I wasn't looking to settle down, and if I was, it wouldn't be in middle-of-nowhere Coal Haven. What would I do? How would I make a living? I wasn't going to bum off my girl like my dad had accused Mom of doing.

Thinking about Mom was a cold splash of water. Not only was I in bed with her client, but her phone call from earlier came crashing back.

Listen, Coy. I need you to distract Isla until Lorraine can get away from the Orlan project.

Why the hell do I need to distract her? Her project was supposed to be next.

Dev needs more time. He's thinking of a different location.

The asshole had gone from wanting to build new to wasting Lorraine's time to evaluate a restoration and now he wants to fucking move locations? And Isla's got to pay for it? *Just send Lorraine here, and Dev can fucking deal. He should've had his location figured out before he hired you.*

I hope that's not how you talked to other professionals. Her censuring tone made it clear my attitude was exactly how I'd wound up with nothing.

Isla had been delayed long enough.

Figure it out, McCoy. I'm counting on you.

Those words got me every time.

"Where'd you go?" Isla asked quietly.

"I'm right here."

She peered over her shoulder. A flush still misted over her cheeks, and damn—I put that there. She gave me a small smile, one that said I didn't have to talk if I didn't want to. The problem was, I wanted to. I was a doer, and normally, I would've trusted Mom to run her shit and not question her, but keeping quiet bothered me on a level I hadn't experienced before.

I owed her something. "I'm content. That's all."

She snuggled into me. It could've been because she was naked and the blankets were on the floor. "Me too, but our food's probably cold."

I'd forgotten about our meal. Her stomach had been protesting all afternoon. Rolling up, I reached for the blankets to cover her. "Stay there. I'll go to the bathroom and then grab the food."

She pulled the sheet to her armpits and sat against the headboard. She hadn't moved after I finished with the condom. I handed her one of the beers she'd brought over and her plastic to-go container.

She opened the lid to some type of chicken sandwich and waffle fries. "The good thing about Rattler's food is that it tastes good cold."

I got my burger and sat next to her, covering my lap with the other half of the sheet. When was the last time I'd been this truly relaxed? Since I'd left home after graduation, I'd been working toward something. Proving myself. I had to get a degree, work harder than anyone else on the jobsite, start my own company, brew the best beer, get the best distribution deals, and when my ex brought up the beer competition scene, that had fit too. I didn't have to do the work for it, other than make beer like I'd been doing, but it was another way to prove myself.

I demolished my food faster than I thought I could, like I'd worked out for days and this was the first solid nourishment I'd had when all I'd done was fix some simple plumbing and have sex.

Fuck, I was getting old. But the burger was that good. Lukewarm and everything. We ate in silence. "I'll miss Rattler's when I'm gone." Uneasiness swirled in my belly. I didn't like the thought of leaving, but it was only because Reservoir Barrel wasn't done. I was a guy who finished what he'd started.

How long would this last? The project was at a halt, and at the moment, it was just me and Isla. We weren't anything to each other, but at the same time, I could leave Coal Haven, never to return, and I wouldn't be the same as when I'd arrived. My time here had changed me, and it was because of this girl. I wasn't sure what she'd done, I just knew I was altered.

"Where are you going after this?" She munched on a waffle fry, her eyes full of innocent questions. She wasn't begging me to stay. This was a fling that seemed more significant than it was. But at the end of the project, I was going my way and Isla was staying.

"I don't know. I have to figure out what I want to do when I grow up." The grumpiness I had when I first arrived in town was returning. I leaned over and tossed my empty container onto the small table.

She licked salt off her finger, and a beat of lust almost had my dick raising the sheet and begging for more. "Are you going back into the beer industry?"

That'd be the logical step, but even as she asked, a dark cloud formed over my head, one that threatened to chase away the sunniness she brought into my life. "I don't know."

She ate the last fry and munched on the pickle spear included with her meal. "You don't like it anymore?"

"I don't know." It was the honest answer. I had enjoyed tasting different beers in Isla's cabin, but I couldn't separate the reason why from spending time with Isla. What had I really enjoyed about that night? The drinks or the girl?

"Is that why you hated the idea of brewing a batch with me?"

Yeah. That. My behavior had been as noticeable as I'd feared. I owed her an answer and talking might help me figure out what it was. "Fergus taught me everything he knew about home brewing, and I scaled up in a way that would've impressed him—and he wasn't an easy guy to impress."

She stayed quiet while I opened the cap of the home brew bottles and took a drink. The beer had warmed but was still fresh and crisp. Isla would've made Fergus proud. He'd probably have tips and get excited about how to riff off the recipe and use other spices and flavors.

"In turn, I had to teach others what I knew to work on

the scale I wanted. I wanted to be the best, the biggest, what-ever it took. I was already outgrowing Tennessee. Hannah and Angus—the guy she left me for—weren't the only ones I'd taught, but they were the most important."

"It's not your fault what they did."

Felt like it. "When I crawled back home, Mom reminded me that a marriage took two people. Hannah might've been ambitious and selfish, but the marriage wasn't working long before she did what she did—and who she did."

"And Angus?"

I bent my knees and draped my arms over them, the bottle held loosely in a hand and the sheet like a tent over my lower half. Never in the last year did I think I'd talk about what had happened this much, but I kept shedding that weight the more I spoke, including accepting my own role in neglecting my marriage. "I called him my best friend, and he was the closest of my friends, but that's not saying a lot. We talked beer. Business. And that was about it. I was all in with work, and he had a more well-rounded life that included my wife. The thing is, I wasn't in touch enough with either of them to think something was off. A guy who lives and works with his spouse should know when she's fallen in love with someone else. If Angus and I were so close, I would've considered he was seeing someone and not perpetually single."

Isla set her container on the nightstand. "Why would you question them if you trusted them?"

I should've. I should've seen what was happening under my nose. Truth was, I hadn't cared enough, and I wasn't proud of that. "I put it all at risk. Fergus would've been so ashamed. Hell, Mom's reaction was bad enough."

"What do you mean?" Isla's tone wasn't simple curios-ity. There was a hint of defensiveness—for me.

Maybe that was what kept me talking. I didn't usually

spill my feelings, but then everything in my life was different than I thought it'd be at this point. "She never said, and she was probably trying to be objective and help me see both sides, but I also think she was a little worried that maybe I was like my dad."

"McCoy, I didn't know your dad, but just from what you've said, you're not like him."

Her support curled around me like a blanket, but I was more like him than I wanted to admit. Unwilling to stop and see how my actions affected those I was supposed to love. "I wasn't invested in the relationship. I went through the motions, and even though I didn't berate Hannah like my dad did with Mom, I wasn't exactly present. Even when I was home, I was thinking about work and how to get better." I took another drink. "That's good beer, though."

"You didn't taste the first batch I made."

"Everyone's first batch sucks."

"I think I could chew it."

Chuckling, I gazed into the amber depths of the bottle. After the conversation we'd just had, I should have been in the pits of despair, but I was feeling as light as the flavor of her drink. "Did you name it yet?"

"No. It's my only crowning achievement. It's not like I have to differentiate different lines."

"Tomorrow, we'll get another batch started. Something you've never tried."

She watched me like she was giving me a chance to back out. "Okay, but I'm doing it. I don't want you to feel like you're training me. You can just hang out and look pretty."

"I ain't never been pretty a day in my life," I drawled.

"You're pretty hot."

I slipped the bottle out of her hand and set it on the nightstand with mine. Dragging her under me, I rolled over her, the sheet bunched between us. "You think so?"

"Mm—I might need to show you."

"By all means, I'm not one to distract a lady." My tongue soured after I said that, but I wiped the concern from my mind. Mom would pull through. She wouldn't screw Isla over just because she was nice and laid back. Because I was coming to treasure that side of her, and I didn't want to be on the wrong side of her hurt if she learned Mom wanted to put her off again.

Thirteen

ISLA

McCoy sat on the dryer, and I was perched on the counter while the wort boiled on the hot plate next to us.

I checked the time. "In five minutes, I can add the zest to the brew." I peeled another clementine to boil and add to the primary fermentation. "You think it'll be too strong to have both zest and fruit meat?" He gave me a look like, *Do you want me to answer that?* Of course he'd know exactly how it was going to turn out. I shook my head. "Never mind. I'll find out for myself."

He tapped his fingers on the top of the dryer, the dull metal sound resonating in the basement. "It's the best way."

I agreed. It would be nice to learn everything from him, but I also wanted to own all my knowledge. "Some people freeze the fruit, and some will even sanitize it with vodka. I might try that next."

"Do it and see. It's how you perfect a clementine recipe."

I separated the segments of the fruit and tossed them into the pot. Good thing I'd picked up more than one hot plate.

I grabbed my notebook, wrote what I was doing, and made notes for what to try next time. "You have to test this with me. It should be done a week after the *A* and *E* team are here. Will you go back when they return to Denver to make plans?"

I selfishly wanted him to stay. I had left the motel late last night, my body humming in all the right places, and not even my deflating air mattress woke me up.

"I don't know. It'll take them a few weeks to draw up the plans. Doesn't seem to be any point in leaving. I'd have to come early to settle before the general contractor gets here, though I'll be taking on a bit of the role for him so he doesn't have to be gone so long."

Yes. "Are you going to rent a place? You'd have more space. Maybe make a meal here and there." The motel was nice enough, but he'd been there six weeks already. Wasn't it cramped?

"Jocelyn might miss me too much if I start cooking for myself."

Laughing, I pictured her doting on him. She hadn't worked at the diner since before I was born because she hated the customers. "There are bigger places."

"I don't need much."

He didn't need much, or he didn't think he should need much? "Aren't you getting sick of motel life?"

"Nah. I had a big-ass house in Nashville, and all I ever used was the bathroom and the bedroom. I didn't use the tools in the garage. Hannah got frustrated and hired out for everything." He continued tapping with his fingers. "How about you?"

He was turning the conversation on me. Was I on the

right track with the motel thing? He didn't think he deserved more than a walking path around a bed to the bathroom? "What about me?"

"No furniture? Don't think I didn't see your flat mattress."

"It's better for my back." I couldn't hold in my snicker. "I need to buy another one. I'll run to the store and grab another."

"They have inflatable mattresses?"

"Lots of hunting and camping in the area."

"Do they have inflatable couches?"

"Isn't the dryer comfortable?" Shame crept in. I was basically camping in my house, and now that he'd pointed it out, I tried to see it from his point of view. It wasn't like I'd bought the place and needed time to move out of somewhere else. I was here with all my belongings, which consisted of clothing, brewing equipment, the tools I'd bought for the bathroom, and the new trailer and mower in the driveway.

"It's fine. I know you're planning to sell the place, but you're living here until then, and I don't think it's a quick turnaround. Why not get comfortable?"

This wasn't the house I wanted to live in. I hadn't pictured where I wanted to live. My mind had been focused on the foundry and what I could convert it into. A little old house that was sorely outdated was not my dream home, but I was in my midtwenties and single. It wasn't like I needed to settle into a family home. Didn't explain why I was sluggish to make it an actual home—my home.

"I don't want to move a ton of furniture when I rip out carpet and paint."

"Got it."

I waited for him to continue, but he didn't. "The entire upstairs needs new carpet."

"Yep."

"And the linoleum in the bathroom and kitchen has got to go."

The slightest quirk curved his lips up. "Hope you took notes with that toilet."

"Why?" It dawned on me, and I closed my eyes. "I'm going to have to remove the toilet to replace the flooring."

"It's best."

His short answers irritated me. "Why do you want me to fill this place up with furniture anyway?"

"Why don't you?"

"I don't know—why don't you rent an apartment instead of staying in a cramped place that you can't make your own at all?"

He stared at me for a moment, and it wasn't the usual look he got. There was no smothered interest. No disgruntled attitude. No question. Just stunned silence. "I . . . don't know."

"Maybe I'm as afraid to put down roots as you are." I dumped the zest into the pot and stirred from my sitting position. A fruity citrus aroma mingled with the grainy smell in the room.

Maybe I'm as afraid to put down roots as you are. Where had that come from? I wasn't scared to live here. I wasn't attached to living anywhere, and this house was as good as any.

"Okay," he said slowly. "I'll admit my baggage might be the reason I'm content in a tiny room. But you have your whole life in front of you."

I rolled my eyes and kept stirring. "You're not an old man, McCoy. You're thirty-six. That's hardly the golden years. It doesn't even count as middle-aged."

"While it's heartening to hear you don't think midthirties is middle-aged, I've still lived a whole life compared to you—and that life bit me. Hard. What's your excuse?"

"This isn't the house I wanted." This place was an investment. It was supposed to be smart.

"Where is that?"

I stirred faster. The pot's contents were getting frothy and sticky. About how I felt inside. "I don't know. Somewhere I have family that talks to me."

"I see." His tone was loaded. What exactly did he see?

I didn't want to know. Our conversation unpeeled me like the clementines. "I should stand and stir."

"I like watching your tits shake like that."

His levity eased the sting the conversation caused. "I've never thought about my boobs while making beer."

"I think about them all the time." A few moments went by. "Isla . . . far be it from me to critique family relations since I have a piss-poor record, but have you reached out to any of them?"

"I don't want to bother anyone. It's not like they're reaching out to me."

"You mean when they invited you to their get-together?"

Frowning, I stared at the light-brown foam as I stirred. I should've stood. My back would be to him. "How do you know about that?"

"I ran into Liam and Archer at the diner. Liam was wondering if you took the news okay."

"That he doesn't want to work with me? Yeah, it's fine." I couldn't take my gaze off my task. Definitely not to meet McCoy's eyes.

"He didn't say he didn't want to. He said he can't."

Both reasons felt the same. I'd reached out to my brother, and he'd stepped away. He had every right to. "Whatever, it was worth a shot."

"And the invite?"

I watched the whirlpool swirling in my pot, willing my emotions would get doused in the liquid. "I overheard them talking about it. Discussing who all was coming. Guess who wasn't on the list?"

"Didn't Kennedy ask you?"

"Afterward. It's not the same. She probably noticed I overheard, and she's too nice to leave me out after that." I chewed on the inside of my cheek. The residual hurt was strong. "Things are just different, you know? I should be used to being on the outskirts. Stetson and Holden did their own thing. Liam wasn't a part of our lives. The others weren't in Coal Haven. Now Nora's moved back. Archer. And except for Nora, they're all settling down and getting closer to each other. It's awesome. It really is."

"But you don't feel included?"

"I had Lyric." I rolled my lips in and inhaled the citrusy, hoppy smell coming from the pot. The beer would be good; I could tell. At least I was decent at something. I wasn't as accomplished in the rest of my life.

"But now she's married to your brother."

"And a mom." If I was happy for her, and I loved having her as a sister-in-law, what actually bothered me? "It happened so fast. I didn't even know she had a fling with Stetson and then she was pregnant and they were married and Rina's here and I'm an aunt. I guess I thought we'd grow into our families together."

"And now she's in at all the family gatherings and you're not."

"Right? I felt horrible thinking that. She didn't have much family growing up. But she's also a mom and works, and I'm bumming around an empty house with no job." Shame didn't sweep in like I anticipated. Saying my thoughts out loud helped.

He pushed off the dryer and went to the sink. There were a couple bags of ice in the cooler to shock my brew. He plugged the sink. I hauled the pot to the sink and carefully placed it inside. We took out the bag of hops, put the lid on, and started the cold water.

We waited for the sink to fill so we could add the ice, both of us staring at the stream of water.

"You're lost," he finally said.

"Maybe a little. This limbo I'm in waiting for *A* and *E* isn't helping." I folded my arms and leaned against the basin, frustrated I couldn't go to Reservoir Barrel and see progress, but the place couldn't be the solution to my personal problems. "I ran across Lyric last night, and she basically accused me of blocking her out of my life. And . . . maybe I have."

"So call her. Message her. Snap. Whatever the kids do these days."

"Now you sound old. She's probably working."

"So are you." When I looked at him, he waved his arm around the room. "This is research. You don't brew for a hobby. This is testing. It's all part of a bigger plan. You're working too. So message her. She'll answer when she's not busy. Same with you. Your lives are changing, but if you don't make an effort to maintain the connection, you'll both move on."

He was too adamant to be speaking about just me. "Is that what you did?"

"They moved on—with each other," he said simply. "I just moved."

But he hadn't moved on. "Do you still love her?" My heart crawled into my throat. His answer shouldn't tear me in two, no matter what it was, but the potential loomed heavy on the horizon.

He let out a resigned sigh. "I don't know if I ever did."

I wasn't prepared for that. "Oh."

"Yeah. Not an easy admission. To be fair, I don't know if she loved me like she thought she did either. Her life was about her, and I didn't make mine about her, so she made me pay." He nudged me with an elbow. "So go ahead—message Lyric."

If I pulled out my phone, I'd have to admit the real reason I was delaying. But McCoy wasn't going to give up. "She'll ask about you, and I don't know what to say."

Understanding and a spark of fear lit his eyes. "And you don't want to lie?"

My stomach didn't bottom out, but it dropped. He wanted to keep us a secret? I didn't think we should go screaming through town that we were sleeping together, but people could wonder. "She's my best friend."

"You trust her to be discreet?" He smoothed over my scowl by tracing a finger between my brows. "I don't care for your big brother knowing what we're doing. It's weird to worry about something like that at my age. And I don't need my mom disappointed in me."

"How would she know?"

"Enough people find out. Shit on social media saying, 'McDaniel Contractors likes to fuck their hot clients.' I don't know, but I don't want to find out."

True. And there were my parents. I wouldn't put it past Dad to call Sylvia and demand to know, *Why did your son put his dick in my daughter? Is that how you conduct business?* I didn't think I'd ever not be a kid in his eyes, but I couldn't be undermined in front of Sylvia. If Dad did something like that, she might quit working with me. Then what?

"I'll think about what you said. How about that?" I could admit I was isolating myself. Lyric and I'd had our share of arguments over the years, mostly petty crap that was resolved in two minutes. This was different. We were different. "But I have to get this primary fermentation going so I can get to the farmers' market."

"Any more issues with the rhubarb glow sticks?"

"No. Becca seems content enough to have the chemical-laden fruit on the other side of the lot. And Dad hasn't brought up restricting what booths we have at the market anymore either. I probably have you to thank." I didn't want to talk about the market. Each Thursday and Sunday afternoon hung over my head. I liked the people. The work wasn't hard. But it wasn't my calling. It wasn't what I wanted to do with my life, and it paid so little it equated more to donating my time. A worthy cause, just not one I was especially passionate about.

What I was doing in the basement—and who I was with? I could do that all day, and I'd be brewing full-time soon enough. But that meant McCoy would be going. He'd move on and figure out what he was going to do with his life, and I wouldn't be a part of it.

I wandered around the market with my clipboard. Shoppers mingled from booth to booth, enjoying the heat and the sun and the wider range of produce selection this time of year. I stopped and chatted with each vendor. July was often the smoothest time of year, but some of the vendors hadn't been their usual jovial selves.

Stopping at Clara's pies, I peered over the options. I'd saved her for last since she liked to chat. I couldn't forget how McCoy had ogled the pies.

She smiled politely when I approached. Lately, she asked about Reservoir Barrel, but today her gaze skated away.

Concerned, I hugged the clipboard to my chest. There

weren't many notes on it. Would that change after my talk with Clara? "How's it going today?"

"Fine." She folded her hands over her overalls. Around town, Clara wore floral shirts, long skirts, and loose pants. At the market, she played up the farmer schtick and wore bib overalls and a big straw hat. She had a boisterous laugh and talked nonstop, and you'd better have an hour if you asked about what kind of shortening was best for a piecrust.

"Is everything all right, Clara?"

"Why wouldn't it be?" Her curt tone startled me. "I just hope I can sell all my pies."

"Why?" I checked the clipboard, paging to the notes I'd made on future markets. "Attendance is up, and you're scheduled for the rest of the season."

She gave me a *duh* look. "Apparently not when August is 'produce only.'"

I frowned, dread churning in my gut. This had all the signs of decisions being made behind my back, and there was only one person with the pull to do it. "I have no plans to change the format. There's no reason to midseason."

"Your dad informed me yesterday when I saw him at the gas station."

"My dad doesn't make the decisions."

Derisive laughter sputtered out of her. "Since when? Your parents are behind everything in this town, and this market is no different. They don't care that the money I make here helps pay for Don's deductible. Or that making pies is the only therapy I can afford for myself."

Tired of this conversation, I kept my tone firm. "No, I'm the director, and there will be no format changes."

She gave me a placating smile. "You're a sweet girl, Isla, but that's not how it works."

I sucked in a measuring breath. *Dammit, Dad.* Why couldn't he leave this alone? Why would he think narrowing what we offered was a good business move? What could I do to convince her there would be no changes?

She wasn't taking me seriously, that was clear. And infuriating. I had to establish my authority, and I couldn't do that without talking to Dad. "Listen, Clara, I'm going to talk to Dad and figure this out."

"Sure, Isla."

I bristled against her flat tone. I'd been undermined long enough. Spinning on a heel, I clutched my clipboard to my chest. I couldn't leave until the market was done for the night. The next hour, I forced a tight grin and kept an eye out for Dad to appear. But his radar for the trouble he caused was accurate. He stayed away, and it was likely because he knew I'd hear about what he'd tried to do.

All the vendors packed and left, many of them ignoring me as they went. Usually, they went out of their way to say goodbye or tell me what a good night they had with shoppers.

Fuck this.

Striding to my pickup, I fumed. No one had thought to approach me? They'd either heard from Dad, or Clara had spread the word, and the rumor flooded the vendors. And no one had talked to me.

I took deep breaths all the way through town to keep my speed down. When I hit the highway, I opened the windows. Heat emanated from the interior, but I needed the sheer noise to diminish the annoyance and anger. My parents had given me a wide berth since they'd kicked me out. So why didn't Dad do the same with the market?

The large picture windows of my childhood home appeared. I turned down the drive. Anxiety fired like my stomach was a wood stove. I was going to park in front of the house, but the shop doors were open. Stetson's pickup wasn't around, or I'd think it was him. The older Dad got, the more he liked working around the ranch, not as a job but as a hobby, and Stetson saved him some duties. The ditches were getting hayed, and Dad was either out in one of the pastures or he was back for the night.

I stopped in front of the shop. The metal clang of tools inside drew me farther into the shop.

Dad was sifting through his stand-up tool box. He glanced over and a pleased surprise crossed his face. I almost let guilt tame my ire, but then Dad's expression went neutral. He knew what I was here for.

I didn't bother with a long rant. He didn't respect those. "Why?"

"It's a smart decision." He grabbed a rag and wiped his hands. People in town wouldn't believe this was Cameron Barron. He was in an old sweatshirt with the name of the refinery he worked at three buyouts ago.

"How?" I folded my arms. "Enlighten me."

His jaw hardened. His chronic leukemia had tempered him, but not by much. "Isla," he said on a sigh, "the city wants to start doing an annual street fair in the summer. Coal Haven won't draw in a crowd when there's a mini street fair twice a week."

"A street fair? That's news to me." It wouldn't be news to Mom. I was left out of the loop.

"The sooner you can adjust the format of the market to produce only, the better it'll adapt and function when the street fair starts."

"That doesn't make sense. An annual fair will attract vendors from out of town. Artists and food trucks. The scale of the farmers' market doesn't compare."

"It's not a farmers' market, Isla. There are pies and home goods. You can't let just anyone in because you're too nice to tell them no."

What could I do, then? Tell them my daddy said no? "Yes, I can. You made me the director, and it's my decision."

He looked down his nose at me. I'd seen him use that stance on everyone in town. Wasn't I different? "What does your data say?"

"That people are satisfied with the growth and what's offered."

"The thing about research, Isla, is that it can be easily skewed if you don't know what you're doing."

"And you think I don't?" He was talking to me like he hadn't paid for all four years of my school. As if I'd been at an adult day care instead of a university. "It's not just numbers. Clara needs that money to live. I make decisions for the people, not just the bottom line."

He tossed the rag on the workbench. "Clara can make three months' worth of sales in one weekend and free herself up twice a week once we start the street fair. She makes what? A couple hundred each week? Maybe five hundred? She can earn five grand in one weekend with one booth fee."

I opened my mouth to argue, but I had nothing.

"Your mom has done research, too, Isla." Irritation fringed his tone. "City street fairs can rake in thousands for each vendor. One big weekend, more money, more time to do what they want. Clara would have to figure out storage, but it would be temporary—and I'd bet after the first year, she'd be fine with the arrangement. Meanwhile, the produce suppliers would still have biweekly markets to attend."

I had no way of refuting his logic. I wasn't prepared for this argument and didn't that make me feel like I was being stubborn for no reason other than to be right. "It doesn't mean—"

"Don't let pride interfere with hard decisions. Sometimes you've got to step on a few toes to make decisions that benefit a larger community. I know you want everyone to like you, but it's not feasible in business."

I was tired of this argument, and people liking me wasn't the issue we were talking about. "It still wasn't your decision to make. Why didn't you bring your ideas to me? Why didn't we sit and talk about them like professionals?"

He dipped his head. "I'll give you that, but you haven't exactly been reachable the last several weeks."

As if they'd tried. The silent treatment was their greatest weapon. "I've been at the markets. At my house."

"I didn't know you'd moved," he snapped, "until my assistant asked if you liked your new house."

I closed my mouth. Dad rarely sounded hurt. It was hard to remember he had feelings that could be hurt in the first place. "Mom kicked me out, and the way you treat me as market director didn't make me think you'd give me any more space or respect with the new house than before."

"So you just don't talk to us? You don't come to us with major decisions?"

I threw my hands up. "You two take over."

"Then take it back!" he roared. Shaking his head, he pressed a hand on the top of the workbench, heedless of the grit on the surface. "Goddammit, Isla. You don't tell us anything after you graduate, so your mom and I arrange something for you to do, a way for you to make money and build your résumé, only you never planned to find a job. You bought a damn building. You want to be upset that I'm taking over the market? How much longer are you going to keep the position?"

My brain skidded out of the rut his yelling put me in. He made it sound like my fault, but in reality, he recited facts. "I haven't decided yet."

"Were you going to give us notice or just quit when you were done with it?"

I scowled. I didn't think that far ahead with the market. It was my safety net. A simple task I didn't have to think about except when there were issues. "I'd be professional about it."

"Like your boyfriend?"

The subject change knocked my mind around like a pinball. "McCoy? He's not—"

"Your pickup was outside his motel room all night. His truck was at your house all day."

My cheeks heated. Hard to argue professionalism when the stroke of his tongue lingered on my skin. "That's only been the last two days. We've had . . . stuff to discuss."

He tipped his head, disappointment shining in his eyes. "Let me ask you this—how will you be able to tell if he's screwing up his job if you're too close to him? If he fucks up or intentionally pulls a fast one, will you be able to confront him like you're doing with me?"

"You're my dad."

"And I know exactly how messy this shit can get."

He'd never talked about his affair. The sordid details were whispered across town but never mentioned under our roof. I'd had to learn about it from Stetson, and he'd probably been told behind the barn by Aunt Kira or Uncle Bruce. I doubted Dad had discussed his dark past with the son who'd still been in diapers when the affair had occurred.

My leg twitched to stomp. I couldn't revert to being a little girl around Dad. I'd come so far. Besides, McCoy wasn't screwing me over. He wouldn't, not after what he'd been through. "It's not like that."

"Isn't it." It wasn't a question.

I wasn't going to lie. He'd accused me of hiding from him and not standing up for myself. "I'm an adult."

"And if he was anyone else, I wouldn't have an issue." My look must've been doubtful because he elaborated. "Did

I say anything when you dated the new electrician in town that had three kids from three different women?"

"I didn't know about the kids when we dated." When I'd found out, thanks to his phone blowing up with a ton of messages asking why he wasn't paying child support, I'd ended it. "It wouldn't have lasted anyway."

"My point is that you didn't work with any of them. Not only do you work with McCoy Cunningham, you're paying him. That can get complicated quickly."

"He's proven competent so far." In so many ways. I couldn't look at my dad when those thoughts bombarded my brain.

"You're refusing to see my point."

He was refusing to see me as a competent business-woman. We could do rounds all night. Sighing, I said, "I get it, Dad, I really do."

He was the one who looked doubtful this time. "Just remember he's more well versed in business in general, in the type of company you're looking to build, and in betrayal."

Each of Dad's points hit the center of my confidence. "The experience behind McDaniel Contractors is why I hired them." My words echoed emptily. The lack of conviction was loud to my ears. I had to save face. "But I'll keep what you said in mind."

His flat stare wasn't convinced. "If you don't want to listen, at least learn from my mistakes."

"It's not exactly the same, Dad."

"Basically, it is. Good sense gets thrown out the window when attraction's involved."

I'd found Dad to talk to him about the market, and we'd circled back to over a month ago when he was warning me about McCoy. But I hadn't been sleeping with McCoy then, and his criticism had been easier to brush off.

So I concentrated on why I'd driven here in the first place. "About the market . . . maybe it's best if I step down." The sheer relief surging inside me was a sign this was too little too late, but the fear lurking underneath thought I'd end up getting fired sooner rather than later. I couldn't handle the controversy leaking onto Reservoir Barrel.

His pause stretched until I twisted my hands together. "Maybe it is," he finally said, harsh but honest. Had he been wishing he could fire me? If I was anyone else, I might've been canned last year.

"Do you want notice? I can work until the end of the month." Then, when the change took place in August, I wouldn't be a part of it. We were both getting what we wanted, but the market would stand as a failure in my mind.

"I'll notify the board."

Just like that, he let me go. Keeping my back straight, I walked out of the shop. Mom was in the house, but she'd have more of the same to say, and I wasn't willing to hear it. I'd hoped to straighten out the market and establish my authority, but I'd had none all along.

Why did it feel like I was going backward in life?

I got into the pickup, and when I turned onto the highway, I drove to the foundry. Reservoir Barrel. I wasn't going backward. My plans were paused and only for a few more weeks.

A few more weeks after that, I'd have the blueprints in my hands, and I'd know I was making the right choices. Even when it came to McCoy.

Fourteen

MCCOY

"And he said what?" I ripped a large and satisfying chunk of wallpaper off the living room wall. I had nothing to do, so Isla's house was like a night-light and I was a moth. Staying away wasn't an option when I was drawn to where she was.

Not only did I hope we'd have sex—I couldn't get enough of her—but I genuinely wanted to be around her.

Isla yanked a scrap of paper off. "An annual street fair."

"Why can't you do both?"

"Exactly. Why can't we?" She dropped her putty knife. "It doesn't matter. I won't be the director after the end of the month."

"I know the income isn't much, but don't you need something?" I'd worked since I was old enough to handle a broom. As soon as Dad could put me on the books, he did as a tax break. The only months of my adult life I'd been unemployed were last year when I was listless in Mom's house. I might still be there if she hadn't pried me up and pushed me out the door to Coal Haven.

"I should be okay. Construction will be starting soon enough, and I'll have paperwork to do. I don't need the market stealing my time. It's taken enough mental energy." She dusted her hands off and stood back to evaluate the wall. "That's so much better."

There were gouges that'd have to be filled from her first attempt at removing the wallpaper, but with the right tools and a few tricks, we'd gotten the rest off without scarring the drywall. The pump sprayer I brought in from the work truck helped. "Looks good."

Her smile was triumphant. "Hungry?"

I crowded toward her. We were dusty and covered in debris, but I didn't care. "Always."

She laughed, and there was the snort I'd heard earlier. She wasn't perfect, but she was real and pretty damn spectacular. "I mean for real food. I'm starving, or I'd be naked right now."

Lust slammed into me, but I grinned. I liked the lightness between us. "Rattler's?"

She thought for a moment. "You know what? The county fair is going on. Want to test out some food trucks?"

The food trucks, yes. People, noise, and loud machinery, no. "I'm not one for big fairs."

She chortled. "McCoy, we don't have big fairs around here. The biggest is in Bismarck, where they set up rides in a parking lot. This is a county fair. 4-H exhibits. Goats, cows, rabbits, and chickens. The biggest spectacle there is probably the bouncy houses."

"I'm intrigued." And it wasn't just because she lit up and her voice filled with excitement that had glued me to her like a sticky trap.

She grinned, and it was like the clouds outside broke

apart at that moment and the sun shone through the picture window. My sunbeam. "I'm going to change first."

I looked down at my worn jeans and gray T-shirt. I brushed the dust off. "What about me?"

"You're fine." She disappeared into her bedroom and came out in the same pink breast cancer awareness shirt, but instead of shorts, she was in jeans and carried an old pair of boots to the door. They weren't the fancy cowboy boots women wore in Nashville—various colors with gems and other decorations. These boots had seen dirt and mud in their time. They were clean but well used.

She stuffed her feet in. "Ready?"

If I needed proof this fair was no Six Flags, her outfit was it. Farmer chic. As much of a relief as that was, curiosity jammed into my chest. This was a side of Isla I'd never seen. She wasn't just a small-town girl, she was a country girl and I was going to get a lesson on the difference. "Yup."

We took her pickup. She drove to a place on the other side of town that I'd noticed getting more traffic than usual the last few days. Now that I thought of it, I'd noticed several more horse trailers going through town.

She hit a dirt road and wound through a parking lot. When she parked, we got out. People roamed to the fairgrounds from the lot. The most popular fashion choices were jeans and cowboy boots. Lots of cowboy hats and dusty ball caps. Several kids milled around the buildings that made up the fairgrounds, and many of them wore green shirts with 4-H on the front.

Isla's hips swayed differently than in her athletic shoes and sandals. A rolling motion that was as natural as her sunny smile. "My favorite is the cow barns—and the chickens. We haven't had laying hens for years, and god, I miss the eggs."

"That good?"

She groaned in a way that made me wonder if I needed to track down fresh farm eggs before I got her in bed. "Nothing like 'em."

Each building had a placard over its big barn doors telling us what animal was inside. Corrals were behind the building, and the rodeo arena and bleachers were to the side. Behind all those were rows of trailers and campers.

"This fair is a thing, huh?"

"People who show animals have to be here at least once a day, usually twice or more, to care for them, and then there's the showing, so a lot of entrants camp out here. Stetson always brought me in."

"You showed horses, right?"

"Yep," she said wistfully.

What would it be like to settle in a small county like this? To raise kids in 4-H who went to horse shows and showed chickens, or whatever the hell they did with the birds?

When I had pictured my life at the age I was now, it'd included a big house, a thriving business, and kids, but I'd never imagined beyond that. What would I do with my kids? My life with my parents had been about work. My dad's job had been the only way to relate to him, and we hadn't had money for more. Then I'd dived into brewing with Fergus when he and Mom married, but it was really his passion. It just worked out that I'd been good and had run with it. I'd made a decent career out of it, and that was how I related to Mom. Our careers. But looking around showed me another slice of life. One I hadn't known was out there. Raising these animals had to be a job, but the energy was different. The people were different.

"It's not like other fairs, is it?" Isla asked.

I must've been slack-jawed, staring at everything. "Definitely. It's busy, but it's relaxed." The one time I'd gone to a theme park with my parents, Dad had yelled at Mom, but I hadn't thought much of it. He yelled at her a lot, and other parents were biting their kids' heads off.

"I'd get so nervous when it was my turn in front of the judges, but then Lyric and I would run around all day and get cotton candy, watch the other competitions, and most years they have a magician. I think there's a concert tonight. Ooh, the rabbits."

She pulled me to a wide-open shed that was little more than a carport. Cages of bunnies, some with giant purple ribbons and others with red, white, or blue ribbons, lined the perimeter.

I fought a smile as she bent and cooed over the rabbits inside. Then she scurried to the shed next door. It was the same but with chickens, and there was considerably more cooing.

She peered at a chicken with a white-and-black pattern on its feathers. "Ohmigod, we used to have this Plymouth Rock hen who used to lay so many double yolkers. Stetson used to tell me he fed her twice as much as the others, and I believed him for months."

Chuckling, I trailed behind as she inspected all of the chickens.

She tugged my hand and towed me out of the open barn and toward another large red barn. "Cows" was on the sign overhead, and the new experience kept me from withdrawing my hand from hers. Holding hands in public wasn't what project managers did with their clients.

A commotion sounded to our left. Laughter and shouts of "Get 'em." I glanced over. What the—

A glossy black cow was darting away from a kid who couldn't be more than five feet tall. His face was panicked and people were darting to grab the lead rope, but the cow was having none of it. It wove through the people like it was late for a flight.

The animal was heading our way, and I tensed to jump after it, not knowing what I would do when I'd never touched a living cow in my life. But Isla leaped toward the animal, snagged the lead rope, and murmured soothing words as she eased it to a stop.

The young boy sprinted toward her, out of breath. "Thank you."

"You betcha." Isla delivered the cow, her eyes dancing. "He looks nice. Good job."

The kid grinned and led the cow away. There were a few chuckles, but people wandered around like nothing had happened. A cow was on the loose, and no one was flustered. "Does that stuff happen all the time?"

"Not really. It wouldn't get far in this crowd anyway. The cattle in the shows are usually pretty mellow—they've been handled so much—but you get some that have their own ideas."

A female voice called behind us. "I see you've still got it."

"Nora!" Delight rang in Isla's voice. If I'd known the fair was going on earlier, I would've spent every hour here with her. She wasn't a different person, but she was more comfortable with herself.

And so was I.

I didn't have time to figure out what that meant. Nora approached us. Dressed like Isla but with her brown hair pulled back in a ponytail and the sun catching the corn-flower blue of her eyes, I could see the resemblance. I doubted they got mistaken for family much, with Isla's taller height and her blonde hair, but their expressions were similar. Naive intelligence. Was Nora as driven and ambitious but as subtle as Isla?

Nora shoved her hands in her back pockets, the move

making her look like she was barely out of high school. "You just missed Stetson and Lyric. Rina wasn't having the heat, and they went home."

If Nora noticed the loss mixed with relief flickering in Isla's expression, she didn't point it out.

Isla waved a hand at me. "McCoy was helping me fix the wallpaper mess I made, and I thought I'd buy him expensive and greasy food from a truck."

It was a small mention but significant. Hannah had never given me credit. Never. She hadn't taken it all herself, but she let people assume. With the design of Nailer's, people would say *I love the modern industrial vibe*. And she'd smile and talk about what inspired the idea—which had been mine, after much research. That part wasn't mentioned, and Hannah passively got the credit. It'd been the same with the names of the beers we'd trademarked. She'd discussed how integral the construction field was to Nailer's, never mentioning my background or that I'd been the one to come up with the names.

Nora's sigh was wistful and reminiscent of the one from Isla when she'd mentioned showing horses. "I miss food truck food." She pressed a hand to her stomach. "But my body has told me no on too many occasions."

"Maybe you need to do your own food truck," Isla said.

Nora leaned over and conspiratorially whispered, "Don't assume I haven't thought of it." Another resigned sigh. "Mom would shit, though. My eating habits have her worked up enough, and then to showcase them in a food truck? She would never survive. So? How's the brewery coming?"

"Fine," Isla answered, like there hadn't been much progress since the middle of June. "McCoy's done everything he can until the engineer and architect get here. Along with the extra task of fixing a broken window from the hail storm last month."

Nora was dismayed to hear about the slight damage the building took and she and Isla continued to chat, but I was stuck on how easily Isla had given me credit. Again, a small difference to what I was used to, but the way she answered might as well be broad daylight to Hannah's pitch black. My ex's syrupy-sweet tone would answer with something like *Everything's taken care of, and that window? What an ordeal! Thankfully, patch materials were on hand, and it'll be good until a custom frame and window are installed.*

There would've been no mention of me. How hadn't I noticed? Because I knew everything she hadn't been saying. Our partners hadn't. The distributors we worked with. The staff. And she'd been fine letting them think she was the force behind everything.

Reservoir Barrel wasn't even mine and I'd gotten more credit for the place than Hannah had given me for Nailer's. I noticed now. I wouldn't forget. Nor would I forget how grateful I would be to Isla for giving me a glimpse of a healthy relationship, even if we had to keep our messing around under wraps and I'd be leaving as soon as her doors opened.

* * *

Isla

McCoy had gone quiet while I talked with Nora. She updated me on Holden and her nieces and nephews. I hadn't been in touch with any of mine since last month. I'd been determined to be a better aunt, yet I was tucked away in my new house and not reaching out, just like McCoy had said.

"Hey." Nora licked her lips and her gaze flittered to McCoy. "Uncle Cameron called me about the market."

My good vibe twanged. A record scratch on an otherwise decent day. "Oh?"

"Are you . . . are you done with the market?"

"At the end of the month. We had a difference of opinion on where the market should go and what it should concentrate on." I sounded casual, but I trusted Nora to read between the lines. She was raised in the same family.

She nodded. "The street fair. He offered me the director job."

Ouch. Fresh hurt rose to the surface, but I attempted to keep my reaction neutral. Did Dad offer the job to Nora to get back at me, knowing it'd sting more than someone not related to us?

"You'd be more of a manager, and he's the director," I warned.

"Oh, trust me. I know what this family is like." She shrugged. "I don't have to, but there's only a month left and I . . ." Her gaze strayed to McCoy again and turned guarded. "I don't turn twenty-five until late next year, so . . ."

Ah. Just like me, she had plans. Would she get her trust and take off? Would she stay in Coal Haven? Would she be living in an empty house with no furniture, waiting on people who hadn't given her a date on when they'd arrive, and sleeping with her project manager who hadn't either?

My stomach clenched. I'd arrived hungry, but anxiety churned in my gut. The *A* and *E* crew were supposed to arrive in a little over two weeks and I had no date. McCoy hadn't mentioned anything, and I'd been enjoying my time with him. Working on the house with him was fun and informative. He knew so damn much and was a ready teacher. When it came to brewing, he hung back and was good company. And with sex, he was phenomenal.

But those last points had nothing to do with Reservoir Barrel, which was the job I was paying him to do.

Nora inspected me, studying my reaction. "Would you be okay if I took the position?"

Her question yanked me out of the pondering that dampened the delight of my day. I hadn't dwelled on Nora getting offered the position. Instead, my thoughts had turned to McCoy and Reservoir Barrel. The market wasn't important to me. "No, I don't mind at all. I'm grateful for the experience but happy to be done with it."

And thrilled to be jumping into a career that didn't include my family lording over me.

She grinned. "Sweet. I'm going for the experience too." An announcement for the roping contest came over the speakers. "Ooh, I wanted to go to that. See you guys."

She jogged off, and I was left with McCoy. I had a niggling question in my head, and after hearing my director job get immediately offered to someone else like they'd been planning for my departure, I couldn't sit on it. "I know it's a weekend, but do we have a date for Lorraine's arrival?"

His expression turned guarded. It shouldn't be a big ask. The date should be his next priority. "I don't have a date. She's wrapping up another project and things have come up—"

Dad's warning echoed in my head. I couldn't let it go because I was sleeping with McCoy. "Two months' worth of things, but six weeks have passed."

He sighed. "The client changed locations, and Lorraine and Halle need to draw up new plans. It takes time."

"But they need to travel."

"We don't take many out-of-state clients, Isla."

"The website says you service five states." I was probably

one of the few North Dakota customers in McDaniel Contractors' lifetime, but Sylvia assured me it wasn't an issue.

His jaw clenched, and he drew out his phone. "I'll shoot her a message. How 'bout that?"

A message? I had a seven-figure project dead in the water. My account had floated out to sea, and the rescue crew was helping another client. I had my shit together, and I'd already agreed to change the first deadline once. Why was I the one waiting? "I'd like an answer. A date."

He lifted his gaze from his phone screen to me. He was back to the closed-off McCoy I'd found wandering the foundry. "I'll get you one, but it might . . . It might be a little more than a couple of weeks."

Since when? I was told two months and hadn't heard anything different. Heat crept up my skin. The blotchy type. "Might or it will be?"

"I don't know yet. Let's see what Sylvia has to say."

Since he was calling his mom by her name, he was in work mode. Did he truly not know? And if he didn't, why wasn't he doing his job and pressuring his boss? "Can I ask you something?"

His face said he'd rather I didn't, but he nodded.

"Have you been lax on your mom? Like, if you were doing this job and the owner wasn't Sylvia, would you have a date for me?"

I knew what it was like working for family. And maybe finding out McCoy was the boss's son should've waved a red flag earlier. The market had been a small position, minuscule in comparison, but working with my parents had caused issues. We all had put up with behavior we likely wouldn't have tolerated in other situations. McCoy was coming off losing everything. Was he afraid to push his mother and risk his job? He said she wouldn't fire him, but was he worried about upsetting her? Sylvia had seemed so nice, so motherly, but she was his boss too. And getting on the wrong side of your parent as a boss hits harder than a falling-out with someone else.

"I'd be working to finalize travel plans, just like I should be doing." His lips flattened. "I can send her a message for updates."

"I know we've muddied the waters, but my entire life's savings are in Reservoir Barrel, and winters around here aren't like Denver. Are your contractors going to be able to do anything when it's twenty below zero with thirty-mile-an-hour winds?"

The muscles in his jaw jumped again. "I'll get you answers, Isla."

Was he upset at himself or with me for pushing the subject? "That's all I ask."

His nod was tight, but the overall tension in him eased. He sent the message and tucked his phone into his pocket. He stepped closer to me, stiffened, and looked around. Did he want to kiss me? To draw me to him? We were in public, and people already thought we were overly friendly with each other.

Like I needed it pointed out how much I risked by sleeping with McCoy. I'd been coasting and so had he. I couldn't continue to be content and . . . I had to prepare myself. If he wasn't going to do the job I needed him to, I'd have to figure out what I would do about it.

MCCOY

I leaned against the kitchen counter in Isla's house and stared at Mom's message. **Call me.**

A damn good day had been ruined as soon as Isla turned the subject to work. She should know Mom was fucking around with her account, but I couldn't bring myself to betray Mom. She thought Isla was a sure thing, and Mom was catering to a guy who had more money than respect. He had McDaniel Contractors on a long leash. Mom would adjust for him, and Isla was stuck before she could get off the ground.

I'd tried to enjoy the rest of the fair, but the fry bread taco—while fucking amazing—had sat like lead in my gut since.

Isla swept into the kitchen, combing her fingers through the hair she'd undone when she'd changed into the shorts from earlier. Her gaze dropped to my phone. "Did you hear back?"

"She wants me to call her. Let me step outside and give her a ring."

On the front steps, I dropped to sit. I stared at the phone for a minute, dreading the call. Then I dialed Mom.

When she picked up, she said, "You know I don't like talking work on weekends."

"Well, you're not talking work to Isla during the week."

"I told you to distract her."

"I tried." If Mom knew how I'd distracted Isla, she'd have a hell of a lot more to say.

"The two months I told her we'd be delayed aren't even up."

"But she's asking, Mom. She wants a date. This is her baby."

A gusty sigh came over the line. "Lorraine's vacation was approved for the end of August."

Shit. And Mom was only factoring this in now? "And what exactly does that mean?" I asked tightly.

"Coy, I'm not pulling her vacation."

"I didn't ask you to." Mom guarded her employees' vacation like a Doberman. One of the many reasons her employees were loyal to her and another reason why I respected her so much. I'd striven to be the same as a boss, but what I dictated had gone through Hannah and she'd gotten the admiration. None of it had affected our clients. "But you've gotta give her something. You moved another account in front of her."

"It's a good business decision, and Lorraine's going to need a break after working with Dev. He's been a bear this go-round."

Dev knew he had Mom over a beer barrel. "You should've factored in Lorraine's vacation."

"Not when a five-million-dollar build is waiting. He said

he'd find someone else if I couldn't start as soon as he wanted."

He'd tested Mom, and she'd shown him she'd treat him with preference, which normally might be fine, but she was abusing Isla's naivety. "What do I tell Isla?"

"Tell her there's another delay. We can't help it; it's business. Hell, tell her about Lorraine's vacation. Isla's got a big heart. She'll understand and approve another change order."

My hand tightened on the phone. She shouldn't have to.

"You need to take care of this, Coy. Everything I've built could get ruined if Dev feels like he had a poor experience with me."

The man had made a name for himself in Denver and his connections overlapped with Mom's. Where Mom was a female in a male-dominated world and earning the senior discount wherever she went, Dev was a little older than me, good-looking, and charismatic. If he was unhappy with McDaniel Contractors, Mom wouldn't get the benefit of the doubt.

Mom's words from when I was a kid invaded my thoughts. *You don't need to take on the responsibility of the world.*

Yet I'd sworn I'd do whatever I could to keep Mom from worrying. To prevent her from being the one to carry the weight of the world on her shoulders. I would be a pillar in her life, not a life-sucking parasite like my dad had been.

"Do you have a date I can give her?" It wouldn't be until September, but damn, I couldn't string Isla along.

"Not until Dev signs off on the plans."

Mom was the type to give her word, and the fact that she wouldn't was ominous. How much crap was she taking from Dev? She could sever ties with him, but like she said, he was a large account and he could influence a lot of would-be brewery entrepreneurs in the area.

I knew how important Dev as a client was to Mom, but I also knew how critical this project was for Isla. I was on a tightrope between two people I cared about. "Fine. I'll take care of it."

I hung up and stared at the pockmarked sidewalk leading to the stairs. *Goddammit, Mom.* She'd put me in a shit position. This was unlike her, but she'd fought an uphill battle since she'd started the company. A woman. And now she was older. If she lost the Orlan account, the consequences would ripple out for years. Who knew what he'd tell others in the industry? McDaniel Contractors didn't value their longtime clients. McDaniel Contractors weren't reliable. Sylvia McDaniel wasn't as sharp as she used to be.

The company would've been at risk, and Mom had sacrificed Isla's timely completion to avoid it. I scrubbed a hand over my face and went inside. Isla was sitting on the kitchen counter, her hands gripping the edge.

Her hopeful expression fell when she saw my face. "Another delay?"

Her flat *I can't believe this shit* tone hit me hard. I couldn't believe it either. Mom was usually better than this, and as a project manager, this resonated as a letdown on my part too. "The main problem is that there was another short delay, but then Lorraine has a scheduled vacation at the end of August."

Isla's eyes flared and her leg twitched. "Vacation? I mean, I don't want to be an ass, but she can't get out here in the month before the end of August?"

I shook my head. There was nothing to say. "I'm sorry. I can get the change order drawn up tomorrow."

Her shoulders slumped. "Yeah, I mean, it's not your fault. And I don't want to demand anyone lose a vacation, but it sucks. That's three months. And then what? Will Sylvia give us a hard date for after the vacation?"

I shook my head again.

She straightened. "Seriously? No date?"

"No, Isla. No date. Not until the other account has signed off on what Lorraine and Halle come up with."

"And no other *A* and *E* team will do. No other *A* and *E* team can work in my state. And Sylvia did me a favor taking me on." Her tone was scornful, and her hair flew with her headshake. "I can't believe this."

"I know." I rubbed my hands together. There had to be more I could do until then. Not to distract Isla but to actually move her closer to her goals. "I'll go through all the possible subcontractors, so when the general contractor gets out here—"

"I'm not—No. Not tonight." Her brows drew together. "I don't feel like doing much tonight."

"Do you want me to go?"

She gave a helpless shrug. "No, but it's not like I have anything to do but more home renovations." Her mouth twisted in a wry smile. "And nowhere to sit."

I wanted to take her to bed and hold her. But her little air mattress wasn't going to allow it. She was holding herself in a stasis in this house, waiting. Waiting for my mom to do the job she'd been contracted to do. The job she should be doing instead of Dev's.

I didn't want to leave, but it was hard to witness Isla's dejection knowing I had some responsibility for it. I crossed to her, put my hands on her warm thighs, and kissed her. The best apology I could give. A simple "I'm sorry" for letting her down. And when her eyes warmed and she softened, I stepped back, using more determination than I'd anticipated. I could take her here, now. But it would be wrong.

I'd already done enough.

* * *

Isla

The news of the extra month or more delay yesterday propelled me through the house. I paced. Stopping, I'd attack the wallpaper in the kitchen, and then I'd pace some more. So I went to the living room and tested a corner of the carpet. Ripping out old Berber might burn through the antsy, simmering feeling in my chest.

Finally, I gave up and grabbed my phone. I tapped out a message to Lyric. **I've been a shit and I need to talk.**

I set the phone down and paced again in short bursts, so I wasn't far from my phone.

Finally, a message flashed on the screen. **I'm at the store. I'll be right over.** And then **I've been a shit too.**

The wave of relief almost took my knees out from under me. I sagged against the counter. I hadn't ignored Lyric so long she'd forgotten me. She might show up and read me the riot act, but I deserved it. I just needed to talk.

I waited on the front step, and when she pulled into the driveway next to my trailer, I jumped up. She got out. "I've been a shit too." She spun to the back door and hauled Rina's car seat carrier out.

"Ohmigod—I've been a crap friend and aunt too." I ran to her and lifted the baby carrier from her fingers. I held it up to my face, and Rina gave me a gummy grin, her chubby legs scissoring. "How's my angel?"

"Cranky," Lyric said. "That's her first smile."

My heart melted. Ignoring my family had gotten me a whole lot of nothing. "I can't believe it's been so long since we've talked."

"Isla—we can go months and still be best friends, but I

knew something was going on and I didn't ask if you needed to talk. I feel terrible, but I'm just so . . . overwhelmed."

We walked into the house. "I don't know if I would've answered. I haven't been in a good headspace, and that's probably when I needed to talk the most instead of shutting you out." Inside, I groaned. "I don't have a single seat in the place."

"The floor is fine."

I didn't want my guests on the old carpet. I spread out a blanket for Rina to stretch out on, and Lyric and I sat on the edges. Everything since the middle of June poured out. How I'd asked Liam to work with me and he'd turned me down, the family gathering when I'd felt like an afterthought, my parents, and finally, McCoy.

"I knew you were into him." Lyric wasn't triumphant—maybe a little. She knew me better than anyone. "But, yeah, that's a problem."

"It's not his fault." But more of my anger was shifting toward him. If I wasn't sleeping with him, I'd have been demanding a project status earlier.

"But you still have to deal with the delay."

"I don't know how." I stretched out and smiled at my niece as she cooed at the treetops visible in the picture window from the floor. "In my gut, I feel like something's not quite right. I don't think McCoy's being completely honest."

"And you're pissed he's protecting his mom over you."

Yes. "She's his boss."

"But you want him to care for you. This isn't just a fling."

I swallowed hard, facing all the realities I'd purposely ignored since McCoy first kissed me. "She's his mother and his employer, but . . . what am I?"

She chewed her lower lip and crossed her legs at the

ankles, bracing her arms behind her. "I think you'll find out when you deal with Sylvia."

"What do you mean?"

She was quiet for a moment, then a surprised laugh left her. "I can't believe I'm saying this, and, Isla—you'll think I've gone to the dark side, but I promise I haven't. I promise I'm being logical and that your brother hasn't dickmatized me."

"You say that one more time, and I'm going to hurl all over the carpet."

"It might brighten up the room. Add some character."

I playfully scowled at her. "The gouges in the wall from removing the wallpaper give it enough character, thank you very much. Hit me. What's your shocking advice?"

"I think you need better tips than I can give you. Better advice than Stetson can give you. You need to talk to people who've been down this road and who've had to deal with questionable contractors."

"I don't think Sylvia is questionable." She couldn't be. "She flew to the state to meet with me after the first change order."

Lyric shot me a quelling look, and I mimicked zipping my mouth shut. After a little pause, she finally said, "You should talk to your mom."

My lungs constricted. I couldn't bring my business to Mom. I'd get an *I told you* so if she even let me in the house. "Dad would've fired me if I hadn't quit first. No—Dad might not have fired me, but Mom would've when he didn't."

"You hated that job."

Hate was a strong word. It was a job. Experience. Something to do, which had been their goal. "She wouldn't have waited for me to resign."

"If you wanted the job, you'd have done what they

asked. And honestly, this is your parents we're talking about. You can't tell me they aren't a little proud that meek little Isla has a backbone."

I never thought of them being proud of me. They were my parents. I had done what I did after college because I knew how they'd act, how they'd try to take over. And when I made it hard on them, they'd lashed out. But both times had been necessary. Both times had been decisions I should've made much earlier.

So did I mope around wondering what to do about McDaniel Contractors when I had highly knowledgeable parents who had worked on similar projects? I'd grown up hearing Mom talk about bids and contractors. Her brother was in construction. He was on McCoy's list of possible subcontractors to approach, only I hadn't mentioned he was my uncle.

"I think I need to talk to them," I admitted. The anxiety from earlier changed, intensified. I was more scared to discuss with my parents what to do than when I thought of discussing my concerns with Sylvia directly.

And that meant I was worried I'd either have to stand up for myself—or face their ire, which had been pushing me in the right direction, however bluntly efficient.

Lyric smiled for a moment before she grew serious. "About that night, Liam and Kennedy's party—We worried about you. Stetson wanted to call you after Kennedy said you turned her down, but I told him not to. I said you'd talk to me if you had a real problem. I'm sorry. I should've called."

"You're a busy mama."

She chewed the inside of her cheek, and her eyes glistened. "I need to feel like myself, and I haven't been."

"Lyric, is everything okay?"

She sniffed. "Hormones and shit. I hate them. But as

happy as I am with Stetson, god, Isla, life is different. Barely a year ago, I had a massive thing for a guy I thought was unobtainable."

"You also thought no one knew."

Lyric giggled and rolled her eyes. "Apparently it was obvious to everyone but him."

"It's not anymore," I said quietly. We'd been missing this. Talking, like we were doing, had been hard while I lived with my parents. And she had her own place and her own life, but it had rarely been just us for a while.

She let out a sigh. "It's not. It's wonderful and it's busy and it's . . . overwhelming at times. Scary even. I went from living with my mom to being a wife and mom. I guess I just need someone to get that, and I was afraid to tell you because it's your brother I'm with."

"And my niece who made you a mommy." I picked up Rina and laid her across my outstretched legs. She kicked and grabbed my fingers. "But I know you can be deliriously happy but overwhelmed. I don't know, but I can understand."

"We're full-on adults, Isla."

I clicked my tongue at Rina and got a droopy grin in return. "With grown-up problems." And that meant I would have to talk to people who had more experience being the bad guy than me.

Sixteen

ISLA

I drove to my parents' house and parked under the big picture windows. The place stared down at me, and I'd never felt like I didn't live here more than I did now. This wasn't my home, but it hadn't been that way for years. It'd been a bunkhouse. A place I wasn't totally comfortable but had refused to leave. I'd bided my time and waited for my opportunity.

Funny I was coming back because I'd tired of waiting.

I found Mom on the back porch. She never spoke about her Sunday evening ritual of having tea on the porch. In the winter, she sat in front of the fireplace, steadily pumping heat onto her while she read. Others might think she'd read literary fiction. Tomes about the meaning of life. Or nonfiction by CEOs on how to be powerful and dominant people.

Mom read mysteries. The darker and more brutal, the better. They were her version of vegging out to murder shows, which she might've done if I hadn't been running around.

I don't know why I suddenly pondered the deeper meaning of it all now. Perhaps because I saw Mom in a new light. She and Dad had made some tough decisions in their lives, often ones that made them unpopular, even unlikable. And she'd owned it. She'd absorbed all the backlash and weathered on, unashamedly carving out the best life for her and her family.

I'd been so determined not to be like her when I should've been taking more notes.

She glanced up, surprise flittering across her features. "Isla. I heard someone drive up, but I thought it was maybe Stetson and he'd go looking for your father."

Mom's Sunday night routine was quiet reading and contemplation before she had to face a week of work with people who actively disliked her or acted cordial while talking shit behind her back. Dad spent his evenings in the barn or shop doing the job I suspected he'd rather have done in his life than donning a suit and going to an office every day.

"No, I came to talk to you. Is Dad around?" My stomach cramped, but I refused to retreat. I could face Dad and ask for help. It was what he wanted, and Lyric had helped me see he was right.

"He's in the kitchen grabbing a bite before he finishes stacking bales."

Dad picked that moment to step out. He seemed just as surprised to see me as Mom had been. He glossed over his expression with neutral interest. Was he afraid I was angry about being fired?

The market drama seemed laughable compared to the foundry restoration. A few bucks lost a week compared to my life's inheritance that happened to be all I had.

"I need to talk to you both," I said. "I need advice."

Neither of them covered their shock. I remained calm, the cyclone in my stomach slowing. There was no heat creeping up my neck. I doubted I was even blotchy. I had thought coming to my parents was a cheat, a sign of immaturity. But it wasn't. They had experience I needed.

"Advice?" Mom set her book on the plexiglass-topped porch table and put her silver readers next to it. "What's wrong?"

Dad's eyes narrowed but not out of menace. He was worried. I pulled out a chair on the other side of Mom and sat. Dad took the spot next to her.

"First, I want to apologize. I used you guys for the last three years and didn't contribute a whole lot. And then I acted like you were the reason I didn't talk to you, when really I needed to learn to stand up for myself."

"You came home from college with no ambition," Dad said. "Or so we thought. We were . . . worried."

Mom nodded. "You didn't talk about what you wanted to do or what you wanted to be. You got a general degree in business and came home and said nothing, but you played around with beer."

I folded my hands on my lap. "I wasn't playing with beer, but I can see how that worried you."

Dad's ironic chuckle carried on the light, warm breeze. "We thought maybe you'd do something with it. Sell it or share it, but I'd find you dumping gallons down the drain."

"It's an art as much as a craft. Those gallons weren't consumable, but I didn't talk to you about it. Also...you didn't ask."

Mom readjusted her position, leaning toward Dad. "I understand we aren't the easiest to talk to."

I didn't mean to laugh as loud as I did, but I didn't snap my mouth shut and pretend I didn't. I wanted them to know I accepted them for who they were. They were scary and they were hard, but they were my parents and ultimately they wanted what was best for me. Maybe if we'd had this talk before Dad's chronic leukemia diagnosis, it'd be different. We'd all changed in the last year. "No, you aren't. But living life like I was scared of my own shadow wasn't the answer. I needed to be kicked out. I needed to be prompted to move on from the market. I also need respect—especially from you guys. You two should be my biggest champions, my most avid mentors. I shouldn't have to fear that you'll belittle me or take over or just generally lack confidence in whatever I do. I don't want to be scared to turn to either of you."

The only sounds were the birds and the breeze. Dad inhaled, long and slow. "I don't want you to fear coming to us either."

"I never thought..." Mom prodded at her temples with her fingers. "I face so much opposition around town, I didn't want to come home to it, and I didn't realize how I was reacting to you. Your father's right. You should be able to talk to us and do it more frankly than you would with others." She gave me a small smile. "What's funny is that I'd be extremely upset if you hadn't apologized first. That was really adult of you and...I'll work on it."

"Me too." It was all we could do. I used to want to be less like Mom, but I could see she was a product of her environment—and there were several times when her reaction was valid. Anything less and she'd be walked on, just like I had footprints all over my business plans.

"You bought a house," Mom blurted.

All Mom knew was that I'd brushed off her advice about renting from her coworker's in-laws and jumped into buying a house. "Yes, and you guys will have to come over. I won't have any furniture, much of anything, really, until I get new flooring in. But I bought the place planning to fix up what I could and sell it. When the restoration is complete and the brewery is functioning, I'll have a better idea of what I can afford for a house, but this way, I should be able to make a good return when I sell."

Mom exchanged a look with Dad I couldn't interpret, and my gut lit up like a nuclear wasteland. If they told me it was a terrible idea, I'd listen. They might not have personally bought and sold much for real estate, but they'd worked with people who had for decades.

"That's not a bad idea," Dad said. "Real estate is rarely a bad option."

"Seriously?" Shocked, I looked between them. The cool wash of relief was welcome, but I wasn't sure I heard correctly. "You really think it's a good idea?"

Mom dipped her head. "Had you told us earlier, I might have had reservations, but I'm starting to see that you really do plan and think things through. You're contemplative, and I didn't see that before."

A little smile tipped up the corner of my mouth. "Thank you. I mean it."

"So what's bothering you?" Dad asked. "The house? The foundry? That project manager?"

I couldn't bring myself to be defensive about Dad's tone regarding McCoy. "About that." I told them everything. Not the steamy details of me and McCoy, but I didn't shy away from admitting there was something between us. When I finished, I lifted my hands and flopped them on my lap. "So, there it is. I need to go into this informed. It's not just money on the line. This is what I want to do with my life. This is how I want to contribute to Coal Haven. To put the money that came from the land back into the area and its people."

I'd had reasons for not talking to them before, but

spilling my goals was easier than I thought. Plans that weren't impulsive, lacking ambition, or selfish. It wasn't exactly charity work, but I had plans for that too. Fundraisers, donations, and charity endeavors, all stemming from Reservoir Barrel and what it could do for the community.

"I also want to be professional. Kind but firm, until kindness no longer suffices." I wasn't Mom, and I didn't have to be. But I accepted that sometimes I'd need to channel her for a good reason.

Mom rubbed her hands together. "Did you have a lawyer go through the contract before you signed?"

"Yes, I went through all the steps, and I swear I researched her company thoroughly. She was professional, but she was also nice. She treated me like an equal. Yet she also wasn't up front about who McCoy is to her." Or the harassment charges. I believed McCoy about what happened, but that added to how she hid the fact he was her son and wasn't a standard employee, and I felt duped.

"People can be nice and professional while they're using all the loopholes to benefit themselves at the cost of others," she said.

I could see her point clearly now. It was time to act more like my parents. "I'd like to know what you'd do."

Her expression turned businesslike. "Here's what I'd suggest."

* * *

McCoy

When Mom called, I was at the foundry, checking on the patch job I did on the window. There was supposed to be another storm tonight with a chance of hail. And it was probably the best place to have this conversation with Mom.

"Why the hell couldn't you have my back on this one, McCoy?"

My full first name. That was never a good sign. "What are you talking about?"

"I just got off the phone with Isla. She spoke to her lawyer this morning, and he had a lot to say about not meeting the deadline."

The brick walls closed around me until I was shrouded in darkness. "What?" I hadn't talked to Isla since I'd left her place on Saturday. I was waiting for her to make the first move when she'd gotten over the worst of her anger about the delay and I could get a sense of what she really thought.

Meanwhile, I'd been planning what I could do. How could I bypass our own *A* and *E* and avoid another change order? Would Mom be willing to let us hire outside of the company? We'd just subcontract out and cross our fingers someone had an opening before the end of the year.

"What exactly did he say?" I asked.

"Isla won't budge on the date. Said if she can't rely on McDaniel Contractors during this early phase, she doesn't think she can count on us for the rest. What did you tell her?"

"What you said. How could I lie?" She was the one who taught me better than that.

"She should understand that we have multiple projects going on at once."

"She does, but hers has been ignored."

"Coy."

"Mom." I didn't have any more answers than when she called last time. Why hadn't Isla come to me? She'd gone right over my head to Mom, and now I looked like the inept one who'd tossed Mom under the bus. But then Isla shouldn't have had to go over me. "What exactly is going on?"

"She's holding firm to the date. No change order, and instead of just letting us incur penalty fees, she's going to terminate the contract, and we'll have to deal with all that entails."

I leaned against one of the walls, letting the cool stone leech heat from my back. My temperature was climbing, and I was sweating under the collar, but not because of summer.

Terminate. I'd be done here. No reason to stay in Coal Haven.

"I had the utmost confidence in you." Mom's disappointment hung heavy over the line.

The one project she'd given me to do, and I'd failed. Isla hadn't talked to me first. I could've reasoned with her. McDaniel Contractors was the best for her needs. Once the plans were done, we'd knock it out and meet whatever bullshit deadline was set in the contract.

"I thought maybe Hannah had exaggerated."

I pushed off the wall. "What?"

"Your customer service. I knew you were a little abrasive like your father, but you built that brewery and restaurant. You claimed Hannah was taking credit for your work, but now I wonder if you didn't need her to keep everyone happy."

"What are you talking about? You know nothing about how I ran Nailer's."

"That's the thing, McCoy. You didn't run it, did you?"

"I . . ." I'd come up with the concept. I'd hired the contractors and worked through the plans. It'd all been my ideas—and then Hannah had been the voice. I'd given the orders, and she'd passed them on. "I ran it," I said tightly.

"And I can see how you lost it." Her office phone blared in the background. "I don't have time for this today. Listen,

McCoy, you need to talk some sense into her. I know she has a soft spot for you."

Hurt struck me hard in the solar plexus. My eyes were open, but I didn't see a thing. When had I traded places with Isla? When had I become nothing to Mom other than what I could do for the company? "Sounds like she has all the sense she needs. I'm done, Mom. Find another project manager who'll lie to clients."

"You can't be serious."

"I am."

"You're making a mess and leaving me to clean it up? It's a little too much like your father for my taste."

"A glitch occurred because of your decisions, and you're taking it out on me? Who's the one acting like Dad?"

An indignant gasp echoed over the line. She hung up, and I was left staring at the phone. Did that conversation just happen?

I heard a car door shut outside and groaned. That would be Isla.

I met her out on the sidewalk. Her gaze was wary, and I hated that she looked at me that way. Nothing like the day she'd invited me to work on a batch of beer with her, like I had all the secrets and all the answers and I might prove her worthy by sharing with her.

How badly I wanted to return to that day and accept her offer. To just be and not worry about how it'd backfire. I'd been doing the best job I could in Coal Haven and had the whole heap of blame dumped on me.

Isla's hair was already in a braid hanging over her shoulder. She wore her work clothes. Did she leave her house to talk to me somewhere she could easily leave?

What was it about me that made it easy for people to toss me away?

"You talked to your mom?" she asked.

"Yes, she called." I scratched the back of my neck, frustrated with the mess the delay was creating. Upset that Isla talked directly to Mom instead of me but steeped in regret because she had tried going through me. I let the client down. And everything was slipping through my fingers—again. "Why didn't you talk to me first?"

"I got the feeling you weren't telling me everything."

"There was nothing to say." The dedicated son in me couldn't help but defend his mom once more, despite how she'd just acted. "Companies like Sylvia's juggle multiple projects every day. Delays are nor—"

"Unplanned delays. Like if the engineer had discovered something about the structure that would hinder making the place into a brewery. Knowingly delaying my job and asking for change orders in order to take higher-earning jobs that benefit her company is exactly the delay the contract protects me from." She tipped her head. "That's what she was doing, wasn't it?"

Mom would want me to lie. Isla wanted the truth. I'd withheld enough, and Mom was already upset with me. Despite what she had said, I had gotten Nailer's to where it was with good business practices. "Yes."

"And you knew it?"

I'd put the hurt on her face, and my answer would cause more. "Yes."

She nodded, her expression hardening further. "You must've thought it'd be so easy to get me to do what you wanted."

"It wasn't like that." Mom had thought so. She'd thought she was a savvy businesswoman, and she'd be able to accomplish what Isla needed but also take on the multiple-million-dollar client thanks to Isla's ignorance.

"How was it? Was the sex supposed to lull me into complacency?"

"I wasn't using you." My tone was harsh but fuck it. I stepped closer, and she took a step back, her eyes as wide as a deer in headlights. "Sleeping together didn't factor into anything with the foundry."

"I'll consider it a lesson learned, I guess." She held her hand out. "I'll need the keys, just in case."

"The contract's not severed yet. I quit right before you showed up, but another project manager will come on. I can fill that person in and hand over the keys." Giving up the keys meant walking away. I'd fucked up the foundry and I'd fucked up us, but I was trying to salvage something with Isla.

Surprise crossed her features. "You quit?" Annoyance chased it away. "So *more* delays." Bitterness stained the air. "Can she produce another project manager out of thin air? Do you think your mom—*Sylvia*—will pay a petty fee over upsetting the other account? And if she does, do you think the *A* and *E* team will be able to get to Coal Haven and have plans drawn up in a couple of weeks?"

No on all accounts. Defeat imprinted into my being.

"The entire team has lost my trust," she said softly.

And that was it. She didn't have to say she was going to have another talk with her lawyer and sever the contract entirely. She'd be within her rights to do so. There was nothing to argue. Losing her trust was like taking a wrecking ball to a building's foundation. I dropped the keys into her hand without touching her. That'd be torture right now.

She stared at the silver glinting in the sun. "Good thing you didn't rent a place. You kept it nice and temporary. Was that your plan?"

"It's just a motel room." There was an unmistakable truth to what she'd said. I'd planned to be here for months, and I hadn't even set down temporary roots.

"Yeah. That's all it is."

The anger I'd been keeping at bay mushroomed. I had no home. None. Not in Nashville. Not in Denver. And there was no place for me in Coal Haven. The two people I cared about the most in the world wanted nothing to do with me. "What about you? The house with no furniture? The beer you don't let anyone try? Have you messaged your friend yet, or are you still isolating yourself from everyone and playing the victim?"

She recoiled. "I had a nice talk with . . . You know what? It's none of your business."

"I guess not. Not anymore. Hope you find someone to give your business to." I stomped away.

But her words carried on the breeze. "I thought I had found that someone."

And the worst part about hearing what she said was that I didn't know if she was talking about Mom's company or me. Because she'd become way more than a job to me, and that was what made this hurt more. I let her down when she'd deserved the best of me.

Seventeen

ISLA

I sat at my new, used kitchen table with my leg curled under me and scrolled through names. Lyric's mom had found a dining room set when picking up consignment items, and she'd messaged me right away. I needed to replace the kitchen and dining room flooring yet, but when Mom and Dad had toured the place, Dad had also commented on opening the wall between the kitchen and living room. Then he'd offered to help.

For once, I took him up on the offer. He didn't take over. My emotions were so frayed, I would've let him, but he was cognizant of overstepping, telling me instead the different ways we could do it. Afterward, he and Mom sat outside on the tailgates of my pickup and Dad's, and we'd each had one of my beers. Mom even complimented the flavor and said she'd love to stock the house with it for her Sunday night reading sessions.

For the last two weeks, Dad had come over in the

evenings, and we ripped out carpet. Stetson had helped haul the remnants to the dump over the weekend. Lyric and I had gone out to eat with Aspen once, and while the rest of my extended family kept their distance, I didn't feel like as much of a stranger as I had over the summer.

After Dad was done with work, I had picked him up from home to help me move the table and chairs. We hadn't done much since but sat at the table and talked about grabbing a bite to eat.

"Do you know this company?" I wasn't a project manager, but I could hire people myself. Several companies in the area had the resources I needed for the restoration, and when it came to the brewery build, I trusted I'd find what I needed. I had to.

Dad peered at the screen. "I'm not familiar with them. Are they out of Bismarck?"

I nodded. "I'll email a query." I'd queried one company already, but they were booked out until next year. Which added another concern—any company with ready availability might not be the best option. "After I check with Mom." She'd vetoed some of the people and subcontractors on the list McCoy and I had come up with.

That man beats his wife. No.

She'll tell you everything you want to hear and then blame you when she doesn't do her job.

The company rebranded two years ago because it had such a bad reputation.

She knew details that weren't exactly put on websites. While she had mentioned her brother, she didn't push but said he was more local than others and had experience in restoration. She tacked on that he might walk all over me. If I hired another project manager, he'd be fine. I ruled him out.

Dad took a drink of my beer from the chilled mug I'd

served it in. Lately, when he sampled my stuff, he asked questions about the process and scaling up. This time, he peeked into the bottle. "So that stuff at the bottom?"

"Yeast. It'd normally be in the cone of the big tanks when the beer is siphoned out."

"This is good."

The way I beamed inside... Dad didn't give praise he didn't think was deserved, and his kids hadn't been exempt. "Thanks. I might try a batch with the clementine rind for flavoring only. Then serve with a clementine slice, kind of like a Blue Moon."

The dynamics between my parents and me had changed since I'd talked to them. When McCoy's truck had quit appearing in the motel parking lot, but I continued with my plans, finding professionals to work with, my parents must've seen I was serious. I hadn't been carried by the big, gruff man, and something like a breakup—a strong term when we'd never been a thing—wasn't going to make me hole up in the basement.

I was in the basement a lot, but I dealt with my broken heart by brewing more beer and sharing it with friends and family.

"You did this . . . by yourself? The recipe?" He was drinking the batch with clementines I'd made with McCoy. I bottled and conditioned the secondary fermentation, blasted country music, and tried not to cry. I missed having him around.

"McCoy hung out with me, but he didn't help me brew or give me any advice about it. I'm sure it's because he taught his ex-wife and best friend everything he knew."

Dad didn't react other than to set his glass down. He hadn't said much about McCoy. "I guess now you know not to make the same mistakes."

I chuckled. "You and Mom have coached me for years.

I've actually been listening the whole time. I might not always follow your advice, but sometimes I do."

He grunted. "I think we're learning our kids are going to do what the hell they want no matter what we think, and that maybe it's better to drop the argument than risk . . . losing you."

The Dad before he got sick, would've never admitted as much.

"Good thing Stetson and I aren't as stubborn as our parents."

Dad's smile was wry. "I'm not so sure about that."

The doorbell rang. I exchanged a confused frown with Dad.

"Maybe it's the mail?" I didn't order any packages. I had a clearance sale recliner in the living room after getting tired of having nowhere comfortable to sit and read when I lied to myself and thought I could quit thinking about McCoy for a few minutes.

Never worked.

The door was closed, but there was movement on the other side. The wrong height and hair for a man who used to wait for me to answer. A falling sensation happened in my gut, as if I was disappointed McCoy hadn't shown up on my doorstep. I knew he wouldn't, but each day I didn't hear from him would eventually hurt less. I hoped.

A navy-blue ball cap shifted in the view window at the top of the door. It wasn't Stetson. I didn't bother peering through the peephole. This was Coal Haven, and chances were low there was danger on the other side.

The screen door was between me and my visitor. "Liam?" Behind him on the sidewalk was another man. "Archer?"

Liam adjusted the brim of his cap. "Hey, Isla. Archer and I wanted to bring a housewarming gift by."

He might as well have spoken another language—any language, I only knew one. "For me?"

His crooked grin made me almost believe him. "You're the only person I know who's bought a house recently." He shrugged and adopted a self-deprecating smile. "Unless it's my wife and three kids, I don't actually pay attention to what everyone else is doing."

"You're more than welcome to come in." A vise gripped my stomach. I wanted to know what the gift was and, more importantly, why they'd gotten me one. But I had to be up front. "Dad's here, though."

Just as I made the announcement, Liam's gaze lifted over my shoulder and grew shadowed.

"Liam," Dad said, his usually hard tone when it came to my brother softer than I'd ever heard. "Archer's here too?"

"Nice to see you, Uncle Cameron," Archer said, not quite jovial but light enough to defuse some of the growing tension.

"I didn't see your truck," Liam said, but his real meaning was clear to all of us. He wouldn't have stopped by if he knew Dad was here.

"I rode with Isla." Dad's almost conversational reply emboldened me.

I pushed the door open and stepped back so the guys could enter. "Come on in."

Liam hesitated before he stepped through. Archer jogged up the three steps and there we were . . . all standing on my living room floor that was down to the plywood.

I might not have chosen the best topic to talk about, but anything was better than silence. "Dad, I had asked Liam to do some ironwork for the brewery. Maybe some stools, light fixtures, or small end tables for the sofa seating area."

Dad's brows lifted. Dismay flitted over his face, but he

smoothed his features over, like the first expression had been a default.

Liam spoke before Dad could. "It was too big of a job. I work with what I get, and planning ahead of time would've been too difficult with an unpredictable supply. Something like what Isla was asking was too important to get wrong."

Touched, I gave him a small smile. His denial had involved a lot of consideration for me, and I hadn't realized it.

Dad studied Liam like he was seeing him for the first time, like he was allowing himself to really see him. "It's hard to pass up a big contract that'd get your name out there."

"Tell me about it," Liam said. "But I have a job with benefits, and this is more of a side hobby that got me through a lot."

"I've heard you do good work." Dad's comment rang through the room like a bell.

Startled and panicked—I'd never heard my dad actually compliment the kid he'd shunned for three decades—I met Archer's gaze. He was just as surprised.

Dad must've thought he was on a roll. Next, he turned to Archer. "How's your dad?"

He was making history right now. Any other year, Liam and Archer would've stomped out, thoroughly criticized and insulted.

Archer's gaze grew more incredulous. "Good. Real good, actually. Delaney and I are going out there this winter to stay for a week. Between Uncle Bruce and Liam, we've got the chores covered."

"And Ansen?" Dad asked. I'd never met Archer's brother, and as far as I knew, neither had Dad.

This time I exchanged a perplexed look with Liam. Dad

sounded sincerely interested, lacking the usual arrogant lift to his tone when he looked for a crack to pry his way into.

Archer's smile fell. "I don't get much more than a message here and there from him. He's still training horses and doin' really well; that's all I know."

"How are the kids?" Dad's words were stilted, like he wasn't sure he was welcome to even ask.

"Good." Liam's jaw tightened like he wasn't going to answer more, but then his gaze filled with cautious resolve. "The boys are excited for school, but I think half the reason is because Kenny works there too. And Ginny is growing big, but I think Rina's going to catch up to her quick enough."

Dad dipped his head, a small ghost of a smile on his lips. "Stetson was a big kid from the start and he didn't quit growing. I wouldn't be surprised if Rina is the same." He lifted his head. "You brought Isla something?"

The friendly, familiar conversation had tapped us all out. The tension—would it turn rude and critical? Would all our days get ruined? How would Dad insult one of them?—was a lot to weather.

"Yeah," Liam said, like he had forgotten why he'd come over in the first place. "I felt bad not being able to help, so I made a little something. Archer, mind running out with me to haul it in?"

"He asked me because I'm more than a pretty face," Archer drawled.

The guys breezed out the door to Liam's pickup parked on the street.

Dad's gaze was stuck on them, something simmering in his eyes that I couldn't identify, but that looked a bit like regret. He'd missed the entire life of his son, and he'd done it on purpose. I doubted if they could be anything more than civil—which would be a huge improvement from how they usually were—they'd never recover what could've been.

I'd take civil. I'd take not having to hide a relationship with my brother. To be as open as Stetson now was.

Archer and Liam carted a large rectangular item up the sidewalk. I held the door open for them. Once inside, Liam crouched by the coffee table and took off the plastic wrap and cardboard protectors he'd taped to the corners. "I thought you might have more in the house this could go with."

"Like carpet?" I joked.

He flashed a smile, and I was no longer the little kid wondering why I couldn't talk to him. I wasn't the person destined to be on the outside of my family because I was too afraid to stand up to my parents. "It matches the subflooring real nice."

He and Archer gathered the packaging, but I waved to a corner. "Set it by the door. It can go out with the linoleum I'm ripping up next." I crossed to the coffee table. It was unique, with wrought iron legs twisting under a wooden slab with a blue epoxy center. Flecks of yellow ran through the epoxy, keeping the piece from being too dark and brooding. Kind of like another man I couldn't forget.

One day, thinking about McCoy wouldn't crack open the fracture lines in my heart.

But it didn't bother me that looking at this gorgeous piece made me think of him. The dark wood was the same brown as the amber bottles beer was bottled in. I pictured McCoy at the island in the cabin, the bottle hanging from his hand, talking about what his stepdad had taught him. "It's stunning."

Liam took his cap off and pushed a hand through his hair. "I thought I'd have to buy the wood to go with it, but Archer came through in the end."

"It's why he recruited me to haul it in," Archer said.

"Thought it was all that muscle Laney gushes about," Liam retorted.

Archer flashed him a playful, confused look. "What are you talking about? She married me for my brains."

Liam snorted. "Wasn't it the way you can't say no when she wants a new goat?"

My cousin's grin was wide. "That's how I keep her. But she's breeding them now."

"You're taking notes?" Liam countered.

Archer snickered. "Nah, but when I get cocky, she threatens to lock me in the billy goat pen."

I caught Dad's wistful expression from the corner of my eye. An amused tilt to his lips and that regret I thought I'd seen earlier. Sympathy welled inside me. He'd dug his own hole with Liam, but maybe he could fill some of it in.

Liam propped his hands on his hips. "Anyway, don't be a stranger." He ran his teeth over his lower lip like he wasn't sure if he should say more. "The boys have been asking about you."

Emotion clogged my chest, squeezing my heart until I thought it'd burst. "They have?" When he nodded, I made plans right then. "I'll make a batch of root beer just for them and bring it over. They'll be my taste testers."

"I'm off next weekend," he said. "I'll see when's good for Kenny." He grinned. "She's the boss."

Archer scoffed. "As if any of us had any doubts."

Liam had a look that said *same*, and Archer shrugged. Laney was the boss.

"All right. I promised Kenny I'd be home by nap time." He waved at the table. "If you find a flaw or a connection comes apart, let me know. I'll run over and fix it."

"I really appreciate this." More than he'd know. "It's beautiful. I'm thrilled to have something of yours, and I still plan to buy something of yours from Hattie to put in the brewery."

"I can always do one special piece for you. When you're ready, let me know, and we'll walk through my scrap and brainstorm." He gave me one last smile, and he and Archer walked to the door.

"See you, Uncle Cameron," Archer said as he went outside.

Liam looked over his shoulder, his gaze wary. "Cameron."

Dad's nod was slight. "Nice to see you both."

Surprise flitted through Liam's eyes before he turned away. I followed them out the door. "Thank you." I couldn't say it enough.

Liam stopped and faced me. "I know what it's like to be on the outside looking in, and I'm sorry if we made you feel like that."

The pressure of tears burned the backs of my eyes from both remorse and gratitude. Not long ago, I was one of the ones keeping him locked out, and now he was apologizing for maybe making me feel that way once. My brother had a big goddamn heart. "You have nothing to be sorry for."

"I appreciate it, but I wanted you to know. You reached out, and I know that took a lot." His gaze touched behind me, but Dad wasn't at the door. "Changing things for my kids is important to me, and that means I'm looking forward to trying your root beer."

I grinned. "I'll have plenty of regular beer I need opinions on."

He tipped the brim of his cap. "Looking forward to it."

He went around his pickup to the driver's side. Archer opened his door. "Laney's had nothing but good things to say." My expression must've been confused. "I know, everyone's always surprised. But she gave me the rundown of y'all when I got here. I'm only tellin' you so you're not afraid to stop by. We can trade some beer for eggs."

That was an invitation I was definitely excited about. "A dozen for a dozen?"

He flashed an unrepentant grin as he hopped in. "Depends on how good the beer is."

Laughing, I waved at them as Liam drove off. Inside, I found Dad standing over the table.

"He does have a gift," I murmured.

Dad didn't reply, but the same emotions from earlier played over his face. He shoved his hands in his pockets. "I give a lot of advice, much of it unwanted. But I had a decision to make once, and I thought I had only two options to pick from. Looking back . . . I had choices, but I was scared. Don't ever let fear limit you. You'll miss out and not know it until it's too late."

I blinked back tears, but I couldn't fight the blotchy heat crawling up my neck. My issue with McDaniel Contractors was nothing like what Dad had gone through with his affair and Liam, but had I been too hard? Too uncompromising? I'd severed the contract when I knew it'd cut the tenuous tie that was growing between me and McCoy. On paper, it was the right thing to do, but my heart still tried to argue.

All I could say was, "I'll try to remember, Dad."

* * *

McCoy

I stretched out on the bed with my arm behind my head. The newest *Predator* movie was on and watching people getting ripped apart was a special form of symbolism I couldn't look away from. My phone buzzed, and I glanced at the screen. Mom again. I didn't answer.

It'd been two weeks since I'd talked to her. I had driven to Denver, dropped off the work truck, bought a pickup of my own, went straight to her house, and moved my stuff out, all before she got home at seven.

Then I'd checked into a hotel. And here I'd been.

The first week, I didn't have the will to figure out the mess of my life. But the last few days, I had actually gone to the gym. From there, I'd searched some job openings, considering anything and everything. There were several jobs open that I had skills for. Construction. Project management. Even a few brewery positions were open.

Except when I hovered over the description, all I could see was the foundry with its conveniently high ceilings and wood beams soaring overhead. The final product, painted so vividly by an invested and enthusiastic owner, formed in my head. I could picture it as clearly as if all the work was done and I stood inside.

The tasks ticked through my brain. All the calls I'd been waiting to make. All the subcontractors I'd actually looked forward to talking to. And the brewing. To see Isla's products in large-scale production and being enjoyed outside of the cabin or her basement.

For almost two months, I hadn't thought as much about what I'd lost. When I had, it was to put things into perspective, to look around the hurt and betrayal and figure out where I was at. To figure out what the hell I actually wanted to do in my life. My careers had been a way to prove something to someone—for myself. But with Isla, I'd wanted her dream to come to fruition. I wanted to see the place when it was done. I wanted to be there when customers filled the taproom, and goddammit, I wanted to see what kind of events booked the back room.

My phone started again. I let out a sigh, and without looking, I answered. "Yeah."

"How long are you going to ignore me, Coy?" Mom asked, exasperated.

I was back to being Coy again. Hearing her voice soothed the little boy inside me, but the ex–project manager was left bitter. "I answered, didn't I?"

"I've been calling for two weeks."

"I thought you said everything you wanted."

A sigh filled the phone. "It was—you know—I . . . I'm sorry. I messed up, and I would've told you earlier, but you wouldn't answer and then I came home from work that day and you were all moved out. Dammit, Coy." She made a choking noise. Was she crying? Mom didn't cry anymore. She used to when Dad was around. Now I was the reason for her tears. Add it to the pile of shit I couldn't do right. "I was upset and mad at myself, and I took it out on you."

"I didn't do my job." Not for her, and not for Isla.

"I made it impossible for you. Look, it's my fault. I catered to Dev when I should've kept to the schedule I had. But he was one of my first clients. Without him—"

"You would've done fine. You would've gotten another client who was happy with your work, who told someone else, and you'd be in the same place you are."

A sniffle sounded. Dammit, she had been crying. I needed a shiny badge that said World's Shittiest Son. I could've answered the phone at least once. Or sent a reply, even if it was that we'd talk later. I was destined to let down the women in my life.

"I might realize that now, but when Dev calls, I feel like that person again. New and being funded by a second husband. I was so scared to let Fergus down in those days."

"Yeah, I know what you mean."

"That's why you built Nailer's, isn't it? I thought you

wanted to show up your father, but after he died, you still worked like a madman."

"Fergus took a chance on me, and I wasn't letting him down any more than you were."

Another choking hiccup. "Dammit, I miss that man." She blew out a hard breath, and her inhale was audible. "The thing is, Coy, he was proud of you before you even had the idea to build and run your own place. He thought you were a good kid with a solid head on your shoulders, and he gushed about my parenting and that you turned out the way you did despite your dad."

"Fergus's recipes were ones I used to start the brewery. And now *she* has them."

"McCoy." Her tone was more understanding. I couldn't hear disappointment, but that was all I felt. "You know what he'd tell you?"

"No," I mumbled.

"That you're more than capable of doing your own thing. Make some more."

Make your own place, kid. Don't wait on people to give you permission. Do it yourself.

"I don't have a place to make more, and I'm not sure I want to."

"Do you like construction?"

I liked making useful shit in the world. "Yeah, but . . . It's not what I want to do for twenty-five more years." I wanted to do more than go to work. I wanted more out of life than monitoring the bottom line.

"Did you enjoy being a project manager?"

"I've had worse jobs." It was fine, but not being in charge ended up slapping my ass. The only slapping I wanted to do was on Isla's ripe flesh when she was naked. I pinched the bridge of my nose as lust nearly strangled me. Was I a glutton for punishment?

"I hear there's a bright girl in a small town with big ideas."

"You're not holding a grudge against her?"

Her chuckle was sincere. "I should, but I was left admiring her steel. I've been in a similar place and I know how hard it is. I never wanted to be the type of person to take advantage of a naive girl. Yet I was, and she called me on it. So no, no grudges here." She paused. "You know, she'll probably need to hire brewers."

"No. That won't—No. Besides, I'm not . . ." It was my turn to let out a heavy exhale. I didn't want to revisit why I would be the last guy Isla hired again. "I was into the craft because of Fergus. Don't get me wrong, I enjoyed it, but I proved what I needed to." And I'd been shown that a whole lot of nothing waited on the other side.

"Then what do you want to do?"

"I don't know."

Silence filled the line, and I wasn't driven to fill the space with needless chatter.

Mom spoke next. "Was there something between you and Isla?"

My lack of a response answered the question.

"Coy." There was the disappointment. "What were you thinking?"

"I don't know." No, that wasn't true. Out of everything I'd done, that part was the easiest to explain. "I do know, actually. I was thinking she's the sunniest person I've been around and it's not because she dances around like she doesn't have a care in the world. She thinks about what she's doing, and she loves her family, but she doesn't know how to show it, and because of some drama, she's not sure who she'll hurt and it makes her cautious. She'll close herself off before she hurts the ones she loves. And she trusted me. She might not have understood how I was feeling, but she accepted it. I didn't have to be anyone but her project manager, and I couldn't do that for her."

"Oh, honey." Mom's tone brought me back to the times I'd broken down when I was a kid. What had I done wrong to make Dad act the way he had? "And she's not talking to you anymore?"

"Why would she?"

"Because you were acting as my employee."

"There was a little nepotism."

"No, if there was, you would've fibbed enough that she signed another change order. Instead, she knew something that'd upset her was going on."

Busted. I hadn't been McDaniel Contractors' best project manager either. "It doesn't matter. She's done with me."

She clucked her tongue. "Could it be 'cause you were just gone, and she couldn't get ahold of you?"

"She has my number." I sounded like a petulant teen. But I'd never been bothered by a breakup when I was that age. I was too busy working to help my parents pay bills.

"You know, when I first got serious with Fergus, we had a misunderstanding." She chuckled and sadness filled the sound. "I don't remember what we argued about anymore. But I do remember when he called, and I refused to answer. So he showed up, and I pretended I wasn't home. So he mailed a letter. Not even an email. Who can resist opening a real letter?"

"It must've worked."

"It did. I hadn't gotten a letter in years, and from a guy? I read it. And he said that he'd hate to see me throw away something he thought was special because a weak man ruined my concept of communication. He vowed to talk things through without yelling, without being controlling, if I was willing to keep the door open for him."

"You think I slammed the door?"

"I think you learned from me. If there's anything you wish you'd told Isla, I think you should do at least that. Open the door, and if she's the one to slam it, so be it."

She had neatly closed the door and had taken the keys, but I didn't want to point that out when Mom shared such a personal detail about her relationship with Fergus. So I deflected. "Aren't you upset with her?"

"I was. So damn irritated that some little twentysomething who hadn't owned anything more expensive than a phone when we first talked fired me. Who did she think she was? And then I got over it. Isla's young, but she's proving herself to be a cautious businesswoman, and while I wish she'd have negotiated more, I didn't do my part and prove my company was trustworthy. But, Coy, that's between her and me."

"It's not, though."

"It is. And if she's as balanced as I think she is, she'll see it if she doesn't already. Talk to her. That's all."

I'd fallen for her. In the last two weeks, I hadn't felt better. What if telling Isla I didn't want to give up what was growing between us made it worse? What if she slammed the door between us and sealed it shut?

"I'll think about it." Only because I couldn't stop thinking about Isla.

"Do that. But maybe figure out what you really want in life before you approach her. What *you* want to do, Coy. Not what you think others want you to do."

Easier said than done. When the call was over, I dropped the phone to my chest and stared at the ceiling. What I wanted was easy. Isla Barron. So the question was—what was I going to do about it?

Eighteen

ISLA

I pulled up to Reservoir Barrel with my trailer and mower. There'd be an official, but temporary, sign soon. I found the company I wanted to create the logo and branding. We came up with a sign to post by the highway. *Future home of Reservoir Barrel Brewery and Events.*

The sign wasn't much progress, but I got a mental boost every time I envisioned it. Paired with the neatly mowed lawn, it was all I could do. I was still searching for a general contractor. If I had to piecemeal this bitch, I would. My name tag would be the one to say project manager. A job I didn't want but suddenly found necessary to do.

Mom and Dad helped with advice. They could identify red flags quicker than I could, but Mom had admitted that she wouldn't have questioned McDaniel Contractors. That was probably the biggest compliment I'd ever gotten from her, other than that she liked my beer.

I hung out with Dad a lot more than I did before. He

enjoyed helping me around the house, and while I had wanted to do a lot myself, it turned out to be more fun to tear out walls and paint with him. I learned a lot from Dad, who took a mentoring role instead of being the boss. It was something neither of us had expected. When was the last time he didn't have to be the boss? I'd heard him laugh more in the last few weeks than in my entire life.

But it was Tuesday, and he was working. Same with Lyric. Aspen and Kennedy were getting their classrooms ready for the start of school, and I'd just picked up eggs from Laney. I'd traded her a six-pack of the vanilla cardamom blend I still had.

I mowed the lawn, zipping around the worst of the rocks sticking out of the ground. I'd hit those with the Weedwacker. Sweat trickled between my breasts, but I wore a long-sleeved shirt, jeans, my cowboy boots, safety glasses, and my headphones for ear protection. The sun beat down on me. The grass was already drying, but enough weeds grew that the lawn looked raggedy if it wasn't mowed regularly. I might have to come out here one last time before Dad walked me through the winterization of the mower.

Sometimes, Mom stopped over with pizza she'd picked up from Rattler's. She ignored the coffee table Liam had given me. I assumed Dad told her the story. The old Mom would've told me to get it out of my house or never talk to her again. But she was slowly accepting that Liam was a part of my life and Stetson's.

Maybe hell had frozen over, or maybe Mom and Dad had finally processed some of the hurt from years ago and found healing. I wasn't questioning it, just reaping the benefits.

I loaded the mower up, tied it down, and grabbed the Weedwacker. I buzzed over the lawn, around the building, and down the sidewalk, my back to the parking lot.

Dang, it was hot. Hair plastered to my face. I had wound my standard braid into a bun since the back of my neck should be safe from debris flying from the mower and Weedwacker.

I shut the Weedwacker off and ran the back of my arm across my damp forehead. Soon enough, snow would be flying, and I'd have to figure out what I wanted to do for snow removal.

I pushed the safety glasses up and spun. I barked out a shout at the unfamiliar pickup that suddenly appeared. The vehicle I'd never seen before was parked next to the trailer, but a very familiar man was leaning against the side, his hands in his pockets.

I drank him in. His hair was shaggier than when I'd seen him a month ago and he had dark circles under his eyes, but neither of those details detracted from his rugged handsomeness.

"McCoy. What are you doing here?" Sylvia wouldn't have sent him. I was done with McDaniel Contractors.

"I need to talk to you."

I was almost soggy after a couple hours of lawn care. I probably had bits of grass in my hair and sweat rings around my collar and pits. The jeans clung to me like a wet rag on a muggy day.

"You could've called." I didn't mean to sound hostile. It wasn't like McCoy was used to seeing me dolled up. He'd never seen me dressed up, actually, but I wasn't prepared to see him again, and I wasn't ready to do it full of grit and smelling like exhaust.

He pushed off the pickup and walked toward me. "This is better in person."

I would've backed up if I wasn't holding a heavy Weedwacker. I was tempted to drop it and run. "Is something wrong?"

"I never apologized for not acting in your best interest."

"Okay." Disappointment curled through me. He'd come to apologize for the way the job ended. But why return to Coal Haven for it? A simple email would've sufficed. I'd have been hurt if that was all I got, but he didn't owe me more.

He stopped a few feet in front of me. "I'm sorry."

He had to squint with the sun so high overhead, but the sincerity was in his amber eyes. "Thank you." Now he could return to Denver with a clean conscience and have a stellar life being a project manager.

"But what I really came here for—" His eyes narrowed more. "Did you think I only tracked you down to apologize for the project?"

Was my dismay that apparent? "I don't know why else you'd be here."

"You."

One simple word and he left it at that. Was it too good to be true? Would I be silly to hope he missed me as much as I missed him? "Me?"

He drifted closer, his chin tilted down like he knew I was afraid to meet his gaze. "I'm here for *you*. I understand if the problems with the company got in the way, but I really hope you're willing to find out just how good we can be together. I hope you think what we had going was special and could've really been something, and it'd be a shame if we just walked away."

"We already walked away."

He took another step closer. We were as close as we could be without touching. "My mom pointed out that I leave instead of communicating. Not that my divorce would've turned out differently, but it'd been my idea to sell the house, to sell my half of Nailer's. I've never . . . talked. And with you, it's easy. I want to hear what you have to say, what you think. I love watching you get excited, and fuck, I love being buried inside of you even more."

"McCoy." It came out in a whisper.

"Isla, I fell hard for you. And while I might've loaded my truck with a pathetic amount of belongings for a guy my age, I still did and came here to show you just how much I don't care about anything else but you. I'll always make you a priority. From now on. If you give me a chance."

"Doesn't your mom hate me?" I couldn't look at him when I asked. My gaze was plastered to his broad chest. I should have been jumping at the chance to make up with him, but I was too scared. I couldn't tolerate something hanging over us, ready to cleave this tenuous connection between us.

"She owns her mistake and the way she tried to manipulate your naivete, and she respects the decision you made." He ducked his head to meet my gaze. "Any more worries about what might make me walk away again?"

"I don't blame you for leaving. I told you to go." I swallowed hard. "And I've been mad at myself ever since."

"Isla." He took the Weedwacker from my hand and set it on the ground. Then he circled his arms around my waist. "You did the right thing, and if you want me around, I promise I won't leave again. But if you send me away, let me finish this first."

I was stuck on his promise to not leave again. "Finish what?"

"Reservoir Barrel. I want to finish the job. You'll be my only client, and I'll work for free."

"McCoy, you can't work for free."

His grin was sly. "Does that mean you're hiring me?"

"I..." Yes. All I wanted to say was yes. He was so close and I couldn't think properly, but I knew I wouldn't feel differently if he was back in Colorado. I'd still want him to be my project manager. "You are the best person for the job."

"I'll make sure of it."

Hope waited in the wings inside my chest, preparing to surge and take over. But I had so many questions. He had no employees. Where would we start? Where would he stay? Would he change his mind? "You sure you want to—"

"Yes." He caught my mouth and the kiss immediately deepened.

I was a mess, inside and out, but I melted into him and it all straightened out. I pulled away enough to say, "You're hired."

"Full disclosure—I want to sleep with my boss."

"Your boss wants you too."

"Fuck, Isla," he growled and picked me up.

I hooked my legs around his waist and swept my tongue across his. It wasn't enough. There were so many clothes in the way, and we were in full view of the highway. When he started walking while holding me, I came up for air.

He was heading for the foundry. "You have the keys on you?"

"I'm all sweaty."

"Isla, I don't care if you've mowed ten lawns before dawn, I want to get between those long legs of yours. Do you want to do it against the door or inside? Because I'll take you right now, anywhere."

Anywhere was tempting, but this moment was between us. "Inside."

He set me down at the door only so I could dig the keys out. When the door was unlocked, he tugged me inside and around the corner. My back was plastered against the cool brick wall in seconds. He hadn't even bothered to close the door.

I was still trying to orient myself when his hands landed

on my waistband. Stepping out of my boots while he was undoing the fly of my jeans and dragging them down was a little stop and go, but soon enough my jeans were off, his were undone, condom on, and I was back in his arms, my legs around his waist.

Reaching between us, I stroked him. "I missed this."

"It fucking missed you." He gave me a hard kiss as his hips pumped into my hand. "The hotel should thank you. I didn't have to waste nearly as much water as I usually would've." He kissed down my neck. "Came as soon as I thought of you."

I did that to him? He didn't feel like I had ruined what had been a second chance for him, and he still wanted me? The feelings going through me weren't just desire but a deep connection. I fell harder in love with him than ever.

He gripped my hips and thrust into me. I groaned, taking him all the way. We were an unsynchronized flurry of movement, and it didn't matter. He stroked into me, and I tried to ride him. The way we were smashed together and how wide open I was spread, my clit was stimulated enough. I'd never orgasmed so fast.

"McCoy!" His name vibrated out of me as he pumped.

"Fuck, Isla. Fuck." He stiffened, and we rode out our climax together. His hands massaged my ass as his hips swayed, the force dying as we drifted down from our peaks.

"That was . . ." I didn't know how to finish. I hadn't thought about the repercussions, the "what nows." As soon as he'd touched me, I'd wanted us to end up here.

"Intense?"

"Yes." I kept my arms draped around his neck. I glanced around at the empty foundry. The cardboard and plastic patch he'd done on the window held firm. The place was quiet and empty. "We had sex in my foundry."

"It won't be the last time."

I needed that to be true. "Promise?"

The look he speared me with was filled with pure determination. "Absolutely. I'm not going to let you down again. Because I love you. You're my very own sunbeam."

My throat grew thick. "You didn't let me down—you came back." We were still connected, and there was perfection to this moment. "I love you too, dammit. I swear, I tried not to, but I think as soon as you protected this place like it was yours, you had me hooked."

His grin was lazy. "I'm going to keep doing that too."

Neither one of us seemed to be in a hurry to move, but we couldn't stay naked in the foundry forever. "Now what?"

"I have to find a place to rent."

"No motel?"

His gaze softened. "Time to put down roots." He rubbed his hands up and down my legs. "Here's what I'm thinking. I'll call that guy who shit on you about the apartment complexes. I'll ask to tour every single empty place he has and then tell him nothing will work."

"I'm all for that plan." I played with the ends of his hair. Should I even offer up my idea? I didn't want to rush him. We'd literally just gotten back together—and we hadn't really been an item before. But this thing between us was worth exploring. "I, um, actually have a bed now. And a chair. A kitchen table even. You can stay with me."

"You won't be able to get rid of me."

"I don't plan to."

"Good. Because I've been wanting to know what it's like to wake up to you."

* * *

McCoy

. . .

Waking up with Isla in my arms was everything I wanted it to be and more. As restless as I was to jump into my new job, I wanted to savor this morning with her. It was past ten, but then we hadn't let each other sleep a lot last night.

Doubts still nagged in the corner of my mind. Was I doing the right thing? I could complete Reservoir Barrel. Could I open an office and build a business that'd thrive? I'd lost Nailer's. McDaniel's was my mom's.

There was nothing left to do but find out. I wouldn't be a bum living with my girlfriend while a business failed.

"Mmm." Isla snuggled into me in her new bed. "Did you sleep okay?"

"Better than I have in a while." Could've been all the exertion from the night before. We'd driven to her place, unhooked the trailer after she backed it in, hauled in my crap, and stayed holed up for the rest of the day. "But I have a job to get to."

"We can stay in bed and research engineering companies."

"I like how you think, boss."

She trailed her fingers over my chest. "I like sunbeam better. So, if we're working together professionally, do you want to work together personally? This house has a long way to go."

"You've done a lot while I was gone."

"Dad and I have been working together."

"I don't want to step between you two."

She thought for a while. "How 'bout this? I'll go get us some lunch. Rattler's opens soon, and while I'm picking up food, you can get us some ideas for the basement. Then Dad and I'll know what we can do."

My time in the hotel room gave me plenty of opportunities to think about how I'd do Reservoir Barrel if I was on my own and also map out an ideal blueprint for her base-ment. "You'll have plans before you get back, sunny."

"That fast?"

"I'm only fast when it counts, sunbeam."

Grinning, she planted a kiss on me, then got out of bed. While she scurried around the room getting dressed, I waited. If I got up, I'd cross to her, and then she'd stay naked and we'd never get started.

With her hair in its braid and her wearing a loose yellow dress with sandals laced up her ankles, she stopped at the edge of the bed. Good thing I'd stayed where I was. She was sexy as fuck, and I was hopeless. She gave me a lingering kiss and then was gone.

I had a task. More excited than I should be, I cleaned up and got dressed. Downstairs, I started jotting down measurements. I was on my third wall when the doorbell rang. Isla must need a hand with the food.

I jogged up the stairs and whipped open the door. I found myself facing her scowling dad and a woman I'd never seen before who resembled an older Isla, and I wished I could rewind time. I didn't want to hide from her parents, but I didn't want to cause a rift between her and them when she'd just gushed about how good their relationship had been. No one knew I was in town, and they'd rather have found out from her.

"Hey," I said, juggling the tape measure and paper with the measurements in my hands. At least I looked useful. "Isla's picking up lunch at Rattler's. You must be Naomi—nice to meet you." Not my smoothest introduction.

"So you're McCoy." Her tone was cool but not cold. I'd take it.

Cameron studied me, his gaze not quite neutral but not hostile. More curious yet cautious. Half turning to look behind him at the new red Titan I didn't see a lot of the farmers and ranchers drive around town, he said, "That must be your truck."

"It's mine. I don't work for McDaniel Contractors anymore."

"And you came back to Coal Haven?" Naomi asked.

Her tone toed the line of interrogating, but I didn't mind. Hiding my past hadn't helped, and I wasn't going to conceal my present. I stepped out of the doorway. "Might as well come in. You're going to be seeing a lot of me."

"Oh?" Cameron let his wife in first, but they didn't move from the entry.

I sat in the recliner I'd spread Isla out on the night before when I knelt between her legs and slaked my thirst for her. But I'd try not to think about that now. I set the measuring tape, paper, and pen on the floor.

"I'm here to stay. I came back for her." I spread my hands apart. "And I'm sure you're going to ask what I plan to do because you're worried I'm going to leech off her. I have some of my own money, and I don't plan to charge her for being her project manager. I have what my mom paid me for my time here earlier. I'll live off that, finish the Reservoir Barrel, then officially start my contractor business after."

Naomi sat on the end of the couch like she was in a board meeting. She was wearing a gray sweatshirt and jeans but held herself like she was in a business suit and heels.

Cameron studied me for a moment. Then he crossed to the couch and sat on the edge of a cushion next to his wife. Running his fingers over the stunning coffee table, his brows drew together. Her gaze traced his hand, her lips slightly pursed and resignation in her eyes. I didn't know what was transpiring between them, so I waited for them to speak. Since Cameron had been so free with his opinions before, the stretch of silence wasn't what I had expected.

"I'm an open book," I said. "Ask me anything."

"I've looked up the work you've done," he said and Naomi nodded.

Not me, but the work I'd done. I didn't cringe like I had with the harassment charges. My past projects were something I thought about with pride. "Followed in my dad's footsteps, trying to be bigger and better than he ever was."

Understanding filled Cameron's eyes. "He was a hard man."

"Yep."

"And did you succeed?"

This wasn't the interrogation I was prepared for. What did he think about me being back on as a project manager? Naomi certainly had to have opinions. What did they think about me in his daughter's house? But if I was a dad, maybe I'd ask those same questions. "I'm sure you saw all my success with Nailer's."

"They've closed their doors."

"What?" When Cameron nodded, not doubting himself for a second, I still had to dig out my phone and look it up. I quit breathing until Nailer's web page pulled up.

The website wasn't down, but the announcement was on the home page and the rest of the web pages were defunct. I slumped in my chair, numb. "Huh."

I stared over his head and out the window. All my work was gone. The building would become another restaurant. Maybe another brewery. Life for the establishment would go on, but Nailer's was gone.

"Are you furious they destroyed your legacy?" he asked.

"My legacy wasn't in Nailer's." I sat forward, propping my arms on my thighs, clarity coming quicker now that the news sank in. "It's in that building. That place isn't ruined. It'll house more businesses, probably even another brewery, and it's up to those people to run their company the right way."

This time Naomi spoke. "What about the beer?"

I laughed, the news that I had been integral to Nailer's continued success causing more delight than I thought possible. I hated to see a business crumble, but Cameron's update showed me I had mattered. I had managed it correctly. Me, the guy my ex had called cold and impersonal. *No wonder your dad's company struggled so much.* Fuck her.

Any residual anxiety about striking out on my own dissolved. "Hannah will filch off some other poor guy if she's not with Angus anymore. And apparently they can't run a business. I don't care about the beer. I enjoyed making it, but only because it reminded me of my stepdad. He loved both the brewery and seeing his recipes being mass-produced and enjoyed by thousands. When he died . . . it was a job more than a passion. I look forward to making beer as a hobby again. But my work will always be in that structure."

I rubbed my hands lightly together. I hadn't been timid with this man the first time we talked. I couldn't start now. Cameron and Naomi Barron would see through anything else. "Isla loves you both. And I love her. I'm not going anywhere whether you want me with her or not—as a couple or in business. The only person who can tell me to leave is her. But I promise you, the people who are important to her will be critical to me, too, because of it."

Cameron's gaze intensified. I was still under the spotlight, and I couldn't tell if I'd upset him or if he'd made his mind up when I opened the door.

He exchanged a look with his wife. "I would think it'd be better to have Reservoir Barrel in your portfolio, regardless of whether my daughter pays you or not."

Stunned, I stared at him. He had no problem with me showing up in town, getting back with his daughter, or taking over as project manager again?

His gaze softened. "I never used to ask Isla to help me with much when she was younger. She seemed accident prone, but I suppose that was from us expecting her to know everything. I don't recall teaching Stetson outright, but he'd always been next to me, watching and learning. I didn't expect the same from her. She's capable of a lot more than I gave her credit for. She has good business instincts and that extends to you."

He didn't seem like a guy to admit that much to a person. Not to me, someone he hardly knew but had scoured the internet about. "She said it's been fun doing projects with you."

"Yes." A nostalgic smile crossed his face. His gaze landed on the measuring tape and paper at my feet. "I guess you'll be taking over now."

"I'm just sketching out plans, but I have to find out what she wants for a design. I won't interfere if that's what you're worried about. Starting my own business will keep me busy enough."

I hadn't realized he'd been holding on to stress until it drained from his eyes. He ran his fingers over the wood top of the table again. "One thing I've learned recently is that I need to accept the people who are important in my kids' lives. I haven't been a good enough dad to be chosen over them." He tapped the surface. "I came at you hard when you first arrived."

"It was understandable."

His laugh was wry. "Not many people describe it that way. Not many people understand me at all. But if you're going to be around, just know I will be, too, and I agree. We should try to get along."

"That won't be a problem," I assured him.

"Isla's going to do what she wants anyway," Naomi said, a hint of pride in her tone.

Isla piled through the front door, plastic bag with to-go containers hanging from one hand, panic written across her features. She glanced from me to her parents. "Mom. Dad. Hi. I guess you saw that McCoy returned."

Cameron nodded. "We've been talking."

I didn't want her to worry. This was nothing like my last talk with him. I jumped up. "Let me get the food for you." Her wide eyes searched mine. I gave her a small smile, and her expression turned stunned. "Go ahead and have a seat. I'll be right back."

As I went into the kitchen, Naomi said, "I was just telling your father we could use more contractors in the area. People coming in to fill out permits always mention how they wish there were more builders in town. Sounds like McCoy will have no issues finding more clients."

I dropped the food on the counter, then went to lean against the entry to the living room.

Isla hadn't sat yet. She looked at me when she said, "His work will speak for itself. Reservoir Barrel is going to blow people away."

"I know. Barrons don't do it any other way." Cameron slapped his hands on his thighs and rose. "We took the afternoon off to see if you needed a hand with emptying the garage, but you two are busy."

I didn't want them to leave because of me. "I can go get more food." I met Isla's gaze. Gratitude and happiness shone in her eyes. I'd make sure to keep that look there for the rest of our lives.

"Let's have dinner this weekend," Cameron said, taking Naomi's hand and walking toward the door. "Otherwise, I've been told I have your old bedroom to paint and build shelving in for a library."

When they were gone, Isla lingered in the doorway.

"I can't believe how much things have changed," she murmured. "I'm almost afraid to be happy."

I draped an arm around her shoulders. The same sensation echoed inside me, like the past trying to rear its head, but I wouldn't allow it. "That's when we need to celebrate the most."

My gaze stuck on her lips when she smiled. "We can put the food in the fridge and go out for a proper meal."

"No, we'll celebrate with that beer we made together while I fuck you again. Then we'll eat lunch."

She shoved the door closed. "That sounds better."

Nineteen

ISLA

Sunlight streamed through the custom-built windows that had been installed in Reservoir Barrel. Large silver fermentation tanks towered in the middle. One side was surrounded by a wall that would soon serve tap beer. Large beams towered overhead, but they'd been cleaned and stained. McCoy used as many original pieces from the foundry as he could. The garage doors we'd use to move shipments in and out were new, like the windows, but matched the aesthetic.

I couldn't believe I was ready for a soft opening of the event side of Reservoir Barrel. And I couldn't believe the timing.

I glanced at the diamond ring on my left hand. It blinked under the light.

"I'm so happy for you," Kennedy gushed. She had Ginny propped on her hip, and her stomach was rounded with a baby due to be born during the winter. "This was a beautiful place to have a wedding."

"Thanks. I'm glad everyone could make it." And everyone in town had made it. "I can't believe how much got done over the summer."

McCoy's meticulous scheduling and attention to detail kept the restoration and installation of the brewing equipment on track. We'd already started brewing my vanilla cardamom on a larger scale to perfect the flavor.

Laney put her hand on the small of her back. Her stomach rounded out. "Figures. I'd finally get pregnant right when you open a brewery."

I grinned. Laney proudly waddled around. I'd gotten to know her more over the winter. She'd shared her infertility journey with me, and now she was due in a couple of months. "I'll be offering root beer. Eli and Owen have had strong input on the recipe, and I promised to name it after them. Something like Twin Roots. Twin Boots? I haven't decided yet."

"Oh my god, that's perfect." Kennedy laughed. "Where are the guys anyway?"

Many of our friends and family had milled around the building when the reception started, taking in the sitting area, looking at the wood and iron stools and tables. A spoked wheel light fixture hung over the bar, and it was one of my favorite pieces. McCoy had found the old wheel when the landscaping crew was cleaning up the trees in the back. He'd hired Liam to make something from it for the place, and it matched perfectly. Sylvia gushed about the brewery as much as if her company had finished it. Her pride for McCoy shone from her and she held no grudge against me. She was giving more of a tour to my relatives than I was.

Dad approached with Mom tucked into his side and Rina in Mom's arms. She'd been open to family gatherings, but they made her anxious. There were too many years of bad blood for everyone to be fully comfortable around each other, but she made an effort, and that was more than any of us thought she'd do. When she and Dad were both at a family function and Liam was there, they stayed for a while, were cordial, and then ducked out so their presence wouldn't make others uncomfortable. As the months passed, they weren't leaving as early as they once had.

"We're going to head out," Mom said, offering Kennedy and Laney a small smile. "Rina needs a nap, and we're giving Lyric and Stetson the night off."

I hugged each of them, gave Rina a kiss on her mop of dark hair, and they left.

Laney shook her head. "Hot damn, I still can't get over it. Did you know your dad actually waved to me on the road the other day? I about drove in the ditch."

"He's loosened up a lot. I think he and McCoy are plotting to buy another house to renovate after he gets ours built." We'd found a quarter of land, forty acres, that was perfect for a house, a barn, and a riding area since McCoy was all about 4-H animals with the kids we planned to start trying for after the grand opening of Reservoir Barrel.

"You're kidding." Kennedy's voice was full of awe. "They really do get along? Liam said he thought so, but I didn't believe him."

"Some days, I think I should be jealous." I wasn't though. I was ecstatic. Dad's chronic leukemia was well managed, and he was hopeful he'd be one of the ones living with the disease for twenty years or more.

Aunt Willow and Uncle Bruce stopped and each gave me a hug. Aunt Willow grinned, wistfulness in her eyes. "If Evander ever returns home, we'll bring him right here."

I hadn't seen my cousin since I was little, but I hoped he would come back someday. "I'll serve you each myself."

As they finished hugging me, Aunt Kira stopped with Nora. "Nice place." She nodded and walked off.

Nora leaned over and whispered. "She stuffed one of your beers in her purse."

Holden stopped to talk with us. "Congrats, Isla. The kids are hopped up on your root beer and haven't quit gushing about it. I'd say it's a success."

My little snort was smothered in my laughter. "I promised to make more root beer. They'll get a batch named after them. I can make a name out of all their initials."

Emery swung by and tucked into his side. Grady was in the event room with Emery's mom. "You'd be their hero if you did that. Every kid at school and whoever they can tell when they're in Arizona with their dad will know about it. You'll get free marketing."

I was laughing when McCoy came up behind me and slipped an arm around my waist. "I think you better come get some food before the guys eat us out of house and home."

We filed into the back room. Large, wooden, beer-hall-style tables were filled with adults and kids. Lyric waved at a couple of spots she'd saved with her and Stetson.

I piled my plate with roast beef and mashed potatoes and sat next to her and my brother. McCoy set his plate down and disappeared. When he returned, he had two bottles of my beer.

"What'd you pick?" Stetson asked. The handmade label on his was the buffalo berry flavor I had toyed with over the winter. I saved it to be a family brew.

McCoy sat next to me. "The vanilla cardamom kind that made me fall in love with her."

"It did not." I laughed.

"Nah, I was in love with you before that."

Stetson groaned. "Christ, is this how you feel with me and Lyric?"

"Yes," I said, unrepentant.

"Do you have a name for it yet?" Lyric asked.

I twirled the bottle. I'd been toying with ideas, but McCoy only offered advice and only when I asked. The brewery was my brainchild. "I think this'll be Sunbeam Barrel."

I exchanged a smile with McCoy. His expression promised he'd show me how much he liked the name later. While I loved hanging out with my family and friends, and I was exhilarated to have a space big enough for us, I couldn't wait for McCoy to get me alone.

———

Thanks for reading!

The Oil Barrons series might be done, but all the Barrons will eventually get their stories. Starting with the first book in my new series Oil Knights and the Oil Barrons Christmas novella!

All Nora wants for Christmas is for Colt to get over their age difference and that fact that he works for her mom. It might take a snow storm and a power outage to make this Christmas miracle happen in Make Me Merry.

Once upon a time, Aggie Knight was a runaway bride, shattered thanks to the man she loved. Ten years later, she's now her ex's boss and her pieced together heart is holding firm. It has to. But seeing Ansen Barron every day will either put her back together, or finish tearing her apart. Find Aggie and Ansen's in A Reckless Memory.

. . .

For all the latest news, sneak peeks, free bonus content sign up for my newsletter and receive an extra epilogue for Isla and McCoy.

Also by Marie Johnston

Return to Coal Haven

Violet Promises

Daisy Whispers

Poppy Kisses

Crocus Valley

A Reckless Memory

A Temporary Memory

An Unfinished Memory

A Fearless Memory

An Endless Memory

Coal Haven

Make Me Whole

Make Me Shiver

Make Me Blush

Make Me Dream

Make Me Exhale

King's Creek

King's Crown

King's Ransom

King's Treasure

King's Country

King's Queen